THE LEFT LEG

PHOEBE ATWOOD TAYLOR

WRITING AS ALICE TILTON

THE
LEFT LEG

A Leonidas Witherall Mystery

A Foul Play Press Book

THE COUNTRYMAN PRESS
Woodstock, Vermont

This edition is published in 1988 by Foul Play Press, a division
of The Countryman Press, Woodstock, Vermont 05091.

ISBN 0-88150-121-2

Printed in the United States of America

THE LEFT LEG

CHAPTER 1

CLUTCHING his cane, his Evening Transcript and his unwieldy brown paper package, Mr. Leonidas Witherall swung off the Boston-bound bus the instant its door opened at the Carnavon Four Corners stop.

As he started to ford the slush-clogged gutter, the burly figure of the bus driver loomed menacingly on the top step above him.

"Don't you forget it, mister! Don't you never show your beard on my bus again, see? Don't you never put a foot on this bus line again, see?"

Mr. Witherall's eyes were glinting behind his pince-nez, and his ears were burning under his Homburg, but he reached the sidewalk and turned down East Main Street without allowing himself to utter a single one of the withering retorts poised on his tongue tip.

"And come back here!" the driver bellowed. "You! You with the beard! Come back here and get your rubbers!"

Ignoring both the command and the numerous repetitions howled after him by delighted bystanders, Mr. Witherall continued to walk rapidly into the March dusk. Not even if it had been his wallet instead of his rubbers that had been left behind, he thought grimly, would he return to that bus! Nothing short of two broken legs would thwart his determined intention to put as much distance as possible between himself and the bus, and its driver, and its passengers. And particularly that predatory blonde female in the scarlet coat and the scarlet wimple.

Long after the mocking, raucous bus horn announced that vehicle's departure, Mr. Witherall continued to stride resolutely on and on, turning corner after corner, crossing one slushy street after another. Heedless of his wet feet, of the knife-like north wind, of the passing cars that splattered him with icy driblets of pasty brown snow, Mr. Witherall kept marching along until the bepuddled brick sidewalks gave way to more suburban paths of gelatinous mud and gravel.

Then he paused, put on his pince-nez that swung from a broad black ribbon, and looked around with distaste at the angular frame houses lining the street on which he stood.

He knew little about the town of Carnavon. He had no idea what part he might be in, or how far he had progressed from the bus stop—not, he mentally added, that he ever wished to see another bus as long as he lived. Rather than take one of those orange buses, he would trudge the twelve miles home to Dalton on foot. Trains were out of the question, too, because trains passing through Carnavon went nowhere near the city of Dalton.

A taxicab was the solution, Leonidas decided. Twelve miles of cab might run into money, but economy was no object in his present state of mind. It would be well worth twelve miles of cab fare to ensure, for the remainder of his trip home, complete freedom from any more predatory females. He would find the railroad station, therefore, and hire a cab.

Raising his cane, he hailed a sedan whose driver had considerately swung to the far side of the street to avoid splashing through the small lake near the sidewalk.

"Could you," Leonidas called out, "tell me where the station is?"

He was a little surprised that such a considerate motorist should merely thrust out a hand and point instead of giving explicit directions, but he signalled his thanks with a wave of his cane, and started slowly back along the brick sidewalk.

Certainly, he thought, this expedition to Tilbury on which he had set out with such enthusiasm was proving peculiar from start to finish. What Professor Colfax had so glowingly described to him over the phone as a genuine first folio Shakespeare proved, in the cold clear light of Colfax's library, to be a facsimile. It was not a very good facsimile, it should never have deceived Carl Colfax for two minutes, and it was absolutely nothing to summon anyone fifty miles to inspect.

And then that bus trip home!

Leonidas bit his lip. That bus trip was going to rankle in his memory for some time to come. That bus trip, and that predatory blonde!

He jumped suddenly at the sharp sound of high spiked heels clicking on the bricks behind him, and then he smiled at his own jumpiness. That blonde in the scarlet wimple had certainly unnerved him! Obviously they were a woman's heels, but of course they could never belong to that woman in scarlet. She never would have been so persistent as to follow him off the bus. She never could have followed him, anyway. No one could have followed his zig-zag course through all that slush without the aid of a pack of bloodhounds and a pair of wading boots.

He still could not understand what on earth had prompted that woman to carry on in any such fashion, or why, of the entire bus load, she should have picked him as her victim. Or why she should have carried it so far. Or—

"Hey, you! You wit' the beard!"

For a stunned second, Leonidas stood like a marble statue.

It was her voice calling him, the voice of the blonde with the scarlet wimple!

She had followed him off the bus, after all!

She was still after him!

"Hey, you! Wait—"

Clutching his cane, his Transcript and his brown paper package, Leonidas turned and fled down the nearest alley.

The next few minutes were never very clear or coherent in his mind.

Alleys, driveways, snowbanks, puddles and fences all played a part, and when he finally emerged from an alley to a street of lighted stores, Leonidas dived into the first one like a man diving into an air raid shelter.

While the steamed windows had given him no clew as to what type of establishment it might be, Leonidas felt vaguely relieved to find it was a hardware store and not a beauty parlor. After a quick look around, he made straight for the paint display on the turntable at the rear. Leonidas was tall, but the turntable was taller.

Panting, he came to a stop behind it.

His ears were pounding so hard that he didn't hear the footsteps of the young man who walked over to him from the counter.

"Can I get you—my God! Shakespeare!" the young man took a step back, and whistled noiselessly. "My God! Did anyone ever tell you you're the spitting image of Shakespeare?"

Leonidas fumbled for his pince-nez and put them on. The lenses were steamed, but he got a blurred impression of a tall, pleasant-faced young man in a brown tweed suit.

"M'yes," he said. "Several hundred thousand people have confided that fact to me."

The young man grinned. "It was a silly question, wasn't it? But it's downright startling to have Shakespeare bound suddenly into a lot of aluminum paint. I almost poked you to see if you were real."

"My—er—midriff," Leonidas said, "is occasionally black and blue from inquisitive prodders. I wonder if you'd sell me a—"

"Now I think of it," the young man interrupted, "I remember hearing of another man who was supposed to look exactly like Shakespeare. I never knew him, but he was a professor at Meredith's Academy. They used to call him Bill Shakespeare. He taught a cousin of mine."

"I am he. I wonder," Leonidas was beginning to get his breath, "if you'd sell me a gallon of paint, please, and—er—would it be humanly possible for you to call me a cab?"

"A cab?" the young man looked at him curiously. "Why, yes. What kind of paint would you like?"

"Any kind. Anything you put a brush into and paint with," Leonidas said. "A gallon, please. And if you could telephone the railroad station or some cab stand, and have a cab sent here for me, I'd be most grateful, indeed."

"Look," the young man said, "d'you feel all right, sir? You're not sick or anything? I mean, you don't really want any paint, do you? You just want a cab. And you seem—that is, you seemed rather upset when you bounded in here just now."

"Upset," Leonidas told him with a smile, "is not an adequate word, Mr.—er—"

"Potter. Lincoln Potter. This is Potter's, Incorporated. Paint, Plumbing, Heating and General Jobbing. What's wrong, sir? Is there any way I can help you?"

Leonidas hesitated.

"Frankly, Mr. Potter," he said at last, "my problem can't even be summed up under the head of General Jobbing. On the other hand, while it is not my custom to saddle strangers with my personal tribulations, I shall probably start having fits if I do not confide this bizarre situation to someone."

"Sit down and tell me about it," Mr. Potter said. "After all, we're really not strangers, Shakespeare. I've read you from cover to cover. I can even quote you: 'I do know him a gentleman, that well deserves a help, which he shall have.' What's the matter, sir?"

"This afternoon I went to Tilbury to visit Professor Colfax, a colleague of mine in the days when I taught at Meredith's. After visiting him, I left Tilbury on one of those orange buses which go to Boston by way of Dalton. A woman—really, she was young enough to be called a girl—got on the bus at the same stop. A girl in a scarlet coat and a scarlet wimple."

"A which?"

"A wimple," Leonidas said. "And—"

"Pimple?" Mr. Potter seemed puzzled. "As a blotch or blemish?"

"Wimple," Leonidas said, "as a head covering. A cone-shaped thing like a small dunce cap, with many folds and drapings. It's probably the only female head-gear I've seen in the last decade that I could epitomize in a word. I once wrote a monograph on the medieval wimple. Anyway, this blonde girl with the scarlet wimple got on the bus at the same time I did. I had never seen her before in my life, and I hope," he added fervently, "that I never see her again. I'm running away from her, now. That's why I dove in here. That's why I require a cab. I wish to get out of this town, and away from her, and as soon as—"

He ducked behind the turntable paint display as the front door of the store was noisily pushed open.

"Hey! Hey, anyone in here?"

At the sound of that throaty voice, Leonidas winced, crouched down on the floor, and sent a mute appeal to Mr. Potter.

"Hey!"

Smothering his impulse to grin, Lincoln Potter walked to the front of the store.

"May I help you?"

"Say, mister, you seen a guy wit' a beard?"

"I beg your pardon?"

"I said," Leonidas could hear the impatient tap of those spike heeled pumps with the scarlet bows, "I said, you seen a guy wit' a beard?"

"That's just what I thought you said," Mr. Potter returned. "Any particular guy with a beard?"

"Wise guy, ain't you?"

"Not at all," Mr. Potter said pleasantly. "I have several customers with beards—only one beard to a customer, of course. I don't mean to insinuate that they have eight or ten beards apiece. Father O'Hara has a Vandyck, and Dr. Leadbetter has—"

"Listen, has a guy wit' a beard been in here?"

"When?"

"Tonight, you dumb cluck! Right now!"

"Sorry," Mr. Potter said. "I had a man with a beard in here last evening, and another about two weeks ago—"

The door slammed in his face.

Lincoln Potter waited a moment, and then he strolled to the rear of the store and eyed Leonidas quizzically.

"Was that," he inquired, "your Scarlet Wimpernel?"

Leonidas managed a wry chuckle as he wiped the beads of perspiration from his forehead.

"An excellent name for her, Mr. Potter," he said. "I wish I'd thought of it myself. Scarlet Wimpernel. M'yes. That's very good. Mr. Potter, I'm profoundly grateful. I've never felt more indebted to any living creature."

"Exactly what happened on that bus, Shakespeare?"

"If you don't mind," Leonidas said, "I prefer not to discuss that episode, Mr. Potter. I should, however, like to purchase that lawnmower over there."

"I bet I know. I bet she decided you'd make a

first-class sugar daddy. She tried to pick you up, didn't she?"

"The lawnmower," Leonidas's voice was cool, but his ears were burning, "and five pounds of grass seed, please. And the green-handled sickle. And the paint. You needn't bother to wrap anything up. I'll take it all with me in the cab. I need a rake, too, and some garden hose—"

"Look here," Lincoln Potter said, "you don't have to prove your gratitude by buying a lot of stuff you don't want! I only wish you'd give me a blow by blow description of the Wimpernel's attack. I can gather that you didn't encourage her—why this intensive pursuit?"

Leonidas smiled as he swung his pince-nez from their ribbon.

"To tell you what is customarily referred to as God's truth," he said, "I don't know. Now, Mr. Potter, if you'd call my cab and get my purchases together, I'll get along home to Dalton."

"You can't take a cab all the way to Dalton, man!" Lincoln Potter protested. "And you know you don't want lawnmowers and all that junk!"

"All my life," Leonidas said, "I've yearned for a lawnmower with rubber tires. And I really need a sickle and grass seed. Urgently. I—er—also need a cab."

"The Carnavon Cab Company isn't a metered outfit, Shakespeare. Bill Maloney'll charge you twenty-five dollars to get to Dalton, if he thinks you're in a hurry.

More than that, probably, when he spots a lawn-mower. Tell you what. I'll drive you over, myself. I've got to go there tomorrow anyway to discuss paint with Mrs. Endicott. Relax, Shakespeare. I'll chaperon you home."

"That's a very gracious gesture," Leonidas said, "which, of course, I can't permit. I'm already in your debt. And you can't leave your store."

"Oh, yes, I can. It's my store, and I keep my own hours. D'you want that lawnmower, really? That settles it, then." Mr. Potter yanked a trench coat off a hook by the counter. "We always deliver lawnmowers. It's a policy of the firm. And I'll deliver you along with it. All I ask, Shakespeare, is that you break down on the way home and tell me how you ever let yourself in for a pursuit by a harpy like the Wimpernel. Wait here, now, while I dash over to the parking lot and get the car. The alley's so full of slush, I'll have to bring it around front—"

Grabbing a plaid scarf, young Mr. Potter hurried out the back of the store.

Leonidas hummed to himself as he picked up a package of lawn seed and stuffed it into one of the patch pockets of his overcoat. Young Mr. Potter would never know it, but he had been destined to act as a transportation agent as soon as Leonidas's pince-nez lenses had cleared sufficiently for him to identify the stripings of young Mr. Potter's college club tie. From his experience with Meredith Academy's Old

Boys, Leonidas knew that the members of Chop and Bone were invariably individuals whose quixotic impulses could be relied upon.

He was examining the plastic material of the sickle's handle when the front door opened again.

Leonidas ducked back behind the paint cans, and then, when he heard the reassuring thud of masculine heels, peeked out cautiously around the side of the turntable display.

At his first glimpse of the man who was walking over to the counter, Leonidas blinked and hastily whipped on his pince-nez.

But even with his glasses on, he still saw the same vivid sight.

The man, now leaning over the counter, was wearing a tall silk hat, and it *was* green. His tight satin knee breeches were green, too. So was his satin coat with the long tails. So were his buckled shoes.

And no matter from what angle you squinted at it, that thing under the man's arm still turned out to be a small gilded pasteboard harp!

Leonidas heard the bell of the cash register ring, and he saw the man draw an envelope from the drawer, but before he could think of anything to say, the man turned and departed as abruptly as he had come.

Completely bewildered, Leonidas shook his head.

For a small and undistinguished town, he decided, Carnavon was one of the most amazing places in which he had ever found himself.

There was a noise in the back room, and young

Mr. Potter appeared in the doorway. He stood there, panting, while little rivulets trickled from his shoes. Obviously he had something to announce, but he seemed unable to decide how to begin.

"Er—is there anything the matter with your car?" Leonidas inquired after Mr. Potter had twice opened his mouth and closed it.

"Shakespeare, there appears to be a slight hitch to all of this."

"Motor trouble?" Leonidas asked sympathetically.

"The parking lot's full of cops."

"Ah, your automobile has been stolen! Too bad! I—"

"My car's perfectly all right, Shakespeare. There's nothing the matter with it. It's there. It goes."

"Then what—?"

"Shakespeare, those cops are hunting for a man with a beard!"

"Ah," Leonidas said. "I see. I understand your agitation, Mr. Potter. You believe I am the person whom the police are hunting, do you not?"

"Aren't you?"

"Mr. Potter, one of the difficulties of wearing a beard these days is that people feel you are unique. Let me assure you that if the police are hunting a man with a beard, it is some other man with a beard. I am not the bearded object of their search."

"The cops," Lincoln Potter said, "are after a man named Leonidas Witherall. They described you from your Homburg and your pince-nez right down to that funny looking brown paper package you've been clutching under your arm. You *are* Leonidas Wither-all, aren't you?"

"Yes. Yes, I am. And the police want me, by name? Er—may I ask what particular grievance the police feel they have against me?"

"They want you on statutory charges, Shakespeare. Scarlet Wimpernel says you annoyed her. She also claims you swiped her purse."

"The police," Leonidas said firmly, "are in error. They have been misinformed. You saw the female involved, Mr. Potter, and aptly described her as a harpy. You should be able to gather that if any charges are to be brought, I am the one to bring—"

Young Mr. Potter reached out suddenly and snatched something from Leonidas's coat pocket.

"I thought," he said with a note of triumph in his voice, "that I saw something scarlet!"

Leonidas took off his pince-nez, wiped them carefully with his handkerchief, then put them on and looked again at the scarlet leather handbag dangling from Mr. Potter's hand.

"Well, Shakespeare, what've you got to say? Isn't this the Wimpernel's handbag?"

"Unquestionably," Leonidas said. "It's the bag she had in the bus. Just as unquestionably, she put it in my pocket, herself. Mr. Potter, this situation has become serious enough to warrant my taking some sort of constructive action. I must be identified to the police, and vouched for, and it has just occurred to me

that a friend of mine who now lives in Carnavon Hills
will be able to do just that—do you know Mr. Marcus
Meredith, the owner of Meredith's Academy? I feel
we had best summon him to—er—are you listening to
me?"

Leonidas paused as young Mr. Potter's eye lighted
on the opened drawer of the cash register, and he
twirled his pince-nez thoughtfully as Mr. Potter
walked over to the counter and inspected the drawer's
contents.

There was something ominous about Mr. Potter's
slow, measured stroll back to where Leonidas stood
waiting.

"M'yes," Leonidas said. "I know what is in your
mind, Mr. Potter. If you'll pause in your sinuous stalk
and listen, I should be only too happy to explain that
empty cash drawer—I assume that it *is* empty?"

"Give me that envelope!"

"I regret," Leonidas said, "that the envelope is
not in my possession."

"Meaning," Mr. Potter said with irony, "that
some little elf sneaked out of the woodwork and made
off with it?"

"As a matter of fact," Leonidas returned, "a man
in a green silk hat and a green satin suit is responsible for the envelope's removal. He was carrying a
harp."

Mr. Potter sat down on the tubular arm of a mod-
ernistic garden chair and favored Leonidas with a look
of intense disbelief.

"Shakespeare, you wouldn't dare look me straight in the eye and say that again."

"A man," Leonidas said, "in a green silk hat and a green satin suit entered this store, opened the cash register, removed an envelope, and departed. He was carrying a small harp."

"I'm so glad," Mr. Potter said, "that it was a small harp. I hate to think of some poor fellow lugging around a *big* harp. No, Shakespeare, I can't take that. It sticks in the craw. But I tell you what I'll do. If you give me back that envelope without any fuss, I'll count five hundred by fives before I call the cops. Come on, now, hand it over before I get actively sore."

"Mr. Potter," Leonidas said, "your attitude is quite understandable. But will you telephone Marcus Meredith, ask him to come here, and wait until he does before you leap to any more conclusions?"

"I want that envelope!"

Mr. Potter's general expression was that of a tiger about to pounce upon its prey. Leonidas, after considering the young man's narrowed eyes and jutting jaw, rather regretfully arrived at a decision.

"Very well, Mr. Potter," he said. "You win. You will find the envelope in your back room. In the large pail."

Mr. Potter got up and grinned. "In the big pail, you say?"

Leonidas nodded. "In the large pail."

He waited until young Mr. Potter was through the door, then he slammed it and shoved home the heavy bolt. Then, tossing his Homburg into a barrel in the corner, Leonidas grabbed a painter's cap from the hook by the counter, and marched out the front door.

A hasty look showed that the street was free of cars and pedestrians. Leonidas crossed to the opposite sidewalk, strode down an alley, and was crossing another street when he heard the whine of a prowl-car siren.

The sound did not particularly perturb Leonidas. He had often heard his friend Colonel Carpenter, the former head of the Dalton police, discourse on the ease with which one man on foot could elude two officers in a prowl car.

But when the siren of a second car was joined by the siren of a third, Leonidas became genuinely worried. A trio of prowl cars would indicate that the Carnavon police were in earnest in their search for him.

Pausing by some ash cans at the foot of an alley, Leonidas took stock.

The police wanted him on two counts, for annoying the girl in the scarlet wimple, and for stealing her purse. Any charitable doubts the police might have entertained as to the veracity of the first charge would be dispelled forever when young Mr. Potter brought forth the scarlet purse and gave a brief account of its discovery. Then, on the basis of Mr. Potter's further testimony, the police would add a third charge of larceny for the theft of that envelope from the hardware store's cash register.

Leonidas sighed.

Never for a moment would the Carnavon police listen to his own version of the Scarlet Wimpernel incident, any more than Mr. Potter would listen to the story of the man with the harp. It was, furthermore, safe to assume that until and unless something of greater interest turned up, the Carnavon police would devote their time to chasing him.

Marcus Meredith was the obvious solution. If he could get hold of Marcus, Marcus could identify him, vouch for him, and force both the police and young Potter to listen to his story. He would have to go to Marcus's house and explain in person; he couldn't take the risk of being arrested while trying to find a public telephone. Besides, this story was nothing that could be adequately told over a phone. This was a story which required gestures. Somehow, with the police hunting him, he must proceed to Forty Bald Pate Hill. And he still had no idea what part of Carnavon he was now in, or by what route he might reach Carnavon Hills.

But it could be done, Leonidas assured himself. He must not run, or give any impression of being worried or anxious. If he took his time and used his wits and kept cool, he ought to be able to settle everything. He had, he thought with quiet pride, done very well up to the present. No man could have been cooler.

His sang-froid was slightly dashed when he suddenly discovered that he was clutching his Transcript, his cane, his brown paper package, and, to his thorough amazement, the green-handled sickle!

He started to dump the lot into the nearest ash can, and then he reconsidered.

The police were hunting someone in a Homburg who should, by rights, be fleeing helter-skelter through Carnavon. He, on the other hand, was a man wearing a painter's cap, a man who was going to stroll calmly along, minding his own business, openly bearing the fruits of his evening's shopping. Better still, he would be a man with a cane, a man who limped slightly. His friend the Colonel had commented more than once on the problem of pursuing anyone alert enough to appropriate a limp or some other apparent physical deformity.

As flashlights began playing around at the far end of the alley, Leonidas adjusted his muffler so that it concealed his beard, and limped casually out to the street.

He found himself on the outskirts of a little group gathered on the sidewalk beside a prowl car. Making his way to a vantage point near the curbing, Leonidas watched interestedly while two officers tilted a search light on the car top to cover the alley from which he had just emerged. The faintest of chuckles escaped his lips when the two finally proceeded into the passageway with drawn pistols.

"What's the matter?" he asked the man standing next to him. "What are they after?"

"Somebody said it was a guy tried to kill a woman or something, and somebody else he robbed a store. They got him cornered in this block."

"Dear me!" the quaver in Leonidas's voice was not entirely assumed. "Er—by the way, can you tell me if this is the right street to take for Carnavon Hills? The bus driver put me off at the wrong stop."

The man gave it as his opinion that those drivers were getting too fresh.

"You're the fourth person this week that's told me they got put off at the wrong stop. You in a hurry?"

"Well, yes," Leonidas said. "As a matter of fact, I am very anxious to get to Carnavon Hills as soon as I possibly can."

"It'll be an hour before the next Hills bus comes. I guess you could probably walk to the Hills in that time. That is," he eyed the cane on which Leonidas was leaning, "if you think you'd want to walk that far."

"A whole hour to wait? I'm afraid I shall have to walk, then," Leonidas said. "If I get too tired, I can always stop and wait for the bus to come along. How should I go?"

Half an hour later, having put the last of the Carnavon sub-divisions behind him, Leonidas was striding along the country road, past snow-heaped fields that shone white in the moonlight.

He was congratulating himself on his good fortune when a car suddenly hurtled out from a wooded side road to his right, and, with a great deal of brake squealing and puddle splashing, pulled up squarely beside him.

"Yoo-hoo!"

At the sound of a woman's voice, Leonidas gripped his bundles and prepared to take to his heels.

Then, as the car window was lowered, he realized with a rush of relief that it wasn't the Scarlet Wimpernel who was leaning out from the driver's seat. It was a girl in a light-colored polo coat, with a peasant kerchief tied under her chin.

"Tell me, did you happen to see a man with a beard—oh, are *you* the one we're hunting?"

"I'm quite sure," Leonidas said firmly, "that I am—"

Before he could add "not!" the girl interrupted. "Get in, hurry!"

"But—"

"Quick!" the girl said. "See those yellow lights down the valley? That's one of those foul police cars, and if they find you here, they'll pick you up! Hurry, hop in quick!"

Leonidas looked briefly at the yellow headlights glowing in the distance, and hopped in quickly, without any further quibbling.

"They'll pick me up too," the girl said as the car shot off like a bullet, "if they think I used that side road. The short cut. It's part of the water reservation, you know, and it's being polluted or something, and the cops are getting nasty about anyone's even being an innocent bystander or passer-by in the vicinity. And they've got me once today for speeding, and Mrs. B.'ll have kittens if I'm picked up again. She's very law-abiding. D'you happen to know the Carnavon police? They're awfully one-minded about things."

Leonidas felt a little dazed, but he managed to pull himself together and answer.

"Er—so I had gathered."

"It's the new mayor," the girl continued. "He's being a new broom. Sweeping clean, and all. Look, this is a tragic mistake!"

Leonidas murmured in complete agreement.

"Were you really making for the Hills? *Did* I tell you Hills instead of Center? Mrs. B. insisted that I must have—oh, those cops! I'm just going to slow down and make 'em go by! I hate having cops trail behind me, don't you?"

"M'yes," Leonidas said. "I do. May I ask—"

"Thank heavens!" the girl said. "They're turning off at that short cut. Inspecting their old water works, I suppose. Well, Mrs. B. said I'd confused you, and I said it wasn't possible after all our phone talk and planning about buses. I said if you'd come early, you were probably going to the Hills on an errand—for my sake, couldn't you tell her that you were visiting a friend, maybe?"

"Gladly," Leonidas said. "In fact, I am."

"Oh, that's fine! We've got time enough. How in the world did Mrs. B. ever find out you'd arrived? Did she see you at the bus stop?"

"A number of people saw me at the bus stop," Leonidas told her truthfully. "Er—I'm going to Forty Bald Pate Hill."

"Marcus Meredith's?" the girl chuckled. "He and Mrs. B. are squabbling violently at the moment. I've been carrying notes back and forth between 'em like a pneumatic tube. I tell you what. I'll leave you at Marcus's, and go on and get the pigeons. Tell me, why *do* you want pigeons?"

"Er—I don't."

"There, that's what I told Mrs. B. I said you simply wanted a stuffed dove, and you weren't adamant about that. And the next thing I knew, she'd grabbed the phone and ordered a coopful from a pigeon fancier. Now," the beachwagon came to a stop at the foot of a driveway, "the turn by Marcus's porte-cochere is simply lousy with pot holes. I don't think I could bring myself to plough through 'em again today, unless you really mind walking in. Should you mind not being delivered to Marcus's very door?"

"I feel," Leonidas got out, "an overwhelming sense of deliverance just to be here. Thank you so much for the—er—lift."

"My dear man, don't thank me. It's practically providential that I found you at all," the girl said. "I never expected to. I thought Mrs. B. had made a mistake—why, it's a *cap!*" She seemed for the first time to be aware of his headgear. "I thought you were wearing a deerstalker!"

"My hat blew away in a gust of wind, and a man on the bus gave me this. He was a churn salesman." In the presence of this girl, Leonidas thought, it was amazingly easy to improvise. "Electric churns, of course. Er—can you see my sickle on the car floor back there? Thank you again. Good-bye."

"Why not leave your stuff, sickle and all, right in the car? By the way, is the sickle a part of your act?"

"Yes," Leonidas said. "But I think I'll take it with me. It's a specially made tool, and I have to be careful of it."

"Okay. I'll toot for you in about ten minutes, after I've collected the birds. Oh—if Marcus hasn't made other arrangements, I'd be glad to take him along, too. I know he plans to go. Don't keep me waiting, will you?"

Leonidas politely assured her that he would not.

"And," he added, "if I am not out here, you may take it for granted that I have gone. Er—with Marcus. Good-bye!"

He drew a long breath as he pushed the front doorbell button of Marcus's vast, old-fashioned, brown-shingled house.

In many ways, the girl in the beachwagon was the most confusing element this expedition had thus far brought forth. There was nothing of the harpy about her, like the Wimpernel. There was nothing furtive about her, like the man with the harp. She was both articulate and candid. But who she was, what she was talking about, who she thought he was, were all questions for which Leonidas had no ready answer. He was not, furthermore, going to befuddle himself by pretending to answer them. In his mind, the girl in the beachwagon would take her place with the Wimpernel and the man with the harp; each would be a fascinating topic to speculate about during some long winter evening in the future.

He noticed, as he thrust out his thumb to push the doorbell again, that the door was open a fraction of an inch. So, instead of ringing, Leonidas pushed at the door, and walked in.

On the threshold of the pleasantly cluttered living room he paused expectantly, and then felt a little anxious when he discovered that Marcus wasn't there in his favorite leather chair by the fireplace.

That Marcus might not be at home was a thought which hadn't occurred to Leonidas before, and it bothered him. Perhaps he had already gone out, as the girl said he planned.

Back in the hallway, he scanned an instructive little note in Marcus's handwriting which was pinned to the servants' bell pull. He had forgotten that it was Thursday, and the servants' day out, which accounted for the lack of attention paid to his door-bell ringing. Marcus was hard of hearing.

Leonidas walked along the book-lined hall to the south wing. If Marcus were home, he would be in his study.

Knocking perfunctorily at the door, Leonidas opened it.

Then he stood in the doorway while his words of greeting and explanation froze on his lips.

Marcus was home.

Marcus was lying there on the rug by the mahogany desk.

Marcus was dead.

And never, either by accident or intent, could Marcus have inflicted on himself the brutally violent blow that had caused that horrible head wound.

Marcus had been killed.

While the thousands of volumes in the book-lined study floated before his eyes, Leonidas forced himself to assimilate that fact.

Marcus had been killed.

With fingers that trembled, Leonidas put on his pince-nez, and suddenly, out of the room's blurred details, two white objects on the floor near Marcus achieved form and shape.

Those white objects were rubbers. They were, furthermore, Leonidas's own, made to order rubbers.

His own white rubbers, that he had left behind on that bus at the Four Corners.

CHAPTER 2

LEONIDAS stood there for a moment, clutching his package and his cane and his evening paper and his sickle under one arm. Then he tiptoed across the room, set his packages down on a chair, and knelt beside the body.

Marcus was dead. And he had not been dead very long, for the stains on the carpet were still wet, and the hands on the shattered face of Marcus's watch, which had fallen out of his pocket onto the brick hearth, had stopped at exactly seven o'clock. It was now quarter after seven.

Apparently, Leonidas thought, while Marcus was sitting at his desk, he had been hit over the head from behind with such terrific force as to knock him out of his chair.

And Leonidas knew what had been used as a weapon, too. It was the loving cup that lay on its side, next to its ebony base, on the mantel. The large silver loving cup with the smear of blood on one of its sharply angled handles.

Without looking, Leonidas knew the inscription on the cup: "Presented by the Headmaster and the Board of Trustees to Marcus Meredith on the event of his sixtieth birthday, and the two-hundredth anniversary of the founding by Elihu Meredith of the institution then known as Deacon Meredith's Lyceum of Latin and Greek, and perpetuated by his family and descendants as Meredith's Academy for Boys."

Irrelevant details of that dinner last October flashed through Leonidas's mind. He remembered the excellence of the fillets mignon, the blushes of the Academy football captain making his first speech in his first dinner jacket. He recalled Marcus's suave, scholarly wit as he accepted the loving cup—which, he later confided to Leonidas, put him in mind of an Etruscan burial urn of the Middle Hallstatt period.

Biting his lip, Leonidas took another look at the rubbers. They were his. He didn't have any need to reassure himself by reading over his name stencilled inside. They were the rubbers he had had made to fit his thick-soled English walking shoes, with a high cut ankle to cope with the Dalton thaws. They were his own rubbers that he had left on the bus, the rubbers that the driver had yelled at him to come back and get.

And now they were here!

Leonidas banished his impulse to take the rubbers, put them on, and go from Marcus's house as fast as his legs could carry him. This couldn't be managed in any such simple fashion. It was not just the certainty of being picked up by the Carnavon police for those charges of the Scarlet Wimpernel and Mr. Potter that held him back. Nor the fact that Marcus was his friend, and to leave now would be unbefitting. The whole hideous truth was that the presence of those white rubbers injected a personal note whose significance could not be overlooked.

For Marcus to be murdered was one thing. It was awful enough. But for Marcus to be murdered by someone who left Leonidas's own rubbers behind as a false clew or visiting card—that was more than awful, Leonidas thought. That bordered on the diabolical.

He would have to find someone whom he could tell his story to. Someone who would listen and believe him and help him convince the police.

The rubbers, to be sure, were nothing but circumstantial evidence, and false circumstantial evidence at that. But this was murder. He had no alternative but to summon the police. And the police were not always as perspicacious about circumstantial evidence as they might be. Even giving them the benefit of every doubt, Leonidas thought, suppose that the police actually did accept his honest statement that he had simply come to the house to see Marcus, and had found Marcus dead on the study floor. It was beyond the realms of human conjecture that they should not immediately request a recital of his previous movements that evening, and a minute description of his trip to Marcus's house. And, of course, the reason for his visit.

And there was the rub.

Any such recital would disclose the whole chain

of fantastic events—his exit from the bus, his pursuit
by the Scarlet Wimpernel, the charges she had made
against him, the incident of Mr. Potter's cash register
and the man with the harp, and all the rest. In the light
of those bizarre items, the police would not be likely
to brush the rubbers away with sportive comments
about circumstantial evidence and the fallacy of be-
lieving what you saw. Nor would the police be inclined to consider his visit as anything remotely akin
to a casual social call.

Leonidas sighed.

Perhaps, instead of leaping into this ghastly blaze,
he would have been wiser to have remained quietly in
the frying pan of the Scarlet Wimpernel. He was even
beginning to look back on the Wimpernel and the bus
trip as the Good Old Days.

Turning his head so that the still form on the
floor was out of his line of vision, Leonidas sat down
and pondered.

Neither Demosthenes nor Patrick Henry could
orate their way out of this, single-handed. He would
have to find someone of force and reputation who
would make the police listen to him.

But Colonel Carpenter, the obvious person to call,
had left by plane that very morning to visit some of
his old Marine Corps friends in Panama. Cassie Price,
the Colonel's sister, would be another ideal person to
summon. But Cassie was in Finland, rehabilitating left
and right with the Red Cross. He had plenty of other
true and honest friends, but not one of them was capa-

ble of grasping this situation. If, Leonidas thought, he
couldn't grasp it himself, he certainly couldn't expect
understanding from his more literal-minded friends.
He ran through a mental list of all the people whose
telephone numbers he knew, and rejected them all.
Not one possessed the mental elasticity to accept the
first and foremost fact, that someone had killed Marcus
Meredith, and left Leonidas's white rubbers behind
at the scene of the crime.

"But who could have?" Leonidas asked himself.
"Who could have!"

In the first place, there were so few people who
even knew that he was wearing rubbers! There was
the bus driver, for one. The bus driver knew he'd left
the rubbers in the orange bus, and had loudly pro-
claimed the fact. But bus drivers drove buses. It was
not the function of a bus driver to follow a rubberless
passenger through alleys, driveways, snowbanks, hardware stores, through the miles of snow and slush that
separated the Four Corners from Carnavon Hills! The
driver was on the bus to drive it, and the passengers
were there to be driven, and Leonidas could not see
that either had any business to become involved with
his rubbers.

On the other hand, there was the Wimpernel.

Could it have been possible that when she left the
bus to pursue him, she took his rubbers with her?

That was possible, Leonidas conceded. The Scarlet Wimpernel was not a one to hesitate at filching
rubbers, if she happened to feel like filching them.

But how in heaven's name could the Wimpernel have known that he was going to the house of Marcus Meredith, at Forty Bald Pate Hill, Carnavon Hills? Until young Mr. Potter had broken the news that the police were hunting him, Leonidas hadn't thought of Marcus. Not until he had fled from the hardware store had he actually made up his mind to go and see Marcus. Unless the Scarlet Wimpernel were wired for thought transference, she couldn't possibly have known his destination.

Then there was young Mr. Potter.

But if young Mr. Potter had ever suspected that he might eventually make his way to Marcus's, Leonidas thought, young Mr. Potter would have forthwith informed the police to that effect.

Besides, how could Mr. Potter have come into the possession of those rubbers?

He might have met up with the Scarlet Wimpernel, who might have had the rubbers, and together they might have accomplished this feat of whisking the rubbers from the bus to Marcus's.

Leonidas shook his head. That would be straining coincidence to the breaking point.

Actually the only person who knew that he had come to Forty Bald Pate Hill was the girl in the beachwagon. But she knew nothing about the rubbers. And Marcus had presumably been killed before she stopped the beachwagon out by the driveway entrance. At seven o'clock, she had been hurtling through the slush of the county road, chatting about pigeon fanciers and a stuffed dove, and someone named Mrs. Bee.

"Maundering," Leonidas said. "Lame, frustrated maundering, all of it!"

Getting up, he took a cashmere shawl from the couch arm and walked slowly across the study to where Marcus lay.

Before he could carry out his intention of spreading the shawl over the crumpled figure, the shawl dropped from his hands.

Unable to believe his eyes, Leonidas stood and looked down, and then he polished his pince-nez again and put them on.

In his agitation he had first looked only at Marcus's face and at that brutal head wound. He had not given more than a brief, cursory glance at the rest of the body.

But now, as he stared down, he found himself faced with the bewildering fact that Marcus Meredith had no left leg!

Incredulous, Leonidas knelt down and found it was true.

Marcus's left leg was missing. The trouser leg was empty to the knee.

And it was no recent loss. Apparently, Leonidas thought as he got to his feet after completing his investigation, apparently Marcus had lacked a left leg for many years!

Had such news been told him by some casual

friend, Leonidas would have questioned its authenticity. But it was true. And now that he considered, there was plenty of evidence from his own experience to prove that Marcus's left leg had been missing ever since Leonidas had known him. For Marcus never engaged in any sport more violent than chess. He had never driven a car. He rarely took walks that might be described as long. He usually carried a cane, and he always had a slight limp. Why, Leonidas could not recall, but it had always been the consensus of the Academy faculty that the limp was caused by his father's gout, which Marcus had inherited along with the school.

He was, Leonidas decided, almost more dumbfounded by this missing left leg than by Marcus's being killed. Sudden death might come to anyone, but few men could conceal a false leg over a period of thirty years!

"Where," Leonidas said aloud, "is it?"

He hunted around the study, under the couch, under the desk, and even in the closet, but he could find no artificial leg, nor any brace, nor any sign of anything which might have fitted that arrangement on Marcus's left knee.

Leonidas frowned.

There must be something. There had to be a leg there somewhere! It wasn't possible that Marcus could sit alone in his study without having a leg, so to speak, at hand. But there wasn't any leg. There wasn't even a cane.

Leonidas made another tour of the room, and then suddenly stopped short in his tracks as a series of metallic sounds emanated from the basement directly beneath him.

Those were no ordinary furnace noises, Leonidas thought. Those were no regulation cracklings of contracting heater pipes.

Someone was down there, moving around, deliberately banging at pipes!

"So!" Leonidas murmured. "So!"

Tiptoeing over to the fireplace, he pulled from its rack above the mantel a six-inch flintlock pistol. Some hundred and forty years before, that weapon had probably been the pride of some former Meredith. Now, Leonidas freely admitted to himself as he slid it into his coat pocket, it was a bit out of date. It was useful neither for assault nor for protection. But if the person roaming around the celler was in any way involved with Marcus's death, that weapon, backed by determination, could conquer the time element. It was, at any rate, the only weapon in sight.

Cautiously, Leonidas crept along the hall to the serving pantry and on into the kitchen, where he looked at the single track of muddy footprints on the linoleum floor.

Then he went on to the entryway at the head of the cellar stairs, and paused.

Having descended to Marcus's dark room on several occasions, Leonidas knew more about the cellar than he did about the upper floors of the ark-like house.

That cellar was hewn out of the rock layers of Bald
Pate Hill, and the door by which he stood was the
only way of entering or of leaving, unless his pipe-
thumping intruder chose to gnaw out a subterranean
tunnel with his teeth.

Flintlock in hand, Leonidas affixed his pince-nez
and waited.

In about five minutes, he heard footsteps coming
up the stairs.

The door swung open, and a man stepped into
the entry.

"Reach!" The barrel of the little flintlock ground
into the small of the man's back. "Reach, if you
please!"

The man reached.

Simultaneously, Leonidas recognized the trench
coat and the plaid scarf.

It was young Mr. Potter!

"Walk towards the sink," Leonidas said, "and do
not turn around."

It would never do for that flintlock to be seen,
he thought, by anyone as stalwartly built as young Mr.
Potter.

"And," he added, "keep your hands high above
your head, please. High. My, how amazing! How
utterly and completely amazing! My, my!"

Mr. Potter's uplifted right hand gripped, of all
things, a harp!

A small, gilded pasteboard harp.

In fact, *the* harp.

"Shakespeare, is that you?"

"M'yes, Mr. Potter," Leonidas said. "M'yes, indeed, it is I. I wonder if—no, please do not force me to shoot you. I dislike bloodshed. Why, exactly, are you lurking in Marcus Meredith's cellar, whacking the plumbing?"

"I was not lurking! And I wasn't whacking any plumbing! I just tapped a pipe to see if it was sound. And I—"

"Mr. Potter," Leonidas said, "don't tell me that you were examining pipes at this hour! Don't tell me that your quest for General Jobbing is so passionate that you habitually slink into cellars and test the efficiency of pipes by hearty thumpings!"

"Listen here, Shakespeare, I came here to get you, because I felt in my bones you'd be coming here sooner or later! And no one answered the bell when I rang, but the door was open as if someone had just stepped out, so I came in. And there were fresh logs burning on the living-room fire, and I thought Meredith would be right back. And in the meantime, I went down in the cellar to have a look at the pipes and the heater. Meredith asked me yesterday about replacing 'em. And why the hell I'm making this lengthy explanation to you, I don't know! You're the lad that ought to be doing all the explaining!"

"Keep your hands up!" Leonidas said. "I'm sorry that it was necessary to trick you at the store, but you were being so stubborn that you left me no other choice. And since you have found the harp, and now realize that I was telling you the truth about that envelope's removal, there is no call for further explanations on my part."

"I found that harp outside in the front hall here!" Mr. Potter protested. "It doesn't explain a damn thing!"

"In the front hall of this house? Marcus's house? Indeed!" Leonidas said. "Indeed! And when, may I ask?"

"When I came in!"

"M'yes. You've been here some time, I take it?" Leonidas asked blandly.

"Half an hour or so. See here, where's Meredith? He asked me to come look at his pipes! He—"

"What time," Leonidas interrupted, "did you come here?"

"Oh, seven or so! Shakespeare, I'm not going to stand for any more of this quizzing! And why you think you have any right is beyond me!"

"As a general rule," Leonidas returned, "the right of an individual armed with a lethal weapon is both unquestioned and uncontested by those not similarly equipped. Precede me, if you please, into Marcus's study in the south wing. At once, Mr. Potter. Don't force me to jab your spinal column, or resort to violent measures."

Muttering under his breath, young Mr. Potter walked along to the study.

"Now," Leonidas said, "if you will step inside, I feel you will find the scene self-explanatory."

He could not see Mr. Potter's face, but he noted that the back of Mr. Potter's neck was changing color with the rapidity of a stage spotlight. The slightly choleric purplish tinge turned suddenly white, and then as suddenly became flaming red.

"My God, Shakespeare! Oh!"

He walked slowly to the center of the room and stood there, looking down, while Leonidas followed with the pistol.

"That silver cup." Mr. Potter seemed to be talking to himself. "That did it. They got him from behind. I suppose the poor man couldn't hear 'em coming. He pitched over and out of his chair—my God! He hasn't any left leg!"

Turning swiftly, Mr. Potter pointed an accusing finger at the sickle and the brown paper package which Leonidas had left in the study.

"That sickle! And that leg-shaped package! Did you—did *you*—" Mr. Potter swallowed.

"No," Leonidas said. "No. Please cause that fantastic thought to perish at once. I did not use that sickle for any such fell purpose. I was not aware of the fact until a few minutes ago, but it appears that Marcus has always worn an artificial leg."

"That package of yours is definitely leg-shaped!"

"And if you will recall," Leonidas said, "I had that package when I came into your store. It contains stocking stretchers. Wooden stocking stretchers that one puts woolen socks on to dry. Of course it's leg-shaped! You'd hardly expect a stocking stretcher to be any other shape than leg-shaped! Touch the package. Tear it open, if you will. Convince yourself. Convince yourself, also, that Marcus has always worn an artificial leg."

Mr. Potter felt of the brown paper package, and then hesitantly touched Marcus's left knee.

"You're right. That's a socket. But if he had an artificial leg, where is it?"

"That," Leonidas said, "is a question I keep asking myself wonderingly. Where? I can't find a trace of it in this room, where it should logically be."

Mr. Potter sat down limply.

"The servants are out. There's a note left for 'em in the front hall. I read it. If he was here alone, his leg should be here! Hey, whose rubbers? Maybe they're a clew!"

"Those are mine," Leonidas said. "When I came here, they were lying beside Marcus."

"*Your* rubbers?"

"Mine."

"You mean, your rubbers were already here?"

Leonidas nodded.

"They were here when you came, Shakespeare? You didn't wear 'em? When'd you have 'em last?"

"On the bus."

"Then how in hell," Mr. Potter inquired, "did they get here?"

"That is another question," Leonidas said, "which I keep asking myself wonderingly. How?"

He still had the little flintlock in his hand, carefully held so that Mr. Potter could not realize its antiquity and general uselessness. But Mr. Potter seemed to have forgotten all about the pistol. Chin in hand, he sat and scrutinized the study.

"Hey, that's his gold watch that's broken on the hearth, Shakespeare! Maybe if it's stopped, we can tell what time this happened."

"M'yes," Leonidas said. "It stopped at exactly seven o'clock."

Mr. Potter's face turned white.

"Seven?"

"Look at it."

But Mr. Potter was already across the room, looking at the watch.

"Shakespeare, that's about the time I came! You think—oh. I see. You think *I* did this! Well, I didn't! I only knew Meredith in a business way! My chief interest in him was this heater job, and I'd hardly be so dumb as to murder a prospective customer in cold blood! I'll admit I shouldn't have gone wandering down into the cellar, but I heard this afternoon that a rival of mine was going after this job, and I couldn't resist taking a look at those pipes. Frankly and in all honesty, I was going to use you as an excuse to call here and see 'em this evening. Be reasonable! If I had anything to do with this business, I'd be over the hills and far away, now! I wouldn't have marched to the cellar and investigated his furnace!"

"M'yes. Quite so. But the fact remains, Mr. Potter, that you possess no alibi."

"I suppose you, personally, have an iron-clad alibi for seven o'clock?" Potter retorted.

"At seven o'clock," Leonidas informed him, "I was in a beachwagon with a girl who was fetching a coopful of pigeons."

"You know what?" Potter inquired. "That sounded just as if you said you were in a beachwagon with a girl who was fetching a coopful of pigeons."

"My very words. I was."

"What girl? Who was she?"

"I haven't the remotest idea," Leonidas told him.

"Well, it's certainly the peach of an alibi!" Potter said with irony. "I've got to congratulate you. That alibi's got everything. It's positive, clear, unequivocal, irrefutable. It's good! Look here, Shakespeare, that watch of Meredith's might have been hours wrong when it was dropped. It might not have been running at all. It might have stopped at seven o'clock three weeks ago!"

"True, Mr. Potter."

"And for all I know, it might even have been set ahead and purposely dropped by someone who wanted people to think this happened at seven. Someone, for example, like you!"

"To allay that suspicious gleam in your eyes," Leonidas said, "may I point out that were I the guilty party, I should have donned my rubbers, picked up my impedimenta, and similarly have departed for far away hills? As you yourself remarked, be reasonable."

Potter thought for a moment, and then he grinned.

"Was it as hard for you, Shakespeare, as it is for me? And don't you think that watch proves *any*thing?"

"That watch will indicate," Leonidas said, "just about what the police wish it to indicate. Since you were here around seven, and I came at quarter past, I think we may assume that the police will claim that the watch fell from Marcus's watch pocket and broke at seven."

"You mean, giving 'em a chance to involve both of us? But when Meredith's examined, the doctor can fix the time of his death, watch or no watch!"

"Not to a split second, the way it's done in the movies and in mystery stories," Leonidas said. "Marcus was killed not very long before I arrived at seven-fifteen. I doubt if any medical examiner will be able to fix the time with any greater degree of exactitude. By the way, didn't you hear me come? Didn't you hear the door bell ring when I arrived?"

Potter shook his head.

"I never heard a thing. And I was listening for Meredith to come back, too. Maybe the acoustics are haywire, with all those rock walls down there. Maybe the bell only rings in the pantry or the servants' quarters, or something like that. Anyway, I never heard you. Shakespeare, pretty soon someone's going to come and poke me, and throw water on me, or the alarm's going off, and I'm going to wake up with the awfullest head!"

"I felt that way myself," Leonidas said. "Unfortunately, this is all quite true."

"How do things like this happen?" Potter demanded. "I didn't have anything to do with this! But if I know the Carnavon cops, they'll have me in chains! And what it'll do to my business! That sounds," he added hurriedly, "as if I didn't realize how grim this is, and as if I didn't care about poor Meredith. And I do! I think you do, too! But you and your pigeons! And me and the pipes! The cops won't ever believe us!"

"Do I gather," Leonidas asked, "that you believe me to be innocent of this?"

"If both of us," Potter said, "weren't innocent fools, we'd never be here."

Leonidas smiled and walked over to the fireplace.

"Under the circumstances," he said, "I can return this lethal weapon to its proper place."

"Is that what you held me up with? That thing? Oh, now I know I'm going to wake up on the floor of the Chop and Bone banquet room!" Potter said unhappily. "None of this happened. If I touch you, you'll vanish into a cloud of smoke, or a herd of cattle. That harp's just a golden figment of alcoholic fancy."

Leonidas picked it up from the floor and fingered it.

"No," he said, "it is still pasteboard. Did you really find this in the hall when you came?"

Potter nodded.

"I had a notion at the time that you'd been here and gone, and left it behind. As a sort of trademark, or something. Honest to God, Shakespeare, did a man come into my store carrying that, and wearing green satin breeches and a green silk hat? Honestly? What did he look like? Can you describe him?"

"When a man is costumed as that man was," Leonidas told him, "it is not possible to describe his personal features. Fully three-quarters of his face was hidden by his hat brim and his white stock. His back was to me, most of the two minutes he was in the store. I have been wondering, Mr. Potter, if—"

"Drop the mister, will you? When two people are faced with a thing like this, the formality of handles is a little stifling. My friends call me Link."

"I have been wondering, Link, if you employ a clerk, or workmen?"

"Two."

"D'you think it might be possible for one of them to have left something in the cash register, and to have taken your envelope by mistake? Because it occurs to me that the fellow opened the register without any hesitation, while I, for example, should never have known which buttons to press down."

"Farr's in the hospital with appendicitis," Link Potter said, "and Frenchy usually wears filthy dungarees and a Mickey Mouse sweatshirt. He's comparatively new, but he's completely honest. I can't imagine his touching the cash register for any reason without speaking to me, and I couldn't visualize him dressed in green satin. Frenchy never swiped that money. Shakespeare, what are we going to do? No one's going to believe either of us, and I don't think the Carnavon cops'll feel thwarted by our lack of motive. They'll just provide motives."

"M'yes." Leonidas swung his pince-nez.

"They'll slap us into the local caboose, and there we moulder till they solve this, if they ever do. I don't know about you, but I haven't the money for lawyers. In fact, most of my assets were in that envelope. I can't afford to be jailed. What'll we do?"

"Solve it."

"Did you say, solve it?"

"Instead of mouldering in jail," Leonidas said, "it seems wiser to solve this ourselves, before the police become obsessed with false ideas. If we present them with the solution, they can hardly incarcerate us."

"There's something about those bland statements of yours that makes me feel the way a hysterical woman looks," Link Potter said. "Like biting the furniture and smashing things. Shakespeare, how can we!"

"Marcus was a friend of mine, and the person who murdered him also attempted to involve me. I intend," Leonidas said coolly, "to apprehend him. The solution of a murder does not require hordes of men and months of preparation, Link, like storming the Maginot line. It doesn't require laboratories, or elaborate paraphernalia. Men solved murders centuries before the G-man was invented, using only their native wit and logic. Er—I've done it before, myself. Perhaps you recall the Brooks case in Dalton last year?"

"No, I wasn't here. I only took over this business of uncle's six months ago, when he died. Shakespeare, those are fine words of yours, and you say 'em with feeling, but what can we do to solve this? What've we got to go on?"

"My rubbers," Leonidas said, "a pasteboard harp, and a missing leg—"

"Reach!"

Leonidas looked at Link Potter, and Link Potter looked at Leonidas, and then the two of them looked at the policeman standing in the doorway of the study.

He was the biggest policeman Leonidas ever remembered having seen in all his life, and in his brawny right hand he grasped a pistol that resembled a small field piece.

"I get it," he said. "You killed him, and now you're cutting him up. Going to toss the pieces away around the county, huh?"

"What!" Leonidas and Link Potter spoke in horrified unison.

"Yeah. I know you guys. You're the ones chopped up that old lady in Bridgefield a couple months ago. And if old Meredith hadn't spotted you, you'd have got away with this one. Turn around. I'm putting you guys in bracelets right now!"

"Spotted us?" Leonidas said. "Er—d'you mean Mr. Meredith saw us, and called you? He summoned you?"

"Yeah. He reported prowlers. Put out your right hand, you! Yeah. You're the one with the beard tried to assault that blonde, ain't you? Well, you're all washed up now, and—"

"One moment, please," Leonidas said. "Do I understand that you were summoned here by Mr. Meredith to investigate prowlers? How long ago?"

"We got the call two minutes ago. Shut up and stick out your hand—"

"It is not your intention," Leonidas interrupted, "to make any sort of investigation before jumping to these—er—visionary conclusions?"

"What've I got to investigate, huh? I know what I see! Turn around before I—"

"Look!" Leonidas cried out excitedly, and pointed toward the fireplace. "Look!"

Involuntarily, the officer looked.

Ten seconds later, Link picked himself up from the floor, and surveyed the inert form of the policeman.

"I hope," Leonidas was blandly polishing his pince-nez, "that he didn't injure you when he carried you down with him? I had no chance to warn you."

"Shakespeare, you knocked that hulk out cold!"

"M'yes. I'm really sorry. I do dislike physical violence. But when one is faced with such a stupid behemoth, one has no choice."

"Out cold! That big hulk!"

"Large men," Leonidas said, "are not always alert. They do not anticipate being hit. Will you be good enough to roll the creature over? I want those handcuffs in his pocket."

"Are you going to put 'em on *his* wrists?"

"Wrist," Leonidas said. "I think, under the

circumstances, we will link the right wrist with the left ankle."

He snapped on the handcuffs, adjusted them to the proper size with a professional flourish, and presented Link with his white linen handkerchief.

"Hey, what's this for? Come back! Where are you going, Shakespeare?"

"To the bathroom for adhesive tape. It's very efficient for gagging purposes. In the meantime, use my handkerchief in case he comes to. The key to the handcuffs," Leonidas added, "is on that key chain of his. I suggest you remove it at once."

He returned with the tape, sealed the officer's mouth, and then bound his left arm close to his body.

"There!" Leonidas stood up. "For the nonce, he's reasonably secure."

"Where," Link asked in an awed voice, "did you pick up these fine points?"

"From the excellent Haseltine."

"Who?"

"Dear me," Leonidas said, "have you never read my—er—the adventures of Lieutenant Haseltine? Or heard them on the radio?"

"You mean, 'HASELTINE! HASELTINE to the RES-CUE!' That merry blood and thunder epic? That one?"

"The worthy Lieutenant," Leonidas's eyes twinkled, "leads a life fraught with excitement and instructive detail. Police invariably turn and look when he tells them to, also. Now, will you roll this behemoth into the closet, please? There are several things I wish to investigate rapidly. The other may present more of a problem, I fear."

"The other what?"

"The other officer in the prowl car. I'm amazed that he has not come in before this. There must be another officer. There always is."

"I hadn't thought of that! What'll we do with him?"

"One of the few features of this vast structure," Leonidas said, "is its staggering stock of closets. The place is a labyrinth of closets. We shall—"

Link held up a warning finger.

"Listen! I hear someone coughing. He's coming! You play Circe and entice him in. It's my turn to biff."

The second policeman appeared presently in the doorway.

He was a diminutive little man with glasses and a head cold, and instead of a gun, his right hand clutched a package of Kleenex.

After pausing just over the threshold to wipe his nose, he addressed Leonidas, who was blocking his view of the room.

"I don't see no prowlers outside, mister. If there was any when you called, they've beaten it away now. They probally seen us—ow."

The little man went down like a log under the force of Link Potter's carefully aimed blow.

"I think," Potter said, "he can truthfully claim he never knew what hit him. Think of that big lug mak-

ing this little shrimp wade around out in the slush,
while he charged in with his cannon! There aren't any
handcuffs in his pocket, Shakespeare. Shall I use tape?"

It was the work of a minute to tape the little
policeman, truss him up, and roll him into a cupboard.

"It's exhilarating, isn't it, once you get into the
swing of this sort of thing?" Link commented. "I feel
I could biff cops, and hog-tie 'em, and roll 'em into
closets all night. I've put some paper tissues into Pee-
wee's hand, and fixed it so he won't choke—Shakespeare, what's the meaning of this prowler business?
You didn't call the cops. I didn't. Meredith didn't.
Who did?"

"Without doubt," Leonidas said, "the same individual who killed Marcus and left my white rubbers
beside him."

Link stared at him.

"You mean that someone put in a fake call about
prowlers, so that the cops would come rushing here
and find you? And me?"

"To assume that the murderer knows of our
presence here is to assume that he is watching the
house, and has had it and us under surveillance for
some time. I doubt that," Leonidas said, "very much.
While he may not be very far away, I am sure he is
well over the hills, so to speak, and well out of sight.
It is my feeling, Link, that this person is particularly
anxious to have the police come here and discover the
murder. And my white rubbers, and the pasteboard
harp. And the missing leg."

"But why? I should think that the longer the period before a murder's discovered, the more chances the murderer has to get away, and cover up his tracks, and stuff like that. Why should he want it discovered right off the bat?"

"Probably," Leonidas said, "because an early discovery best suits his purpose. One might even conclude that the murderer is very sure that he himself will not in any way be involved. Or, conversely, that someone else most certainly will."

"Now," Link said, "you're putting this into the conspiracy class."

Leonidas smiled wryly as he swung his pince-nez.

"If you will recall, Link, you will remember that the Carnavon police not only had an accurate description of me when they were hunting me on those charges manufactured by the Scarlet Wimpernel. They also knew my name. She did not know my name. But the name is stencilled on my rubbers."

Link ran his hand through his hair.

"Shakespeare, I can't think of words to say, I can only make noises! I don't get this! What's it all mean?"

"It means that someone gave the police my name, and that by this time, my name has been wafted over police radios and tapped out over police teletypes, and very likely, the Dalton police are camouflaged as snowbanks, waiting to pounce on me the instant I start up my front walk."

"Shakespeare," Link said, "I think we'd better give up right now! What can we do?"

"We have so much to work with," Leonidas said, "that the problem is not so much what to do, as what to do first." He walked over to the desk. "Shall we investigate the rubbers, or the harp, or the leg, or shall we delve into the possible identity of this person who is so actively anxious to set the police to work?"

"Personally," Link said, "I don't see how you can do anything about any of 'em. The only thing I can deduce is that the murderer's a man."

"Indeed," Leonidas said. "Er—why?"

"Why, it would take a man to deliver a blow like that. And it would have to be a man, if he called the cops and said he was Meredith, reporting prowlers. A man can sound like a woman over the phone, but it's almost impossible for a woman to sound like a man. Isn't that so?"

"M'yes."

"And you wouldn't be likely to have any cherchez-la-femme angles involved, anyway. No Scarlet Wimpernels would ever tackle Meredith. Not even from acute hunger. Women are definitely out."

"But I wonder," Leonidas said, "if it—"

He broke off abruptly at the sound of a siren whining out front.

"Shakespeare, that's another police car!" Link said. "Another!"

"Not another," Leonidas returned. "Several, I think. Let us investigate."

Hurrying into the darkened dining room, the

two of them peeked out from behind the long window draperies.

At the foot of the driveway were the yellow lights of a prowl car which was apparently stuck in the slush.

Behind that was another.

Behind the second was a third.

Behind the third, and under a streetlight, was a patrol wagon.

As they watched, each vehicle began to disgorge policemen.

CHAPTER 3

IT seemed to Leonidas that even the running boards and the fenders were sprouting policemen.

"Riot guns!" Link said. "And look! Tommy guns! Shakespeare, it's a blitzkrieg! What do we do now?"

"I fear," Leonidas said regretfully, "that we have not enough closets to accommodate all of this vast swarm. Hm. I think that we—"

"Look! They're forming a flying wedge, or a hollow square, or a phalanx or a buttress—they're going to make a sortie! Nope, they're not either. The boys from the paddy wagon forgot something. Tear gas, I shouldn't wonder. Maybe they mislaid their halberds. They've got everything else but a battering ram and the kitchen sink!"

Leonidas took him by the arm.

"We have," he said, "just about two minutes. Let us utilize them to the fullest."

"Going to beat it out the back way? My car's parked in the lane—"

"No. Put the chain across the front door, and come to the pantry. Quickly, please!"

Out in the pantry, Link watched in bewilderment while Leonidas divested himself of his coat and necktie.

"Strip tease?" he inquired.

"Help me on with that butcher's apron, please. I am going to be William, Marcus's butler. Tie it carefully."

"You can't, Shakespeare! They'll spot your beard and grab you! Let me—"

"William has a beard, mercifully. Now, the white coat behind the door. Isn't there a bow tie on an elastic? William always wears one. There! On that hook. And get that pair of shell-rimmed glasses from the sink ledge. Now, find me a broom."

Link rushed out into the kitchen and rushed back with the glasses and the broom.

"There is nothing so disarming," Leonidas said, "as a broom. Now, you comb your hair, Link, and get that harp, and that stuffed moose head in the study. Quick."

"What?"

"You heard me. Quickly!"

"What'll I do then?"

"Linger in the background and provide local color if I'm successful. Otherwise," Leonidas smiled as a series of peals on the door bell was accompanied by a series of thumpings on the front door, "otherwise, you run, and find someone to bail me out."

At the door, Leonidas purposely paused and

fumbled with the lock and the safety chain, as William always did. Aside from the fact that he had a beard, Leonidas thought, he did not resemble William at all, but William's shaky voice would not be hard to approximate.

"Coming!" he said. "Coming!"

"Open up!"

Leonidas swung the door open wide and stood there, broom in hand, gaping at the array of weapons aimed at his person. If any went off, he thought, he could hardly escape being shot in one vital portion or another.

"Oh! Oh, dear!" he said in a voice that was almost a squeak. "Oh, dear me! What's wrong now, gentlemen?"

"Where's the men?"

"Men, sir? What men would you mean?"

"I men the mean—I mean, the men attacking Mr. Meredith! What's going on?"

"On, sir?" Leonidas cupped his hand to his ear. "Did you say on, sir?"

"Yes, on!" the sergeant on the top step prodded Leonidas with the barrels of his sawed-off shotgun. "What's going on? We got a call Meredith was being attacked, and the men was trying to kidnap him! Where are they?"

"Dear me!" Leonidas said tolerantly, "it must be more of the lads' work!"

"What lads? Listen, who're you trying to kid, huh? Who are you, anyway?"

"I know him, sarge," one of the policemen from the lower step spoke up. "He's Meredith's servant. Butler. I seen him around. I think he's a little deaf, sarge."

"Deaf, hell! He's dumb! Listen, you, what lads you talking about?"

"Mr. Meredith's the owner of Meredith's Academy, sir, and this is initiation night—my, what a time we've had, sir! What a day we've put in! What an evening! Two coffins were delivered here about an hour ago! And the calls—oh, the telephone calls! And the telegrams! It's been horrible! Let me call Mr. Link! Mr. Link'll explain it all to you, sir. He's one of the masters at the Academy, and he's been trying to quiet poor Mr. Meredith."

Link came forward.

"Mr. Link," Leonidas said earnestly, "this calling the officers is more of the lads' pranks—will you explain to them about the initiation? And show them the moose head, sir. And the harp, and all. Tell them what's happened!"

Link's momentary hesitation worried Leonidas. A member of Chop and Bone, he reflected, ought to be quicker on the uptake.

But Link rose majestically to the occasion.

"I've just called the doctor," he said in a hushed voice. "Mr. Meredith's very upset. Could you—I hate to ask you—but could you be just a little quieter out there? Thank you. It's the annual initiation at the Academy, you know, and although we always expect a certain amount of horseplay, and make allowances for it, the affair has simply overstepped all bounds today. They're annoyed with Mr. Meredith for having changed the dates of the spring vacation, you see. Look at this moose head here!" Link held it up. "We found this in the refrigerator!"

Leonidas took heart from the couple of snickers rising from the rear ranks of the police. But the sergeant was still far from satisfied.

"Yeah?" he said. "Yeah?"

"And this harp." Link displayed it. "We found one kid in Mr. Meredith's bathtub, with this harp in his hand. He was dressed like an angel. With paper wings and a smile. We had to send him back to the Academy in a blanket!"

The sergeant's face softened.

"The coffins were the worst," Link went on. "The kids had even ordered a man sent along to measure Mr. Meredith for one. His blood pressure's pretty bad, you know, and he can't stand that sort of thing. If he finds out about you, I'm afraid he'll have a stroke. It's going to distress him."

"Well," the sergeant said, "well—"

"I'll see," Link said, "that you're put at the head of the list of people he's going to apologize to tomorrow. He has—was that his bell, William?"

"Yes, sir," Leonidas said. "I'm afraid he's heard the gentlemen, sir. Will you go to him?"

"I'd better," Link said. "Sergeant, if I were you, I'd disregard any further calls you may have to come

here, unless they come from me, or William, personally. Tell him about the other officers, William."

"Yes, sir," Leonidas said, as Link retired along the
hall. "There was two officers come here a few minutes
ago, sir. Said they had a call about prowlers. A big
man and a small man. Mr. Link asked if they'd hunt
around through the woods and make sure none of the
young devils—beg pardon, sir, I mean the lads—was
there. Between you and me," he lowered his voice confidentially, "it wouldn't be a bad thing if the whole
bunch of 'em got a good tanning, working Mr. Meredith up like this! And—"

A bell, which Leonidas recognized as the little
silver bell on Marcus's dining room buffet, tinkled
twice.

"Oh! He wants me, sir! Will there be anything
else, sir?"

"Well, no," the sergeant said. "If he's sick, I won't
bother him, but tomorrow—"

"Yes, sir. Didn't you drop that?" Leonidas pointed
to the neatly folded bill which he had been treasuring
in his moist palm throughout the interview. "That's
yours, sir. Mr. Meredith will see you tomorrow.
Oh, there's the bell again! Good night, sir!"

He closed the door hurriedly, and quietly affixed
the safety chain to prevent any possible skeptic among
the group from making a surprise entrance.

Then, creeping into the dining room, he watched
with Link while the swarm departed.

"I have a nasty feeling," Link said, "that one of

those paunchy ones in the rear was the fellow that got me for speeding—Bill Shakespeare, what's this fatal charm you exert? How d'you manage to make people do what you want 'em to? How'd you get away with that?"

Leonidas smiled.

"With the possible exception of the adventures of Lieutenant Haseltine," he said, "I know nothing so instructive as teaching small boys over a long period. It is rarely possible to make a person do what you wish, but if you provide a certain amount of atmosphere, you can occasionally suggest what you wish a person to feel. Is that the last car going? Good. Now let us prepare to leave."

"After all that, you're going to leave here?"

"M'yes," Leonidas said. "If two or three of those officers pause and ponder, they may conceivably figure out that they have been duped. The simple expedient of telephoning the Academy for corroboration would put us in a most embarrassing position. We have succeeded in forestalling our friend who wishes this to be brought to light, and I like to think that if he summons the police here on some other pretext, he may find them sufficiently annoyed to take some steps toward discovering his identity. Will you take these—er—props back to the pantry, and bring me my things? I want to take one more look around the study."

He was examining the date pad from Marcus's desk when Link returned to the study.

"Look, Shakespeare, you're going to take those rubbers with you, aren't you?"

Leonidas shook his head as he put on his coat and necktie.

"I should like to," he said, "but the rubbers were here, and I don't feel I have any right to touch anything that was here. By the same token, we shall leave the harp where you found it. Actually," he reached out for his overcoat and painter's cap, "I do not really wish to leave here at all. But then, we have observed both the spirit and the letter of the law, and left policemen in charge. Perhaps we had best take a look at those two before we depart."

Both officers were secure, and neither had made the slightest headway towards freeing their adhesive bonds.

"I think, myself," Link commented, "that Pee-wee's cold sounds better. Maybe it's the moth stuff in the cupboard. I've got an aunt in Bangor who always uses moth balls to cure snuffles. Shakespeare," he shut the cupboard door, "just exactly how do we start tracking down this fellow?"

"Er—I am not so sure," the corners of Leonidas's mouth were twitching, "that we have a fellow to track."

"I see," Link said. "You've decided it's all a matter of mirrors?"

"Look," Leonidas said, "at Marcus's date pad on his desk. I was about to call your attention to it when those sirens sounded."

Link grabbed the pad and hastily read the list of names written in Marcus's small, scholarly handwriting.

Then he blinked and read it again.

"Er—you perceive," Leonidas said, "what I mean."

Link put the pad down on the table top and felt it carefully. Then he picked it up again and shook it.

"It's real," he said. "It has length, breadth and thickness. And it says Thursday the fourteenth. That's today. Or is it? I seem to have lost all sense of time. Bill Shakespeare, did you read this list of names? Did you see the same names I see? Myrna! Topsey!" he looked at Leonidas and raised his eyebrows. "Myrna. Topsey. Judy. Ellen. Evelyn. All listed on his date pad for this evening!"

"M'yes," Leonidas said. "I feel we should consider that list before assuming that Marcus's murderer was a man. A woman could strike that blow, Link. The cup itself is heavy enough so that a great amount of force behind the blow would not be necessary. And there would be ample time to take careful aim, because the chances are excellent that Marcus never heard the person creeping up on him. And there are plenty of contraltos who sound quite masculine over a telephone. The order girl at my grocery store is virtually a basso profundo. M'yes. I do definitely feel we should consider that list."

"Myrna," Link said. "Topsey. Judy. Ellen. Evelyn. Well, there's just one solution to all that! Meredith was naming a grandchild."

Leonidas pointed out that Marcus was unmarried, and, to the best of his knowledge, possessed no children.

"Or—er—grandchildren."

"It's horses, then. These are his selections for five races."

"I considered that possibility," Leonidas said. "Marcus had a weakness for betting on horses. But don't you feel they're rather normal names for horses? Besides, Marcus preferred horses with five or six syllabled names. Tulsamundle Toothpick was one of his particular favorites."

"He was naming someone's child in a radio contest," Link said firmly. "Or a new cold cream. Or toilet soap."

"Perhaps you will notice that there are no radios in the house?"

"Boats, then. A yacht. Or dogs. Or maybe a batch of Pullman cars. I tell you, Bill Shakespeare, he was naming *something!*"

"Marcus was not a man to clutter up his date pad with irrelevant and extraneous data," Leonidas returned. "If Marcus troubled himself to put a name on his date pad, I think we may assume that Marcus had some sort of engagement with the designated person."

Link tugged at his hair.

"But five women! Five! Look here, Bill," Link said, "Meredith's come into the store, often. I've spoken with him. He was a pillar of the church, and all that sort of thing. Maybe you've known him for years, and maybe you know him better than I do, but you'll never be able to convince me that he had dates with five different women, beginning with someone named Myrna! If Meredith ever even saw anyone named Myrna, it was purely by accident at the movies! Myrna! Topsey! Judy! Ellen! Evelyn! No, Bill. Never. Not in fifty million years!"

"I suggest," Leonidas said, "that you observe yesterday's page."

"My God!" Link said. "Evelyn and Topsey!"

"M'yes. On Tuesday," Leonidas told him, "Topsey and Judy are both mentioned. On Sunday, Topsey and Evelyn. In this month's pages, you will find that everyone but Ellen is noted at least four or five times."

Link tossed the pad on the desk, and shook his head.

"It's incredible," he said. "Simply incredible. As my aunt in Bangor says, you just don't ever know, do you? A man lived next door to her for seventeen years, and when he died, they found he was a woman. In a small way, I know how she felt. Where are you going with that sickle and package and stuff?"

"I hope," Leonidas said, "that you are going to get your car so that we may start out without any further delay."

"And where are we starting to? How do we begin? What do we do, go to the Four Corners, and yell 'Myrna! Topsey! Judy! Ellen! Evelyn!' at the top of our lungs?"

"No," Leonidas put on his pince-nez. "No, we

are first going to find the girl with the beachwagon,
I think."

"The girl in the beachwagon? You mean the one
that'd be your alibi if you knew who she was, or what
time Meredith was killed?"

"M'yes."

"What fun!" Link said. "What peachy fun! Do
we lasso every beachwagon we see, or do we just
tramp from garage to garage, trying to pick out the
right machine? Listen, Bill Shakespeare, how can we
ever find that girl?"

"It seems to me," Leonidas said blandly, "that in
a place the size of Carnavon, we should have no un-
surmountable difficulty in finding a beachwagon that
was transporting, or had recently been used to trans-
port, a coopful of live pigeons."

"And if we don't," Link said, "I suppose we can
just snoop around and find out who keeps pigeons,
and then find out who took some? I can just see us,
meandering from dove cote to dove cote! And what
do you want the girl for anyway?"

"She knew Marcus, she'd been here before today,
and she knows someone who was squabbling with
Marcus and writing him notes. I like to think she will
cast some light on those names. Now," Leonidas said,
"before we go, I think we should formulate some sort
of program in the event of one of us becoming separated, by some trick of fate, from the other."

"Separated," Link said. "Separated. That's a lovely
way of phrasing it. In crasser language, come the cops,

and one of us gets pinched, we ought to have a plan?"

"In so far as it's possible, I feel that the—er—free one should carry on. If we are separated by chance and not by the police, suppose we arrange to meet again at your store. Have you an extra key that I might have?"

Link took one off his key ring.

"Here you are. Now, I'll go and get my car and bring it to the foot of the drive. There's no sense in your wading through the snow and slush to that back lane."

"Perhaps, on your way," Leonidas said, "you had better toss the cannon belonging to that large policeman into some handy snowdrift. I'll meet you by the driveway post."

"Okay." Link rushed off.

After a final peek at the policemen and a final survey of the study, Leonidas walked slowly out and stood in the shadow of the tall stone driveway post.

Below to his right, Carnavon Center and the Carnavon valley stretched out, peaceful and twinkling in the moonlight, and looking, Leonidas thought, for all the world like a village on a greeting card. High above, to his left, a New York–bound plane droned across the sky, and somewhere in the hills behind him he heard the chugging of a freight on the Boston and Addbury circuit.

A car flashed along the county road, and Leonidas idly watched it swerving around corners as it mounted Bald Pate Hill.

The car slowed to a crawl as it passed by Marcus's driveway, and it seemed to shrink to the edge of the road, as if some invisible obstacle were in its way.

Something began to click in Leonidas's mind.

Once before that evening, another car had done just that, had gone through that same maneuver of circling far to the side of the road.

It was the car whose driver he had asked the way to the station, when he had been hunting a cab, before he had fled into Link Potter's store. That was the car that had circled out of his way around a puddle, the car whose driver had pointed, but had not let his voice be heard.

Leonidas leaned against the driveway post, and pondered.

Not more than four minutes after that car went by, the Scarlet Wimpernel had reappeared on his trail.

And now that he thought of it, in his rapid retreat from the orange bus, he had a sense of the same car having passed by him several times. In Dalton, it was customary for drivers who couldn't find parking spaces to circle endlessly around the same block, while one of the car's occupants shopped frantically.

But this was in the evening, Leonidas told himself. Carnavon matrons would not be likely to be shopping madly after six on a Thursday evening, nor would their long-suffering husbands be block-circling at that hour. You couldn't explain away that car as simply as all that.

Could it be possible that someone was actually

watching him, following him, trailing him, and that the Scarlet Wimpernel was really a part of all this?

Leonidas shook his head.

The viscid, fluctuating tentacles of the octopus of fate, he thought, could be stretched just so far.

But it *was* possible.

He hadn't intended to get off the bus at the Carnavon Four Corners. His ticket was for Dalton. So was the Wimpernel's. He had seen it. When she first sat down beside him, and before she had begun to exert her wiles, Leonidas had even gone so far as to help her tuck her ticket stub into the metal slot of the seat ahead.

Still, the Wimpernel had followed him off the bus.

And if she had any connection with the ubiquitous sedan, that meant that the sedan must have been following the orange bus, all along.

He rejected his next thought.

He had rejected that same thought before, and he was going to continue to keep it out of his mind until he had gone through the list of names on that date pad.

Those names came first.

Leonidas's eyes opened wide at the sound of someone approaching.

That would be the Wimpernel, he thought. The sedan had dropped her off, and now she was tripping back.

But it was only a spotted setter who trotted up the drive. He sniffed at Leonidas, and trotted down the road again.

Feeling thwarted, Leonidas peered out between the drive posts. It was time for Link Potter to be getting back.

At the end of ten minutes, Leonidas impatiently set out to find him, prudently keeping inside Marcus's evergreen hedge.

He had progressed some fifty feet through the snow when a beachwagon, coming from the direction of Carnavon, swerved into the driveway so sharply that a rear fender grazed the stone post. Leonidas could hear the crunching sound from where he stood, but the mishap was ignored by the driver of the car, which bounded along over the pot holes in the driveway and finally rocked to a stop with a tremendous screeching of brakes.

Leonidas smiled.

He recognized those strident brakes.

But the woman who got out of the car was not the girl with the peasant kerchief tied around her head.

She was older. And wider. And differently dressed.

She bustled up the steps, pushed open the door, and disappeared inside.

Leonidas followed her.

He had thought, when he came out, that he had shut that door securely. But apparently the metal weather stripping was so jammed that the door popped open again. Which, he decided, accounted for much of what had gone on.

He walked in and stood in the doorway of the

study, to which she had at once gone. It was pleasant, for a change, to stand there and look accusingly at someone instead of standing within and being accusingly stared at.

From what he could see of the woman as she knelt on the floor, she was dressed like the other women he saw shopping at home in Dalton every day. There was nothing unusual about her dark blue coat and dark blue dress. Nothing unusual about her in any way. Except, he amended as she turned around, her hair. Her jet-black hair had one of those startling white streaks running through it.

"I was here in this house at half past six," she said, "and he was alive. And now he's dead, and he hasn't any leg!"

Leonidas found himself slightly taken aback by her announcement. Here was a woman at the scene of a murder who didn't instantly assume that she would be considered guilty by the first person who appeared. Conversely, she took it for granted that the first person who appeared was equally innocent.

"Are you," he inquired, "Myrna?"

"What!"

"Ellen, perhaps? Or Evelyn? Or—"

"I know you!" the woman said. "You're Cassie Price's Bill Shakespeare, aren't you? The one who used to teach at Marcus's school. Thank heavens, you'll know what to do. What *do* you do in a case like this, call a doctor, or a policeman?"

"You're a friend of Cassie's?" Leonidas demanded.

"Yes. She told me all about you at lunch one day last spring, just before she went abroad, and when I was in the throes of moving out here. I'm Mrs. Beaton."

"Topsey!" Leonidas said. "Topsey Beaton! You're the one who crossed Tibet on a bicycle, and kidnapped a gang of Chinese bandits!"

"It was a camel. And only one bandit. Cassie exaggerates so! You should have heard what she told me about you. Fantastic things. And she said she'd tell you to call—"

"She did. I forgot. And if only," Leonidas said, "I'd remembered you earlier!"

"Well, I told her I'd have you to dinner, but I forgot you, too. Shakespeare—I can't remember your name—this is simply frightful!" She crossed over to where he stood. "What shall we do? I came here at half past six, and he was alive and well! This is too frightful!"

"M'yes. Er—why did you come?"

"About that silly forsythia."

"What?"

"Marcus and I are both on the park commission, and he wanted a formal garden for the station park—it seems hideous to talk about this now! Anyway, he had a fixed idea about making it a formal garden. Maybe you've had some experience with Marcus's fixed ideas? You know what happens?"

"Marcus became suddenly very deaf," Leonidas said promptly, "refused to discuss the problem because of his infirmity, and bombarded you with notes in an effort to make you capitulate out of sheer exhaustion. Colfax told me today that he was taking a terrific barrage about the Academy's next Speech Day. So Marcus has been writing you notes about formal gardens?"

"About twenty a day for the last week," Mrs. Beaton said with a little sigh. "But today's have been more about domineering women who come to a town and try to run it than they have about formal gardens. It's so absurd, because what I said or thought wouldn't matter a whit! We had a forsythia budget. I came here tonight after that last vituperative gem of his, and told him so. I simply held him in his chair and screamed at him. I said, 'We have a forsythia budget, and stop writing those foolish notes!'"

"Er—why did you return?" Leonidas asked.

"Oh, that rummage!"

"I'm so sorry to keep asking you why and what, but what rummage? Why?"

Mrs. Beaton sighed again.

"You don't really want to go into that now, do you? It's all so involved! Shouldn't we call a doctor or the police right away?"

"If you don't mind, I should like to know now."

"Well, I'm chairman of the rummage sale and entertainment at the church tonight, and when Judy came for that last note, she forgot to get the rummage Marcus had for me. I came back for that. And to make peace. I like Marcus, and he was furious at me for screaming at him. I don't often lose my temper, but I lost it at him tonight. I felt badly about it before, but

now I'm simply wretched! Shakespeare, this is awful!
Oh, I need a handkerchief, and I haven't got one!"

Leonidas presented her with his.

She wiped her eyes and blew her nose.

"Tell me," Leonidas said, "is Judy the one with
the kerchief over her head?"

"Yes. She's my son's secretary, but I borrowed
her when I was running the Community Fund last
fall, and she's so useful, I kept her. Judy Brett. I sent
her for you and the pigeons and the rummage, but—"

"For me?"

"Yes," Mrs. Beaton said. "I told you this was involved! You see, I saw you get off the bus at the Four
Corners, and I thought you were Gregory Hornblower. You know him."

"I'm afraid," Leonidas said, "that I don't. I—oh,
please keep the handkerchief!"

"Thanks. Hornblower's the one that's been divorced six times. Of course," Mrs. Beaton added
hastily, "I only saw your back and your hat. I was in
the center lane, waiting for the red light."

"Do I look like a man who's been divorced six
times?"

"It was the hat. Hornblower wears a Homburg
in his publicity pictures. Anyway, I thought you were
Hornblower, and then I decided you weren't, because
you didn't act like a stranger. You just marched away
as if you knew where you were going. Then I saw
you again on Ridge Road when I came back from

Marcus's, later. And when I got back and found Hornblower wasn't there—"

"Er—at the rummage sale?"

"No. I'm chairman of the Foreign Events committee of the Club, and Hornblower's tonight's lecturer. I didn't realize that the lecture and the sale collided—Judy kept a last year's desk calendar because she liked the picture on it, and she's completely disorganized my social life with it."

Leonidas put on his pince-nez. "Er—you're running two things at once?"

"I warned you this was involved! But it's working out. The Club meets in the auditorium across from the church. Anyway, when I found Hornblower hadn't come, I decided you were Hornblower after all, and I sent Judy to get you."

"But she was hunting a man with a beard!"

"Hornblower had a beard in his publicity pictures," Mrs. Beaton said, "but it seems he shaved it off. He came a few minutes after Judy left."

"Where is he now?"

"Lecturing. Judy's handling that, and Evelyn's taking care of the sale."

Leonidas sat down.

"Evelyn—you call it *E*velyn, and not *Ev*elyn. I gather Evelyn is a man. Er—would he know Marcus?"

"Evelyn simply knows everyone. He's goaded Marcus to exasperation, trying to wangle old gym equipment from the Academy for his Boys' Club. Evelyn's our rector."

"M'yes," Leonidas said. "Evelyn is the rector, you are Topsey, and Judy is your secretary. M'yes. Does Judy—"

"Will you believe that she came back not only without Marcus's rummage, but without you, and with ducks?"

"Ducks?" Leonidas said.

"Ducks."

"Er—I thought she was fetching pigeons."

"She said the pigeon fancier had flown the coop, and there wasn't anyone there but some small chickens in a yard, and some ducks in a slatted box. So she brought back the ducks instead of the pigeons. Shakespeare, we ought to—"

"Why pigeons, anyway?" Leonidas inquired.

"Shakespeare, I don't resent your asking me all these questions. After all," Mrs. Beaton said, "you came on me in a frightful situation, and I think you showed control in not denouncing me. But don't let's waste time with pigeons. We ought to call someone!"

"Those birds," Leonidas said, "have been haunting me for an hour and a half, and I should like to have them cleared up. Were they rummage?"

"Rummage? Of course not! They were for Hornblower's lecture. 'Peace in a Troubled World.' He wanted a stuffed dove, but I thought live pigeons would be more effective."

There was just a touch of defiant self-righteousness in her voice that made Leonidas look at her sharply. Cassie Price sometimes used that tone when she was on the defensive.

"Well," Mrs. Beaton said, "if you want to know the truth, I didn't want Hornblower. I think he's a windbag and a humbug. But the rest of the committee thought he was glamorous—those six divorces, of course! So they voted me down. So I ordered Hornblower. And the pigeons."

"But why?"

"Oh, dear, it's one of those things Cassie would understand," Mrs. Beaton said, "better than you probably will. I met Hornblower's third wife in Bombay last year. She was charming, and I liked her, and Hornblower had treated her very badly. She told me, and the fact stuck in my mind, that he was allergic to pigeons. They give him hives. There, now you know! And now, let's call—what's that funny noise?"

She pointed toward the cupboard.

"That," Leonidas said, "is a policeman with a cold."

"A what?"

"A policeman with a cold. Er—if you listen very carefully, you may hear an occasional rustle from the closet. That is another policeman. Should you care to see them?"

Mutely, Mrs. Beaton watched while Leonidas opened doors and displayed the trussed up police.

"You see," Leonidas said, "I was here first."

"*You* did *that* to *them?*"

"Only the big one. Link Potter accounted for the other. You see, Mrs. Beaton, when I came here at quarter past seven, I found Marcus lying there, and my rubbers, those white rubbers, lying beside him."

"Those rubbers were here? Your rubbers?"

"M'yes. Er—would you care to hear the whole story?"

"I certainly should," Mrs. Beaton said. "I certainly should!"

"Then perhaps," Leonidas said, "you'll come into the dining room? I want to watch for Link Potter, who should have been here fifteen minutes ago."

Mrs. Beaton silently followed him along the hall.

"Now," Leonidas said as they came to a stop by the dining room window, "will you listen very closely? I'm going to begin with an urgent phone call from Professor Carl Colfax in Tilbury, begging me to come and inspect his first-folio Shakespeare which had just arrived, and which turned out to be a facsimile, and not a very good facsimile. Er—are you ready?"

"Go on."

Three minutes later, Leonidas concluded his precise summary.

"There," he said. "That is the jist of what has taken place. You know everything."

"I owe Cassie an apology," Mrs. Beaton said. "She doesn't exaggerate. What she told me about you is a miracle of understatement. Shakespeare, this is a lot worse than I thought anything could be. Hm. So that folio was a copy?"

Leonidas nodded. She had pounced unerringly on the thought which had kept occurring to him, and which he had been rejecting until he could clear up the other minor points.

"Hm," Mrs. Beaton said. "Hm. That harp was in the hall here when I came. The front door was ajar, too. I told Marcus a month ago to have that weather stripping fixed. We'll have to find that man with the harp, Bill Shakespeare, and we'll have to find that leg. Or do you have a horrid suspicion that the leg may find you?"

"Somehow," Leonidas swung his pince-nez, "I picture that leg in my house at Dalton, don't you? I'm sure it will be left in some place where the police can most conveniently find it and implicate me at the same time. It will be very hard to explain the possession of someone's left leg. It will be equally hard to dispose of a left leg. But those are bridges we can defer crossing. Can you be of any assistance on Myrna, or Ellen?"

Mrs. Beaton shook her head.

"I thought of servants, but William's wife is named Geraldine, and I'm sure she and William do all the work. Marcus never has laundresses or cleaning women. I don't know a soul in Carnavon named Myrna. The only Ellen I can think of is Mrs. Spoffard's new grand-daughter. Was your first idea to go through those names on the date pad, and eliminate them?"

"More or less," Leonidas said. "If the people had called, or phoned, or spoken with Marcus, I thought they might provide some sort of clew. Possibly Myrna might have seen someone bearing white rubbers in as she left, for example."

"Hm. Those rubbers," Mrs. Beaton said. "I was working up to them. By the way, why white rubbers?"

"They're easier to identify," Leonidas explained. "They save me the nuisance of being given the wrong rubbers in check rooms, and I don't have to grovel around the floors of people's closets, trying on a dozen pairs before I find mine."

"Shakespeare, I saw a man pick up those rubbers at the Four Corners!"

Leonidas surveyed her through his pince-nez.

"Were you saving that fact for a—er—rainy day?" he inquired.

"I told you I saw you and thought you were Hornblower. I was in the center lane, waiting for the light to change. The Boston bus was drawn up by the curb at the bus stop, about two car lengths ahead. You rushed away, and then the bus driver flung something white after you. And then a man got out of a sedan parked directly behind the bus, and picked the rubbers up. Only of course I didn't know they were rubbers, then. It was too dark to tell."

"Then what? Did you see the girl, the Scarlet Wimpernel? What happened then?"

"The light changed."

"D'you mean that you just drove on!" Leonidas said.

"Certainly."

"How could you?"

"Why, I'd already decided you couldn't be Hornblower," Mrs. Beaton said, "and I didn't know they were rubbers. I didn't give the matter a second thought. I just drove on. I know it's tantalizing not to be able to add anything more, but that's all I saw."

"Can't you," Leonidas said, "even describe the man?"

She reminded him that it was dusk.

"He was simply a man in a dark overcoat. I think he had a moustache, but I'm not at all sure. I was really more interested in the red light, because I was terribly late getting back from the orphanage. I'm chairman of the Visiting Committee, and this was Visiting Day. What did you say?"

"Er—nothing," Leonidas said. "I just cleared my throat. Mrs. Beaton, I'm getting very worried about Link!"

"He's probably having to dig his car out of the slush in that back lane. Judy got stuck there yesterday, and it took a troop of hiking Boy Scouts to pull her out. Shakespeare, at least we know that the sedan that's been dogging your footsteps must have been trailing the bus. And the man in the sedan got your rubbers— d'you know what's going to involve me in this just as surely as your rubbers are going to involve you? It's simply tragic!"

"Er—what?"

"Evelyn," Mrs. Beaton said. "Evelyn saw me leaving the church when I set out earlier to come here and yell at Marcus. And he rushed out and asked where I was going. And I told him, to Bald Pate Hill to pound some sense into Marcus Meredith's head if I had to use a club, and that I was going to stop that nonsensical note-shuttling if I had to do it over Marcus's dead body. And a lot of other things, all on the same order. It's simply tragic that Evelyn, of all the people in the world, should have heard me say those things!"

"But certainly he wouldn't take it seriously, would he?" Leonidas asked. "For example, I've often heard Cassie say she was going to murder her cook and quarter her maid, but if the cook were murdered and the maid quartered, I should never feel that Cassie was the person responsible for the deeds."

"You don't know Evelyn! He took me seriously," Mrs. Beaton said. "He grabbed my arm and read me a little lecture about loving my neighbors and not putting forth my hand in anger. Oh, of course I didn't mean a single, solitary word of it, and I shouldn't have said it, and I wouldn't have, if I hadn't lost my temper at Marcus's last note! But I tell you, the minute Evelyn hears that Marcus has been killed, he'll rush straight to the police and denounce me."

"Practically no one," Leonidas said, "could be that idiotic!"

"You just don't know Evelyn! He reports unlicensed dogs. And over-time parkers. And the number plates of cars that don't stop before entering Stop-before-Entering streets! You can always count on that boy to do his duty at all costs. He believes that the laws of God and man are firmly interwoven. He'll tell you all about it at the drop of a hat. And the police adore him. He tumbles with them. He boxes with them. He's Honorary Chaplain to the police department. Oh, dear," she drew a long breath, "we've simply got to get started and get this thing straightened out! Come on!"

"As soon as Link comes—"

"Shakespeare, we can't waste time waiting for that boy to get his car unstuck! And don't suggest that I drive up that lane and get him. We'll just get stuck there, too! When he gets out, he'll come here, and when he finds you've gone, he'll just go to the store and wait for you, as you planned. I don't know the boy, but his store's just around the corner from the church. It'll all work out beautifully."

"But," Leonidas said, "I—"

"Judy can pop over at intervals, and bring him to you when he comes. Now, I've really got to get back and see that everything's running smoothly. Evelyn and Mrs. Spoffard can cope with the rummage and the entertainment at the church. Nothing can go wrong there. But I'll have to keep a guiding hand over Horn-blower's question period. Someone's sure to bring up divorce. They can't miss it. And I've got to check up on the caterer. He hadn't sent the spun sugar when I left, and we were short three dozen cakes. Come on."

"Er—what," Leonidas asked, "do you plan to do with me? Perhaps I'm wrong, but I had the idea that you and Link and I were going to see what we could do about this murder. And—"

"My dear man, we are!" Mrs. Beaton assured him. "We are. But I can't just let these other things slide. If I don't put in an appearance at the church or the Club, people will start hunting me, and Evelyn will be sure to see if I've come here, and that will simply ruin everything!"

Leonidas suggested that she might possibly succumb to an imaginary headache, and use that as an excuse to withdraw from both functions.

"And then have people—and Evelyn—see me bustling around half an hour later? Certainly not. We've got too much ground to cover. People are used to seeing me bustling around all over the place. We can bustle all over town and no one will say a thing. With a headache, I'd have to keep out of sight, and that would be much harder. Now, you must go to the church."

"I beg your pardon?" Leonidas said courteously.

"You'll be safest there. You can't stay here. There's no telling when some policeman might take it into his head to drop back. And you can hardly wander around the streets of Carnavon with the police hunting a man with a beard. And besides, the man in that sedan might catch up with you. You can't tell what might happen. The church is the best place."

"M'yes, it's the traditional refuge and all that sort

of thing," Leonidas said, "but I think, myself, that I had best go to Link Potter's store—"

"And have some eagle-eyed citizen report you as a marauder? I wish," Mrs. Beaton said, "that you wouldn't deliberately try to make things hard. If you go to that store and put the light on and sit there, the police have only to stretch out a hand to get their man with the beard. If you roam around the store in that half light, the way they leave stores, someone will be sure to spot you. Just you let Link Potter go there first, and Judy'll bring him to you. St. Anselm's is definitely the place for you."

"You mean, I'm just to sit there?" Leonidas said.

"After all this rushing and dashing and racing and chasing around that you've done tonight, you ought to welcome the chance to sit quietly and think. When Link Potter turns up, we'll send him to your house to see if anyone really did put Marcus's leg there. Now, come along!"

Leonidas found himself being propelled toward the front door.

"That weather stripping," Mrs. Beaton continued, "is disgraceful. Take the key out, and let's see if we can't manage to lock the door from the outside."

"You can't," Leonidas said. "The door won't come to enough."

"Oh, well, we'll just have to leave it, then." Mrs. Beaton started down the steps. "Merciful heavens, look at that fender! Did I do that, or did Judy, I wonder?"

"You hit the post," Leonidas told her as he followed her down the steps, "when you turned in the driveway here. Is it badly crumpled?"

"Yes. See? It isn't the denty kind of thing where someone just hammers it out. It's torn. I don't think cars are as good as they used to be, do you? Not as sturdy. Cassie said it seemed to her that she just bought one fender after another."

Leonidas smiled.

"Radiator grilles are her particular specialty," he said. "The garage gives her wholesale prices on them —Mrs. Beaton, duck! Here comes—"

"More police?"

"The Wimpernel!"

CHAPTER 4

DUCKING down beside Mrs. Beaton, Leonidas slowly edged along the side of the beachwagon and peered over the hood.

It was the Scarlet Wimpernel, without any doubt at all, picking her way through the slush and the puddles, her pointed hat bobbing jauntily in the moonlight, the folds of her wimple wafting to and fro in the wind.

"Let's grab her!" Mrs. Beaton whispered over his shoulder.

"No! Wait!"

"Why?"

"See what she does!"

"I want to grab her."

"No!"

Mrs. Beaton shrugged.

Leonidas knew how she felt, for it was his impulse to grab the girl, too. But it was wiser to bide their time and find out exactly what this wench was up to.

Humming a little tune under her breath, the girl tripped past the beachwagon and up to the front door.

On the top step, she reached out her hand toward the doorbell, and then she paused and proceeded to renew her lipstick and powder her nose. Then she straightened out her stocking seams, and rearranged her wimple, and smoothed out the shoulders of her tightly-fitting, cossack-like scarlet coat. Then, after drawing her wide scarlet belt up another notch, she gave one final hitch to her girdle, and rang the bell.

She waited a moment, and rang again.

Finally she descended the steps, and started back down the driveway.

Leonidas, who had crept up behind a small hemlock, was waiting for her as she jauntily tripped past.

Jamming his cane tip between her shoulder blades, he barked out a gruff order.

"Stick 'em up!"

At once the girl let out a noise resembling the death call of a banshee.

"Help!" Her throaty voice achieved a resonant crescendo. "Help! Murder! Police! Help! Murder! Police!"

As if in response to her clamorous appeal, the yellow lights of a Carnavon prowl car promptly headed into the driveway.

Mercifully, the car stuck in the slush at the turn, just as the first car of the previous police detachment had stuck.

"Help!" the girl rushed toward the car. "I been shot at!"

Two officers jumped out.

"Where?"

"I been shot at! Help! I been shot at!"

"Where?"

In soft snow up to his knees, Leonidas crouched behind the hemlock and hoped that Mrs. Beaton was out of sight behind the beachwagon. He kept one eye on the car as he listened to the conversation between the girl and the officers.

If, he mentally amended, one could accurately term it a conversation. It was more like listening to a badly scratched phonograph record that repeated the same thing, over and over again. The girl continued to reiterate her original statement, with the insertion of a trilling little giggle, that she had been shot at. And the two policeman kept asking interestedly where.

When the girl had been thumped with obvious relish by both officers, and the fact established that no lethal wound had been sustained, the atmosphere cleared at once.

The atmosphere, in fact, became practically jovial.

"Well, toots, you're okay! Sound as a dollar!"

"Say," the girl said, "you won't never know how gratified I am to you, Mr.—er—"

"Harrigan. But just you call me Butch, huh? This is my cousin Skinny."

"I certainly am pleased to meet your acquaintance," the girl said. "And I got to say, you come in the tick of time! Honest, I was so petrified, my knees was just like water!"

"I guess it was pretty lucky I forgot my flashlight when we was up here before," Harrigan said. "Say, Skin, you know what I bet? I bet this is more of them kids' work."

Skinny agreed.

"What kids?" the girl asked.

"The kids at this school of Meredith's. They're having an initiation, like."

"An what?" the girl asked.

"An initiation, sort of. Like you get initiated. Like riding the goat, and wearing funny costumes, and all sort of crazy stuff like that. You know. Skin, ain't that young Dr. Bailey's beachwagon up by the door there?"

"Looks like it. He must have come to see the old man."

"But nobody's home!" the girl said. "I rang the bell, and nobody answered. Nobody's home."

"They probably didn't answer because they thought it was the kids, I bet," Harrigan said. "Say, Skin, let's run them kids the hell out of here, huh?"

"Yeah. Let's. Where you suppose they are, hiding?"

"Sure," Harrigan said. "Probably behind some of these trees. Let's get 'em and run 'em in. I'm sick and tired chasing guys with beards. If you want to know what I think, I think there's something phony about

all this guys-with-beards stuff. Let's show the little
girl here some action. Just you watch us, toots, and see
the way we do it in Carnavon."

"Go get me a flash, and let me help you!" the girl
said. "Gee, this is thrilling. Just like G-men!"

Leonidas heard something moving behind him.

He twisted around.

It was Mrs. Beaton, who had apparently circled
the house and made her way to him through the screen
of bushes to his right.

"Well?" she whispered tartly.

"Make for the hedge."

The two of them progressed from the inadequate
shelter of the small hemlock to a clump of arbor vitae,
and were well on their way to the evergreen hedge by
the road when the Scarlet Wimpernel dropped her
flashlight.

And the pencil-like beam focussed directly on
Leonidas and Mrs. Beaton.

Without any ado, the pair took to their heels.

Leonidas's only consolation, as he punctured his
way through the soft snow, was that the police would
probably still think they were roistering Academy
boys, in costume, and not start blazing away at them.

White things flapping in the breeze yards ahead
of them puzzled Leonidas momentarily.

Then he diagnosed the fluttering objects, and
forthwith received a sudden and brilliant inspiration.

It might well not work out, but it had worked

out very well for the embattled Finns. And after all, Leonidas thought, he and Mrs. Beaton could not plough on forever, being pursued by determined policemen, through knee-deep snow the consistency of Jello.

It all depended on the clothespins. If there weren't any clothespins, he would at least try.

There weren't!

"Swerve right!" he said to Mrs. Beaton, and snatched the flapping sheets from the clothesline as he passed between the posts.

Then he swerved to the right, grabbed Mrs. Beaton's arm, and hustled.her along towards the lattice work of the drying yard beyond.

"Here!" Leonidas held out a sheet.

"What on earth—"

"Finns," Leonidas said. "Put it on. Fall down. Quick!"

He helped her, hurriedly swathed himself in his clammy sheet, and flopped heavily down into the snow.

Holding his breath, Leonidas waited.

"Hey, Skin!" Harrigan sounded as though he were on top of Leonidas. "Skin, where'd they go?"

"Hell, I don't know! Look in the clothes yard!"

"I did."

"Where's their tracks?"

"Hell, I don't know! This place is all trampled up here. They must have cut around you, Skin, and gone over to the woods."

"Okay. Let's go there, then."

Leonidas heard the sound of them ploughing on in the direction of Bald Pate woods.

When he dared to lift his head, the pair had disappeared from sight. Presumably they were forging on through the woods.

"In all the days of my life," Mrs. Beaton said, "I never went through anything like this! Never! Never even anything remotely resembling this!"

"Cassie told me," Leonidas returned as he brushed the snow from the back of his collar, "that you once spent two days on Mount Washington in a February blizzard, with a lost guide and a party of sixteen, all of whom you personally conducted back to safety. If that is true, I'm sure that was immeasurably worse than this."

"Six," Mrs. Beaton said. "Not sixteen. Cassie does exaggerate! Shakespeare, if we had grabbed that girl when I wanted to grab her—"

"We should promptly have been grabbed by Harrigan and Skinny," Leonidas said. "Bear that in mind. And now, let's cautiously go back and get her, and whisk her off before those two come back from the woods. Very cautiously, because if she makes any more of those banshee noises, we'll have this to do all over again."

"God forbid!" Mrs. Beaton said. "And I've simply got to get back to Hornblower. Sneak along, quickly!"

Leonidas obediently sneaked along, with Mrs. Beaton at his heels.

Finally they made their way around to the side of the house, and Leonidas peered out from behind a pine tree.

The Scarlet Wimpernel was nowhere to be seen!

"Where is she?" Mrs. Beaton demanded.

"Gone. Look, there's the light she dropped. It's lying right there, still going."

"Hm," Mrs. Beaton said. "If she didn't even bother to pick that up, then she raced right away from here the minute those cops started after us. I wondered if she wasn't rather running with the hounds. Hm. Well, let's be on our way. I've no doubt that someone's got Hornblower going full steam on free love this very minute back at the Club."

But Leonidas refused to be propelled toward the beachwagon.

"Mrs. Beaton," he said firmly, "it is my desire not only to hunt for that girl, but—"

"My dear man, if the Scarlet Tanager or whatever you call her came in that sedan that's been following you, then she's gone away in it. There's nothing we can do about it. If she came here on her own, I've no doubt we'll find her again, sooner or later."

"Er—what gives you that impression?" Leonidas asked.

"Sometimes I think you're not quite as quick as Cassie claimed," Mrs. Beaton said. "She told me your brain worked like chain lightning. Look, didn't you tell me that the Potter boy has her scarlet pocketbook,

the one he found in your pocket, back in his hardware
store?"

"I assume it's still at his store," Leonidas said. "I
don't know. I didn't ask him."

"The point I'm making isn't where the pocketbook is," Mrs. Beaton said. "My point is, the girl hasn't
any pocketbook now. She has a lipstick and compact,
but no pocketbook. No money. No funds. She isn't
going to get awfully far from Carnavon, if she's on
her own and broke. And she's not going to be difficult
to trace, in that outfit, even if she does manage to pick
up a ride from some truck driver or other. Now, will
you please come along?"

"Link Potter," Leonidas began, "is—"

"Is probably frothing at the mouth, to use Judy's
expression, at his store this minute! Now, Bill, come
along before those police get back! There's absolutely
nothing constructive you can do about the Scarlet
Woman or the Potter boy, and I'm sure you don't
want to go through any more nonsense with Harrigan
and his cousin, do you?"

Leonidas sighed, and walked over to the beachwagon.

"When, at some future date, Cassie Price asks me
what I think of her friend Topsey Beaton, I am going
to be able to say with perfect truth that she is an ad-
mirable woman, with a distressing tendency to be
right."

"Pooh!"

"But," Leonidas added as she hit the other rear fender going out the driveway, "but not completely infallible."

"I skidded!"

"Er—that's the point I'm making," Leonidas said. "One does skid sometimes, doesn't one?"

"It was the slush," Mrs. Beaton said, and proceeded down Bald Pate Hill with a certain disconcerting directness.

It was not, Leonidas thought, that she cut corners and shaved curbings. It was rather as though she had drawn a mental line between the place she was in and the place she intended to go to, and in so far as it was physically possible, she followed that line.

She finally pulled the beachwagon up at the curb in front of a large, imposing, and brightly lighted edifice.

"Dear me!" Leonidas put on his pince-nez. "Is that a church?"

"Evelyn loves floodlights," Mrs. Beaton said. "And since he installed that neon cross, people are always dropping in and asking what the feature picture is. Now, I'm going across the street to the Club. Hm. Nine-fifteen. Not as late as I thought. Hornblower should be through by half past. I'll see that he is, and take over, and send Judy for Potter. Hm."

"Don't you think that—"

"Wait, I'm thinking about this. Then the question period, and then food. I'll have to stay during the questions, and then I'll pop over here and have a look at things before food. Then I'll pop back, and handshake, and then come over here to wind things up. People always leave the Club early, but they hang around here until the last gun is fired. We've got dancing in the East Room. Well, I can finish off the Club by quarter to eleven, and we should be able to get away from here by eleven, or a few minutes after. Hm. The youngsters will be dancing in the East Room till five minutes to twelve, but Evelyn will have to take care of them and shoo them out. There! Now, what were you going to ask me?"

"Er—ask you?"

"You started to ask me if I didn't think something or other."

"Oh," Leonidas said. "M'yes. Back there, near the question period. Frankly, it's been—er—dashed from my mind."

"Well, then everything's settled. Judy will get Potter, Potter can go to Dalton to your house, and if anything comes up, Potter or Judy can take care of it. Now, you go along in. Just take a seat in the rear of the hall, and listen. There's entertainment, and music—"

"Sopranos?" Leonidas inquired.

"Only one. And—"

"Will she be the kind who hangs appils on a lilock tree, and yopens wide her lettuce?" Leonidas demanded. "If so, I shall wait in the alley."

Mrs. Beaton laughed.

"She's a good soprano. You won't resent her. And there's a dulcimer."

"What *is* a dulcimer?" Leonidas asked. "I never was sure."

"As far as I'm concerned, it's an instrument owned by a deserving man Evelyn knows. You run along in, and sit, and listen, and think how we're to go about this. If anyone strikes up a conversation, just say that you're a friend of mine, waiting for me, and you wonder how I ever find time to do so many things. The other person will carry on the conversation from there. You can spot Evelyn. And Mrs. Spoffard, the subchairman. She looks like a penguin with a stiff neck. Go along!"

As Leonidas slowly started along the wet sidewalk, she called to him.

"And do take off that silly cap!"

Leonidas, who had completely forgotten all about his painter's cap, removed it and thrust it in his pocket.

Mrs. Beaton waved at him, and bustled off across the street.

She was right, Leonidas thought as he started up the shovelled flagstone path that led to the church vestibule. It was wise and sensible for him to stay there quietly until something could be thought out and organized.

He knew it was right and sensible, but he still owned to an irresistible desire to slip around the corner and make his way to Link Potter's store.

Leonidas paused on the flagstones. Then he turned.

As he turned, he saw a policeman watching him curiously from the corner he had intended to slip around.

And, at the same time, a vigorous young man in clerical clothes burst from the vestibule and leapt down the steps toward him.

"My dear fellow, we'd almost given you up entirely!"

The policeman, apparently having lost all interest in Leonidas, strolled off down the street.

"My dear fellow, come in!"

Leonidas disengaged his elbow from the young man's grasp, and put on his pince-nez.

If this were Evelyn, he was a younger, heartier and far more ebullient Evelyn than he had expected to find.

"Er—you are Evelyn? The rector?"

"Yes, yes, dear fellow, come in!"

"Er—I am a friend of Mrs. Beaton's," Leonidas said. "She—"

"Yes, we know!"

"Er—you know?"

"Yes, yes, dear fellow! We got the message about you."

"From Mrs. Beaton?" Leonidas demanded.

"Yes, dear fellow, yes! We know all about you! Everything!"

"Indeed?" Leonidas felt sure that Evelyn didn't

begin to know everything, but this certainly was no time to delve into the matter at any length.

"Come in, dear fellow." Leonidas found himself led inside the vestibule and trundled toward a carved oaken bench. "Sit down, and I'll call Mrs. Spoffard."

He went up the wide, red-carpeted stairs two at a time, and almost at once he leapt back and pressed a pink handbill into Leonidas's hand.

"The program! I'll be right back!"

He bounded up the stairs again, paused at the landing, and bounded back.

"I say, perhaps you'd care to wash? May I help you tidy up a bit?"

"Thank you, no," Leonidas said firmly.

He was mussed, and his feet hadn't been dry for hours, but he did not intend to have this hearty young man valet him.

"Quite sure, dear fellow?"

"Quite. Er—definitely."

"May I take your bundles?"

Leonidas looked down at his brown paper package and his paper and his sickle and his cane, which he had automatically brought in from the beachwagon.

"If you refer to these—er—chattels," Leonidas said, "I prefer to keep them here, thank you. I look on them as old friends. We have been through much together."

"Oh. Oh," the young man said dubiously. Then he brightened. "I see. Perhaps it's all your make-up?"

"Yes," Leonidas felt it was simpler to concur than to discuss the situation. "M'yes, indeed."

"Oh. Then you're all ready to go on. I see. I'll tell Mrs. Spoffard."

Once again the young man bounded up the stairs.

Hastily putting on his pince-nez, Leonidas examined the pink handbill. Now that he had committed himself, he thought, it might be wise to see for what.

The handbill was both an advertisement and a program for the Colossal Rummage Sale, sponsored by the Women's Friendly Society of St. Anselm's, and under the direction of Mrs. Sebastian Beaton.

Colossal, Leonidas decided after a preliminary survey, was the word.

He had not suspected from Mrs. Beaton's casual remarks about rummage that she was referring to anything quite so colossal and stupendous. Clearly, the sale, which had begun at eleven o'clock that morning, was only a flimsy excuse for volcanic activity on the part of the Friendly Women.

At noon there was a special luncheon for children, followed by movies, games, and a circus. Then there was a cake sale. At six-thirty there had been a chicken-pie supper.

Then things really got under way.

The supper was followed by three two-minute talks on "Our Building Fund," "Our Boys' Club Treasury," and "Our Larger Monetary Needs." Then members of the Boys' Club, under the direction of the Reverend Evelyn Leicester, were scheduled to give a tumbling exhibition. Then Mr. Leicester led a brief Community Sing.

Leonidas drew a long breath. He was already beginning to feel tired, and he hadn't even got to Part Two, Entertainment and Music.

He ran through the list of performers. There was the soprano whom Mrs. Beaton had mentioned, and the man with the dulcimer. Then there was a string quartet, a barytone, and someone billed as Todestriano, Maestro of the Violin.

"Dear me," Leonidas murmured. "I hope I'm not supposed to be Todestriano! Or a barytone, either!"

He couldn't find anything else on the program that Evelyn might have mistaken him for. Certainly no man in his right mind would take him for Mickey's Swing Four, which concluded the entertainment!

Concluded it, that was, except for The National Anthem, whose verse was to be rendered by the Reverend Evelyn Leicester.

Probably, Leonidas thought, Evelyn would be the only person with that much breath left in his body.

He looked up to find himself being sharply scrutinized through a platinum lorgnette.

Laying aside his packages and the pink handbill, Leonidas got to his feet, bowed from the waist, and spoke to the woman standing before him. She was obviously Mrs. Spoffard, for she fitted to a T Mrs. Beaton's description of a penguin with a stiff neck. The resemblance was accentuated by a white vest-like strip of lace in the front of her black velvet dress.

"Er—good evening," Leonidas said.

"Good evening."

She continued to stare at him.

Leonidas bowed again. It had always been his impression that the boys of the Lower Sixth at Meredith's could excel a reviewing general when it came to a head-to-toe inspection, but this woman's contemplative stare outdid the Lower Sixth's. This stare bordered on espionage.

"I didn't expect you to look like this," she said at last.

Leonidas was spared the necessity of answering by Evelyn, who bounded up.

"The Bard!"

"What?" Mrs. Spoffard said.

"The Bard!" Evelyn's 'a' was very, very broad.

"I beg your pardon," Leonidas said, "but I trust that you are—er—referring to me?"

Mrs. Spoffard looked confused, and Evelyn looked shocked beyond words.

"I said, 'Bard,'" he said. "'R,' you know. Barrd. I hadn't quite placed you before, although you looked very familiar to me. Don't you think it's clever makeup, Mrs. Spoffard?"

"Well, yes, I suppose it is," Mrs. Spoffard said in an aggrieved voice. "But I don't understand what it's for! I don't see why he needs any makeup or anything!"

"I'm sure," Evelyn said, "that it must be another of dear Topsey's inspirations. Now, shall we get

started? Bring along your packages and things, dear
fellow, and put them in my office. Come along, Mr.—
er—er—"

"Budenny," Mrs. Spoffard said.

"Er—what?" Leonidas asked.

"Well, that's the way it kept sounding over the
phone," Mrs. Spoffard said plaintively. "It must have
been an awfully bad connection. I thought you were
some sort of foreigner. Budenny. That's what I *told*
everyone it was. Isn't Budenny near enough? I hate
explaining everything all over again. It was bad
enough, just explaining Budenny once."

"Budenny," Leonidas told her, "will do beautifully!"

He still wished that he knew what it would do
beautifully for.

"Well, then, come on," Mrs. Spoffard said. "Just
bring your things with you. The quartet's using the
office. At least, they were supposed to. I *told* them to.
You can leave them on a chair."

"Er—the quartet?" Leonidas said.

"No, no, your clothes! And Evelyn, I don't understand what's become of that friend of yours with
the dulcimer. You'd better hunt him up. Come along,
Mr. Budenny."

Leonidas followed her from the oak-panelled
vestibule through a door into a long narrow corridor.

"I don't understand," Mrs. Spoffard said over her
shoulder, "how Mrs. Beaton wants this done. She
didn't tell me. There's not a word about it on her list.

Not a word. I've had to figure you out, all by myself."

She sounded, Leonidas thought, as though he were a project on the order of Boulder Dam.

"And I thought and I thought," Mrs. Spoffard continued, "and I finally decided to have a bit of you, and then a bit of music, and then to keep sandwiching you in. Pauline thought it might confuse you to be sandwiched, so I suppose I'd better ask you if you *mind* being sandwiched."

"At this point," Leonidas said with perfect candor, "I shall hardly notice it."

"Well, I suppose it's all right then," Mrs. Spoffard said. "Wait here, and I'll introduce you. You understand about all that, I suppose? When I say your name, you come in."

She opened a door leading into the side of a large rectangular hall with a raised platform at one end.

The place was crowded with people, and the noise was terrific. Groups sat around on folding chairs and on settees, and talked. Other groups talked as they hovered around the long tables that ran the length of the room. Still other groups just stood and talked.

The objects displayed on the tables caught Leonidas's eye as he looked around. They were, even at a distance, the most colossal rummage he had ever seen.

And what part he was to play in connection with it all, Leonidas still couldn't imagine. There was no one whom he could ask. Everyone was far too busy talking with someone else.

He watched Mrs. Spoffard make her way towards

the platform. It was a slow, tedious, zig-zag process, punctuated by many conversational detours and digressions.

But she finally reached the platform, mounted it, and walked cautiously to the mathematical center. Rather, Leonidas thought, as if she were the boy on the burning deck, and expected it to collapse any second.

She clapped her hands several times, and then she made a sort of clawing gesture at the air, which Leonidas diagnosed as a plea for quiet.

No one paid the slightest bit of attention to her until a kindly fat man took pity on her and bellowed for quiet.

After half a dozen bellows, some of the noise diminished.

Mrs. Spoffard thanked the fat man, cleared her voice, patted her hair, and asked if someone would please open the east window. Not too much, but just a wee crack.

A few people clapped, and everybody started talking again, evidently feeling that Mrs. Spoffard was through.

The fat man rushed to her aid by thumping a chair on the floor, and at last quiet was achieved.

In her most plaintive voice, Mrs. Spoffard said that everything was doing very well, very well indeed, and she was sure that everyone was having a simply splendid time buying these very useful and very lovely things that everyone had been so kind to bring. And she was sure that it was nice to think that it was all for such a perfectly splendid cause, and she thought that everyone deserved a great deal of credit.

"And now," she said, "Mr. Budenny."

She beckoned violently to Leonidas.

Still a little confused as to his role, Leonidas started from the side door only to be sent back by a shooing gesture from Mrs. Spoffard, who mounted the platform again.

"I forgot to say," she announced, "that he's going to start selling. He's the auctioneer. *Now*, Mr. Budenny!"

Turning around, she beckoned to someone off stage.

"Now, boys!"

At once two boys in grey flannel shorts and grey sweaters—clearly members of the tumbling team—shoved a heavily loaded trestle table from the wings onto the platform.

"Come, Mr. Budenny!"

Leonidas, feeling that it could be much worse, stepped forward and was greeted by a polite but none too enthusiastic smattering of applause.

He bowed to Mrs. Spoffard as she passed him, and then he smiled his blandest and most charming smile at the audience. They were just slightly hostile, slightly annoyed at having their chatter interrupted, and slightly resentful of the possibility that they might have to buy something.

None of which disconcerted Leonidas.

If he had been called on to sing some rousing barytone solo, something about stout-hearted men and Burgundy, he would have been completely floored. But talking to an audience was a tonic to Leonidas. He had spent much of his life talking to an audience. If he could sell education and English literature to Meredith Academy boys, he thought, he certainly could manage to dispose of some of this colossal rummage.

A hat on one of the long tables to his right caught his attention.

Leaving the platform, Leonidas strolled over to it, picked it up, and strolled back.

Then he put it on.

Five minutes later he had sold the hat to the fat man for twelve dollars and forty cents, and his audience was rocking with laughter.

He sold, in the next ten minutes, a broken concertina, a purple glass tea set, six dishtowels with crocheted edges, and two umbrella stands shaped like fish.

Ten minutes later, Leonidas was beginning to feel like the man who broke the bank at Monte Carlo. The trestle table was empty except for heaps of bills and coins.

"Now," Mrs. Spoffard's voice came plaintively from the side door, "while the table is being replenished with some more st—I mean, with some more useful and lovely things, and while Mr. Budenny is having a rest, we shall have some music. The String Quartet, and Miss La Fleur."

Leonidas gallantly relinquished the platform to a stout lady in pink who announced that she was going to sing a group of Old English Folk Songs, and before he reached the side door, she was well into the inevitable hey-nonnys.

If that soprano was quite good, Leonidas thought, then that was still further proof that Mrs. Beaton was not infallible in her judgments.

Mrs. Spoffard motioned for him to come out into the hall.

She looked unusually aggrieved, to the amazement of Leonidas, who thought he had carried things off rather well.

"I trust," he said, "that you are satisfied with my sales, Mrs. Spoffard? How, in the vernacular, am I doing?"

Mrs. Spoffard raised her lorgnette and stared at him.

"Er—don't you think," Leonidas went on, "that twelve dollars and forty cents was a magnificent price for that hideous straw hat with the violets?"

"I paid thirty-five dollars for that hat yesterday," Mrs. Spoffard said plaintively. "Thirty-five dollars!"

"Then, dear lady," Leonidas returned imperturbably, "I have done you a great service!"

"I don't understand how you can call it doing me a great service to sell my new hat to that fat John Robbins for twelve dollars and forty cents, when I paid thirty-five dollars for it in Boston yesterday!"

"Dear lady," Leonidas said smoothly, "I saved

your peace of mind. By tomorrow you would be asking yourself, 'Was that thing worth thirty-five dollars?' And being an honest and a—er—clear-thinking woman, you would have been forced to admit to yourself that it was not."

"But it *was!*" Mrs. Spoffard said sulkily. "It was marked down from fifty!"

"Dear lady, ask yourself why!"

"Why what?"

"Why it was marked down," Leonidas said.

"I couldn't understand why it should have been," Mrs. Spoffard said. "It wasn't torn, and it didn't have a spot on it, or anything. It looked like a fifty-dollar hat. It *was.* And now you've gone and sold it to fat John Robbins!"

Mrs. Spoffard had an air of being ready and willing to battle it out on the topic of hats if it took her the rest of the evening, Leonidas thought, and hastily racked his brains for some means of nipping her in the bud.

"I don't understand," Mrs. Spoffard went on doggedly, "how you could take that hat for *rummage!*"

"Dear lady," Leonidas had finally remembered the strategy employed by Colonel Carpenter when the latter was once frustrated by one of his sister Cassie's hats, "dear lady, it was *not* your hat. How shall I say it? Not *your* hat."

"It *was* my hat! Oh. You mean, it was too *old?*"

"Not old," Leonidas said. "But it was a hat more suited for the—well, for the dowdy type. To tell you the truth," Leonidas lowered his voice confidentially, "my cousin's sister has a hat almost exactly like that, and she's known far and wide as the dowdiest woman in Dalton."

"Who is she?" Mrs. Spoffard asked. "I wonder if I know her?"

"You need something small," Leonidas said swiftly. "Small, and black. Chic. No, dear lady, I've done you a great service—by the way, who is seeing to the replenishment of the trestle table?"

"Pauline, or someone, I guess. Really, I think this is going quite well," Mrs. Spoffard said. "Aside from the hat, I mean. And it's possible you may be right about that hat. There *was* something about it I couldn't quite put my finger on. Yes, I think this is going quite well, Mr. Budenny, considering that I didn't understand Mrs. Beaton's message very well at first."

"M'yes, that message," Leonidas said. "Er—what about that message?"

"She left a note saying that if things didn't sell, we should have an auction and get rid of them. And so when we hadn't sold a single blessed thing from supper till eight o'clock, Evelyn and I decided we'd better have an auction. So we wondered who to have as auctioneer—she didn't tell us who. And then I thought of the back pages of the phone book. It's really wonderful what you find in those colored pages, isn't it? And there was your name!"

"Er—Budenny?"

"No, no, the business name. The Carnavon Auction Company. You were the only auctioneer there, so we felt sure you were the one Mrs. Beaton wanted. I still don't understand why I was so sure you were a foreigner. Do you think you can really get rid of all the rest of that stuff? And what do you think of blue? Something small, with just a dash of color. Like a red feather."

Leonidas had to drop his pince-nez twice before he grasped the fact that Mrs. Spoffard had returned to the topic of hats, and was asking his advice about one.

"M'yes," he said. "Dark blue. That deep, dark blue. Excellent. And just the merest touch of color. M'yes, indeed. And now—er—the table. Don't you think that perhaps you really should oversee the replenishing of that table, yourself?"

"I suppose so. You wait here."

Mrs. Spoffard departed.

Leonidas leaned against the rough plastered wall of the corridor, and drew several long breaths.

Then he walked out to the front vestibule.

Certainly it was time for Mrs. Beaton to be rushing over. Or for Link Potter to come. Or Judy to report. Certainly, out of all of Mrs. Beaton's intricate and involved plans, at least one thing should proceed according to schedule!

As he started to open the vestibule door to take a look outdoors, Leonidas was buttonholed by the fat man, who was wearing the Spoffard straw hat.

"Brother," the fat man said, "I want to tell you

I'm still splitting my seams over the thought of you in this hat!"

"Er—thank you," Leonidas said. "I—er—appreciated your co-operation."

"By the way, here's my card. I'm John Robbins, of John Robbins, Incorporated. I'm in cement."

"Are you," Leonidas said, "indeed!"

"And say, if I don't get a prize with one of 'em, my name's not John Robbins!"

Leonidas put on his pince-nez and looked at Mr. Robbins's card.

"Er—one of the cement blocks?" he asked.

"No, the pictures! I got twelve shots of you with this hat on." He indicated the three cameras dangling from straps around his neck. "Didn't you see my cameras?"

"Er—no." Leonidas couldn't think of any tactful way to tell Mr. Robbins that on his vast person, three cameras made as little impression as three stones on the side of a large hill. "So you took pictures?"

"Honestly," Mr. Robbins said, "this kind of show is a field day for me! I got the padre in a full tumble, tonight. Right on his fanny. I'm going to enlarge that one. And I got old lady Vandivart chewing a drumstick. Oh, boy! Do I eat up these shows!"

"Certainly," Leonidas said, "you are provided with a rich and fertile field of subjects."

"Boy, am I!"

Mr. Robbins sat down on the oaken bench, pulled out his cigar case, and offered it to Leonidas.

"Thank you, no," Leonidas said. "I don't smoke."

"Doctor tells me I shouldn't." Mr. Robbins lighted up. "Damn fools, doctors. Wanted me to give up the concrete game, and retire, and have a hobby. I fooled 'em. I got a hobby and kept right on in concrete. Say, do you know Topsey Beaton? I got her today while she was getting hell from a cop for sloughing into a safety island. And I got—"

Just the thought of what he got amused Mr. Robbins so much that he sat there on the bench and rumbled with laughter for several minutes.

"What?" Leonidas asked, with his eye glued to the vestibule door.

"Boy, was that funny! I'm coming along Main Street, see, and all of a sudden in a snowdrift ahead, here's a man with a harp!"

"What!"

"Yes, sir. I nearly died. Here's St. Patrick himself, with a harp. Green silk pants, and a silk hat, and a silk coat with tails. Smack in a drift. He'd slipped, see? Faw down and went boom. He was sore as a boil when he spotted me taking pictures, but then I bought him a drink and slipped him a few bucks, and he let me take all I wanted. I posed him playing the harp on top of a lamp post, and then like a drunk wrapped around the post, and then I took him into the Star Store and had him pretend he was playing for a dummy. You know. One of the window dummies. Say, I never laughed so much in my life! St. Patrick on his knees, playing a harp for the dummy! She was a lady dummy, see, and—"

"Mr. Robbins," Leonidas said, "did you happen to find out who this man was, the man with the harp?"

"Oh, he's a fellow that works for Potter over at the hardware store. And we took the dummy's dress off, see, and—"

"Why was he dressed like St. Patrick?"

"Oh, he was going to some party up the line. The St. Alphonsus Chowder and Marching and Athletic Club, or whatever they call it, is having a St. Patrick's Day party. Sunday's St. Patrick's Day, you know. I'm going to drop in there later on and take a few shots. Boy, could I do wonders with you, too! If I could have a day with you, wouldn't I have fun!"

"Mr. Robbins," Leonidas said feelingly, "any day next week you wish, come to my house and shoot me to your heart's content. Arrive for breakfast. Stay to lunch. For dinner, I'll broil you the biggest steak I can find in Dalton. You can shoot me from dawn to dusk, from all angles, in any costume from tails and a top hat to bathing trunks and a solar topee."

"Say, that's very decent of you! I'll save you some of the shots I got here tonight. For your memory book." Mr. Robbins started rumbling with laughter again as he got up from the bench. "Call me Monday and tell me when to come. I got to go in now and get that girl, if she's through talking with the padre. Boy, she's a corker! You certainly get all kinds at a show like this, don't you? I thought when she first came in that she'd got St. Anselm mixed up with the St. Alphonsus Chowder and Marching gang. I only wish I had some Kodachrome! If I could get a shot of that baby in front of that stained glass window with all those saints! Those saints and that red dunce cap, boy, that would be something! See you later!"

Mr. Robbins heaved over to the door that led directly into the rear of the auditorium, and disappeared inside.

For a moment Leonidas paused, and then he hurried back along the corridor to the side door, opened it a crack, and peeked into the hall.

There in the rear, talking to Evelyn, was the Scarlet Wimpernel!

CHAPTER 5

AS Leonidas watched her, the Scarlet Wimpernel made the unmistakable gesture of pulling at the space below her pert chin that indicated that she was discussing a beard.

And Leonidas greatly doubted if she was discussing just a beard, or beards in an abstract sense. As surely as a forefinger twirled round and round indicated a spiral staircase, that girl's gesture meant that she was talking about a man with a beard. Leonidas was under no delusions that she might be chatting about bearded ladies. She was talking about a man with a beard. About him.

And to Evelyn!

Of all the people in that hall, she had to pick Evelyn!

Mrs. Spoffard trailed up to him.

"We're all ready," she said. "I don't think there's any sense in my introducing you all over, do you? Can't you just go right in there now, and take charge, Mr. Budenny?"

"No," Leonidas said. "Er—no. What about those tables over there, dear lady? They're laden with—er —beautiful and useful things. Don't you think all those beautiful and useful things should be carried up on the stage?"

"I thought we ought to keep those till later on," Mrs. Spoffard said.

"Dear lady," Leonidas said, "let's have them put on the stage now, and save any more delays!"

"But there isn't anything going on now. I'm sure Mrs. Beaton wouldn't like that. I can't understand why, but she always seems to want something going on all the time. She doesn't like hitches, she always says."

"Where's that fellow with the dulcimer?" Leonidas asked. "Run him on now, and clear the tables while he's playing. Then you'll have no hitch later."

"Well—"

"Get the man with the dulcimer," Leonidas very gently shoved her into the hall, "and clear those tables!"

Mrs. Spoffard trailed away, and Leonidas closed the corridor door and leaned against the door jamb.

He had at the most ten minutes to settle this problem, and he couldn't possibly settle it without the aid of Mrs. Beaton. He'd have to hurry across the street and get her.

Judy collided with him in the vestibule.

"Oh, hello," she said. "I can't find that man at the hardware store. What *is* this all about, anyway?

Mrs. B. didn't bother to enlighten me. And why didn't you tell me you weren't Hornblower? And—"

"Go," Leonidas said, "and get Mrs. Beaton. Tell her the Scarlet Wimpernel is here, talking to Evelyn—don't interrupt me! And Mrs. Spoffard has made me into an auctioneer named Budenny. Tell Mrs. Beaton to get over here just as quickly as her two legs can carry her!"

"Who is—"

Leonidas repeated his message, and opened the vestibule door.

"Hurry!"

He walked back up the corridor and stood by the side door.

A sallow man in a brown suit was hammering away at what seemed to be a very small coffin. He stopped suddenly, made a funny little bow, and started hammering away in a different tempo before the audience had time to realize that he had finished one piece and begun another.

Mrs. Beaton appeared beside him.

"Here." She pulled two petit fours from her coat pocket. "They're awfully good. I think the caterer made a mistake and gave us someone's wedding food. What's wrong?"

Leonidas put on his pince-nez.

"Didn't Judy tell you?"

"Oh, she gave me some sort of garbled message about Evelyn being in a rash, and Mrs. Spoffard having an auction—but that's all right. I left a message telling them to have an auction if things didn't sell. What's Evelyn in a rash about?"

Leonidas sighed. "Judy must have thought I said scarlet pimples," he said. "I didn't! I said Scarlet Wimpernel! Listen to me!"

He explained swiftly how an auction to Evelyn and Mrs. Spoffard indicated a professional auctioneer, and how they had inspiredly picked one from the classified telephone directory.

"And they took me for the auctioneer when I came! I'm Mr. Budenny, the auctioneer! And—"

"How *do* you let yourself get into this sort of thing?" Mrs. Beaton said. "Cassie was right. I never heard of anything quite so rash! Why in the world did you let them wangle you into it!"

"I challenge you," Leonidas said, "to have done differently. Now, please, thrust your head in that doorway and look at your friend Evelyn talking to the Scarlet Wimpernel!"

"Is she here? I told you," Mrs. Beaton said with satisfaction, "that she'd turn up again!"

"Does it occur to you that she is pursuing me, that she knows my name, that Evelyn knows me as Mr. Budenny, and that if her actions on the bus are any indication of her nature, there are practically no lengths to which she will not go?"

"What *did* she do on the bus?" Mrs. Beaton asked. "You never really told me."

"The least of it was sitting on my lap, pulling my beard, calling me daddy, and then yelling in an affronted and horror-stricken voice that I'd made improper advances," Leonidas said. "That will give you a brief idea. Now, I want to get hold of that girl. She mustn't see me. She's been telling Evelyn about me—"

"Well, then, we're lost right now!"

"No," Leonidas said. "I'm the Bard in makeup to Evelyn. As far as I can judge at this distance, she's been telling him that she wants a man with a beard, and he's telling her that he has a man with a beard, but it's makeup."

"Makeup?"

"M'yes," Leonidas said. "Mercifully, Evelyn thinks my resemblance to Shakespeare is a matter of grease paint. And—"

"Why?"

"I am not one," Leonidas told her, "to inquire into the idiosyncrasies of Evelyn's mental processes. He's being very helpful and polite and democratic with the Wimpernel, and she probably isn't understanding more than one word in ten of what he's saying."

"Why?" Mrs. Beaton asked again.

"Don't you remember the difficulty she had understanding Harrigan when he spoke about initiations? And then they're both probably having trouble understanding the other's accent. Now, Mrs. Beaton, I want that girl. I want to get her away from Evelyn. I don't want her to see me. And I want to get through this auctioneering without being unmasked or arrested. I suggest that—perhaps, though, you have some suggestion from your wealth of experience in infinite chairmanships?"

"My dear, good, crazed man, I never stagemanaged a murder before, or anything as complicated as this! This is your own mess. You figure it out all by yourself!"

"Then," Leonidas said, "you go back to the vestibule, and enter the hall through that door at the rear. Then seize Evelyn and tell him to make an announcement. Then—dear me, we mustn't allow that dulcimer man to get through now! Dash in here, Mrs. Beaton, and seize Mrs. Spoffard first, and have that dulcimer man play an encore!"

Mrs. Beaton marched in and took Mrs. Spoffard by the shoulder, and almost at once Mrs. Spoffard ran for the man with the dulcimer. In the same manner, Leonidas thought, that a new boy at the Academy might run an errand for the star halfback.

"There," Mrs. Beaton said. "Have Evelyn announce what?"

"Anything. I'm sure he's bubbling over with two-minute talks. He can touch lightly on 'Peace in a Troubled World,' for all I care. Just get him on the stage. Now, isn't there a place where we can put that girl until we get a chance to leave quietly, taking her with us? Isn't there a ladies' room, or a ladies' parlor, or some place where she can be—er—held in comparative restraint?"

"Hm," Mrs. Beaton said. "Hm. Yes, I know just the place. I don't know exactly what you call it, but it has something to do with the acoustics and the organ. It's a box-shaped room, metal lined and sound proof, and it has a spring lock. The janitor got shut in there for a day and a half at Christmas time, and he'd be there yet if the organist hadn't happened to open the place to show it to some musical friend. Hm. And it's opposite the ladies' room. I can manage that, all right."

"Be careful," Leonidas said. "I don't think that the Wimpernel is any mental colossus, but don't underestimate her. Now, after you've disposed of her, get Judy and tell her she simply must find Link Potter. By the way, the man with the harp is a man who works for him."

"What was he doing at Marcus's?" Mrs. Beaton demanded. "Hm. I think that's definitely queer!"

"For all I know, he too was tapping the pipes," Leonidas said. "Now, tell Judy she must find Link! And—ah, our friend with the dulcimer's getting through. You take care of Evelyn and the Wimpernel, and perhaps you'd best have him introduce me when he finishes his announcement. I'll stall him a minute by the platform, so you can get up the corridor with the girl before he has a chance to tag you."

"Right. Shut this door behind you, too," Mrs. Beaton said. "Don't worry, I'll handle things, and I'll be back as soon as I wind things up at the Club."

It seemed to Leonidas that she had hardly disappeared before Evelyn was up on the stage, announcing in bell-like tones that he wanted everyone's attention for just two minutes.

As he launched into a forecast of events to take place in St. Anselm's for the coming week, Leonidas edged into the hall and closed the corridor door behind him.

Mrs. Beaton and the Wimpernel had already gone.

Ten minutes later, when Leonidas was in the throes of auctioning off an ancient phonograph with a bulging horn, he finally caught sight of Mrs. Beaton standing at the side door, casually munching another petit four. She waved at him reassuringly, wiped her mouth, and departed.

With renewed vigor, Leonidas disposed of the phonograph.

There weren't a dozen items left on the trestle table when Mrs. Spoffard plaintively said she thought it was time for more music, and introduced a strapping barytone, who tramped up onto the platform and started right in, to Leonidas's inward pleasure, urging the sons of France to break the chains that bound them, and demolish Burgundy.

As he returned to his vantage point by the side door, Leonidas noticed that Evelyn was wandering uneasily about the hall.

"You didn't do badly at all," Mrs. Spoffard informed him. "Though I must say I don't understand how you could ever let that green cloisonné jardiniere go for only twenty-one cents! Aunt Annie brought that home to mother from the Columbian Exposition, and I know for a fact she must have paid at least ten dollars—I wonder why Evelyn's craning his neck around that way for? Do you suppose he's lost something? Maybe I'd better see if I can help him."

Ignoring the barytone, who was still busily involved with the chore of settling Burgundy once and for all, Mrs. Spoffard trailed directly across the hall and spoke with Evelyn. Then, after a moment's conversation, she trailed back.

"Sometimes I don't understand Evelyn," she said to Leonidas. "I don't understand what the matter is with him tonight. He's been so restless. I think he must have hurt his ankle tumbling with the boys."

"Er—has he lost something?"

"That man sings *loud*, doesn't he? Oh, I guess that's the end of that song." She clapped, without making very much noise, and flung a smile toward the platform. "Evelyn said something about a girl in red. He was talking to her, and now he can't seem to find her. I wonder who it could have been? My Dorothy's wearing yellow. I haven't *seen* any girl in red, have you?"

Leonidas made no effort to answer her over the rousing declaration of the barytone that he was the master of his fate and the captain of his soul. Swinging his pince-nez, he watched Evelyn pop out of the vestibule door.

A second later, he popped up at Leonidas's elbow, and spoke in Leonidas's ear.

"I say, my dear fellow, have you seen a girl in red?"

"Red?"

"A red coat," Evelyn said, "and a sort of pointed cap. You haven't seen her, either? I wonder where she possibly could have gone. That was the most puzzling incident, Mr. Budenny!"

"Really?" Leonidas said. "What do you mean, puzzling?"

"Dear fellow," Evelyn moved up the corridor, away from the noise, and the door, and Mrs. Spoffard, and beckoned for Leonidas to follow, "may I tell you about it?"

Evelyn was plainly bursting to tell someone about the Wimpernel.

"Of course," Leonidas said. "Please do. I'm always interested in puzzling incidents. One might go so far as to say, that I collect them."

"That's fine," Evelyn said heartily, "because I really would like to tell someone else about this, and I am afraid that they," he nodded his head toward the hall, "are sometimes inclined to misinterpret any interest I may show in younger women. Like Mrs. Spoffard just now. She thought I was hunting her daughter Dorothy. This girl in red, Mr. Budenny—didn't you really notice her? She was *very* striking-looking. Different. Vivid, if you know what I mean."

"Yes," Leonidas said encouragingly. "You mean vivid."

Evelyn nodded. "I noticed her at once when she came in the door, and since she was a stranger, I thought it was only proper for me to greet her, and she asked me if I had seen a man with a beard!"

"Dear me, a beard?" Leonidas said.

"Yes. I thought of you, naturally, and started to find you—you'd just finished selling the first table load. And then I remembered your beard was only makeup, so it couldn't be you she was searching for. Then I looked around and found several men with beards. There was old General Masters—perhaps you noticed him? He bought that antique musket. And Judge Kingsley, and some others. I pointed them out—unobtrusively, of course, but none of them appeared to be the man with the beard whom she wanted. Finally I asked the man's name. And what do you suppose?"

"Er—what?" Leonidas asked.

"She didn't know it!" Evelyn said.

"Er—you mean," Leonidas said, "she wouldn't tell you?"

"She actually didn't know his name. Really. She had no idea who he was. Naturally that surprised me, and I asked why she wanted this man with a beard, anyway. And she said that the man had her pocketbook!"

"Ah. He stole it, I suppose?" Leonidas inquired.

"No, that what what I assumed, too, but she said he hadn't stolen it. She said that he just happened to have the pocketbook, and he didn't know that he had. Now, don't you think that was very puzzling, Mr. Budenny?"

"I think," Leonidas said honestly, "that it's incredible!"

"She said she had spent hours hunting this man,

who had been on the bus with her, and who got off at the Four Corners. And she, herself, was most anxious to get home to Boston. But you see she couldn't, without her pocketbook. She had no money. So I told her that if she'd wait, I'd be very willing to take her to the bus, and buy her a ticket, and escort her home—don't you think," Evelyn asked rather anxiously, "that was the proper thing to do?"

"I think," Leonidas said, "that depends very largely on your previous experience with buses, and —er—girls in red. For my part, I most certainly and assuredly would undertake no such expedition. Under no circumstances. Not even at gun point."

"What I mean, Mr. Budenny," Evelyn said with great earnestness, "is that I always think you can tell if a person *means* that sort of thing, if you offer to help that way. I mean, if someone asks you for a dime for a cup of coffee, and you offer instead to take them to a restaurant or a cafeteria and buy them a cup of coffee, then you can always find out if they really *do* want a cup of coffee, or if they've just been trying to get some money out of you. Do you understand what I mean? I mean—"

"M'yes," Leonidas said, before Evelyn explained what he meant all over again, "I understand. M'yes. Quite. And—er—this young girl in red agreed to your suggestion?"

Evelyn nodded. "Yes. She said she thought I was very kind. She seemed very grateful." He smiled tolerantly. "What she really said was that she was gratified, but I suppose in her nervousness and distress, she meant grateful."

"M'yes." Leonidas recalled that the Wimpernel had also told Harrigan that she was gratified. "M'yes. And then the girl disappeared?"

"Mrs. Beaton asked if I'd make an announcement," Evelyn said, "and I did. I lost sight of the girl then, and now I can't seem to find her anywhere. I'm rather worried about her."

"Er—you don't suppose," Leonidas said, "that perhaps she just went out for a moment, possibly for a breath of air?"

"I looked outdoors," Evelyn returned.

"Perhaps she saw a friend," Leonidas suggested. "Er—had she no friends in town?"

"She said the only person she knew in Carnavon wasn't home."

"Indeed," Leonidas said. "Indeed. The only person she knew wasn't home. Did she tell you who the person was?"

"No, Mrs. Beaton came along just then," Evelyn said, "and the girl didn't have a chance."

"Tch, tch." Leonidas clucked his tongue. "That is too bad. How did this girl happen to come in here, I wonder?"

"I don't know, but I got the impression that she was wandering from place to place, poor child, trying to find her pocketbook and that man with the beard. She was so sure he hadn't stolen it!" Evelyn shook his head. "The poor, trusting child!"

Anyone less like a trusting child, Leonidas thought, would be difficult to find. It seemed incredible that Evelyn could even think such a thing, let alone say it.

Evelyn laughed a little self-consciously.

"She said that I reminded her of Spencer Tracy."

"Er—what?"

"Spencer Tracy. It seemed she'd just seen a moving picture where he was a minister. I—well, of course, he's usually an idealized type, but it made me feel—well, proud. Proud to be spoken of in that manner."

Leonidas dropped his pince-nez, and took his time about picking them up again.

"Do you think I should try to find her," Evelyn went on, "or should I go to the police? Perhaps it would be better if I went to them and enlisted their aid. There's no telling what might happen to that poor child if she happened to fall into the wrong hands. I think I'd better call on the police."

"There," Leonidas hurriedly put on his pince-nez, "there I disagree with you. Such a girl as you have described, kind and trusting and—er—naive, would be frightened to death to find herself suddenly accosted by an officer of the law! Why, think of some great hulking policeman seizing her by the shoulder! Of course," he remembered Mrs. Beaton's remarks emphasizing the fact that Evelyn and the police were on the best of terms, "I concede that the officer would be inspired only by the kindliest of motives, but this poor child would not know that! Definitely, I should not call the police! No. That would be an error."

"Well," Evelyn said, "what do you think I should do?"

"Your duty," Leonidas told him, "is plainly here. Here with your—er—flock. Until this sale and this entertainment are over. Don't you really feel, Mr. Leicester, that your duty lies here? After all, as Mrs. Spoffard said, it's such a splendid cause!"

There was not only a faintly dubious look in Evelyn's eyes.

There was also a dreamy look.

Leonidas drew a long breath, and mentally girt himself to erase both.

It took several minutes, and a long, moving and moral narrative which he recalled from an old McGuffey's Reader before Leonidas felt that Evelyn's feet were firmly re-established on the path of duty, and all his notions about calling the police obliterated from his mind.

"Actually," Leonidas concluded, "I feel that the girl will come to light. Probably she will come back later. Who knows? And—Mrs. Spoffard wants you. She's beckoning. Dear me," he put on his pince-nez, "who are those four boys?"

"Mickey's Swing Band, for the East Room dancing. We always try to have an interval of dancing for the young people, right here. We feel it's better for them to dance here than to visit questionable establishments." Evelyn straightened his shoulders. "Thank you, Mr. Budenny. You've been very inspiring. I assure you that I shall remember your little homily. If you want me, I shall be in the East Room with the young people."

Evelyn marched off.

Leonidas sighed, and went along the corridor into the vestibule.

Judy was just coming in.

"Every time I step foot in this place," she said, "I collide with you here!"

"Did you find Link?" Leonidas asked anxiously.

"I have not found Link," Judy said. "As far as I'm concerned, he's the original missing Link. If you want to know my opinion, I don't think there's any such person." She sat down wearily on the oaken bench and lighted a cigarette. "Mrs. B.'s finally managed to break down and tell me what's happened. And what's going on. And I think it's all horrible, and I think you're both stark mad, and I think—"

"Judy, won't you take the beachwagon and hunt for him in that lane by Marcus's?"

"I've been to that lane. Twice!"

"Go to the store again. You must be able to find him!"

"I have been to that damned store so many damned times," Judy said, "that I can give you a verbal inventory just from peeking in the windows! I tell you, he isn't there!"

"Link Potter," Leonidas said, "is somewhere in

this town. I'm sure he is. Can't you get into the car, and drive around—"

"I did something like that once this evening," Judy interrupted. "Remember? I picked you up. And see what happened! And besides, I don't know Link Potter from Adam!"

"You couldn't miss him. He's—"

"He's got a beard, I suppose?" Judy inquired acidly. "If anyone asks me to pick up any more strange men with beards, I'm going to start kicking and screaming!"

"Link is tall, well-built, and he's wearing a trench coat and a plaid scarf. He has brown hair, and no hat. Judy, we've got to find him! Won't you please try again?"

"Well," Judy said, "all right. All right, Mr. Hornblower-Shakespeare-Budenny! I never knew a man to have so many names! All right, I'll try again. I'll drag my weary bones out on one more search! And then I'm going to hide in a hole until you and Mrs. B. come to your senses!"

"Go to the store before you go anywhere else," Leonidas said. "He may have returned since you've been there. Do try to find him, please!"

A squat little man wearing a derby hat came into the vestibule as Judy left.

"Plizz."

Leonidas, who had started back for the corridor door, wheeled around.

"Oh," he said. "I beg your pardon?"

"Plizz, is it the auction?"

"The what?" Leonidas asked courteously. "Er—this is a church, you know."

The squat little man produced a grubby slip of paper from his breast pocket.

"Here is the name, like it is outside on the sign, yes?"

"St. Anselm's," Leonidas said. "M'yes. This is St. Anselm's."

"At five minutes past eight, I am getting the call I should come to this place to auction. Plizz, where is the auction?"

"Oh, the auction!" Leonidas said, as though the fact had slipped his mind. "Oh, yes. M'yes. Of course. You're Mr. Budenny?"

"Simon Budenny is the name. Where is the auction, plizz?"

"My dear man," Leonidas said, "we had to give that up! We waited for you and waited for you, and you didn't come! It's nearly half past ten, you know!"

Mr. Budenny shrugged.

"The car is breaking down once, it is breaking down twice, it is breaking down three times! I come as soon as I can!"

"Well, I'm very sorry," Leonidas said. "But an auction at this time is out of the question entirely. Owing to your tardiness, we regretfully relinquished all thoughts of utilizing your services as a vendor, Mr. Budenny."

"Plizz, no auction?"

"No auction," Leonidas said. "Because, however, you have been torn from the warmth and comfort of your—er—couch, allow me to present you with this bill as a token of my latent gratitude for the part you have unwittingly played."

Mr. Budenny looked suspiciously at the bill, and then he tipped his derby.

"Thanks, mister."

"And now," Leonidas said, "good evening to you, sir. Allow me to open the door for you."

The speed with which Mr. Budenny scuttled down the flagstone walk, hopped into a car parked by the curb, and hurriedly departed, indicated that he was taking no chances on having Leonidas change his mind about that bill.

Leonidas smiled as he closed the door.

That he should be the one to meet the real Budenny seemed to him more than mere fortunate coincidence.

He chose to regard it as a good omen, a sign that the tide of trials and tribulations was turning, and that from now on, fate might think twice before inserting more obstacles in his path.

Almost at once, he was accosted by Mrs. Spoffard.

"I don't understand what you're doing out here!" she said plaintively. "What are you out here for, anyway?"

Luckily for him, Leonidas thought, her question seemed to be purely rhetorical.

"Come on," she continued, "and finish things up.

We've found two more baskets full of stuff. Pauline thinks it's the stuff nobody thought was worth the effort of putting out on the tables. I don't understand how you can ever sell any of it, but you might as well try, I suppose."

Leonidas sold it all down to the very last item, a moth-eaten Indian war bonnet, at the sight of which fat Mr. Robbins let out a whoop and started bidding. He was instantly confronted by spirited opposition from old General Masters, whose wife had removed the war bonnet from the general's den without either the general's knowledge or his consent.

The resulting battle excited everyone, and Mr. Robbins's winning bid of twenty-one dollars and fifty cents put people in a tremendous good humor.

Evelyn appeared with the soprano and the barytone and the string quartet and the violinist and the man with the dulcimer, and the National Anthem was rendered with terrific gusto.

Then Mr. Robbins took pictures of Evelyn in the war bonnet, of Mrs. Spoffard in the war bonnet, of both the soprano and the barytone in the war bonnet, and even one of the man playing the dulcimer wearing the war bonnet. Then, in a final burst of good will, he gave the war bonnet back to General Masters, and devoted his last bit of film to a picture of the general in his wheel chair, wearing the war bonnet.

The evening, everyone thought, was an unqualified success.

Leonidas noticed suddenly that the disorderly

milling towards the vestibule door had turned miraculously into a neat and orderly line. It was due, he discovered, to Mrs. Beaton, who was standing with Evelyn at the door, busily shaking hands and wishing everyone a cordial good night.

It somehow didn't surprise him a bit to find that all the credit for the evening's success was being laid at her feet. No less than half a dozen people, in his hearing, said they didn't see how Mrs. Beaton ever thought these interesting things up, or how she carried them through so efficiently, without ever a single hitch of any sort.

Mrs. Beaton motioned to him.

"There's a plate of cakes and some ice cream for you out in Evelyn's office," she said. "It just occurred to me that you couldn't have had any dinner. Where's Judy, still hunting?"

"Er—I hope so," Leonidas told her.

"Well, run along and eat. I'll be with you in a moment."

Leonidas just managed to get the ice cream and cake before it was seized by two small boys in grey shorts.

"I'm sorry," he said firmly. "My need is far more pressing than yours!"

He was finishing the last of seven pink-frosted cakes when Mrs. Beaton appeared.

"My, you were hungry, weren't you? I'm sorry I couldn't bring you any more," she said, "but people were terribly piggish tonight. I've noticed before that there's something about a talk on peace that just seems to turn people into a pack of ravenous wolves. Where is that wretched child?"

"If you mean me," Judy spoke from the doorway, "I'm here. I yelled at you coming down the corridor, but you were too busy glad-handing Mrs. Murgatroyd to hear. I haven't got the missing Link, but I'm proud to say I don't return empty-handed, Shakespeare. I've got—"

"Ducks?" Leonidas inquired.

"I've got the man with the harp," Judy said with pride.

"What?"

"That is, the man who had the harp. He's out in the beachwagon. I left him there."

"Indeed!" Leonidas said. "And you expect that he will stay there, like a dear good fellow?"

"Of course! He's very nice. Of course, his grammar skids a bit, but on a basis of sheer sanity, I'd pick him over you two, any day in the week."

"Indeed!" Leonidas said. "And where did you find the man? Had he changed into a trench coat and a plaid scarf?"

"No, he's got on his green satin," Judy said with a little giggle. "Just wearing his green. I found him just now in Link's store—I call him Link, you notice. I feel as if I'd known him always."

"What was he doing there?"

"Bending over the cash register. I thought at first he was a burglar, and started to yell, and then I noticed his hat and tail coat. So I rapped on the glass, and he let me in. He's sweet. His eyebrows grow together over his nose."

"Er—what was he doing?" Leonidas asked again.

"Putting an envelope back in the cash register. He told me all about it. He asked Potter to leave his pay check on the register—on it, you know. Like on top. And when he hurried in earlier and found it wasn't on top, he just opened the register and took out the envelope he saw there. And he opened the envelope just a few minutes ago and found it had nearly nine hundred dollars in it! Potter's interest money, or loan money, or something. So he whipped right back to the store and put it back in the register. He was still panting. He'd run all the way from the St. Alphonsus Chowder and Marching party. He's pretty worked up about the whole thing."

"Er—did you invite him to come in?" Leonidas asked.

"I suggested it to him, but he said he'd feel too silly, coming in dressed like that, with all those people —there certainly was a mob here tonight, Mrs. B.! Anyway, he said he'd just wait out in the beachwagon."

"I wonder if you'd get him, now? Thank you. If," he added to Mrs. Beaton as Judy left, "if he's still there, I shall send a large anonymous donation to Evelyn's Building Fund."

"So," Mrs. Beaton said, "shall I. I shall also feel that I was very definitely right in my first suspicion that Potter has something to do with all of this."

But, when Judy returned, the man in the green satin suit was with her.

He looked at Leonidas, and then he lunged across the room at him.

"Bill!" Leonidas discovered that he was being hugged, and not throttled. "Bill! For the love of God, it's Bill Shakespeare!"

"M'yes," Leonidas said. "Er—"

"Bill! Good old Bill! I ain't seen you since—say, how long ago was it? Remember, when you was janitor in the bookstore?"

"My dear man," Mrs. Beaton said, "you're sadly mistaken! He never was a janitor in a bookstore, or anywhere else!"

"But I was," Leonidas said. "After my trip around the world in nineteen twenty-nine, I janited for a long time. Now, let me think—"

"Cassie said you were a professor at Meredith's Academy!"

"M'yes. Then I retired, and after that trip, my bank failed. I worked at a variety of things. Including janiting—I have it! Giacomo Santelli!"

"That's it! That's right! Good old Bill!"

"You lived," Leonidas said, "in a room on the top floor of the Pemberton Square building where the bookstore was. M'yes. They called you—"

"Frenchy," Judy said. "He told me so."

"Not in those days. Then you were known as Easy. A name derived, if I remember correctly, from

the ease with which you—er—handled a trigger. Er—
how is your brother?"

"Bat's in Alcatraz, Bill. They got him on his income tax. Those was the days, huh. Bill? Remember
Snake-eye? He's in Atlanta. So's Whitey. Remember
the guy they called Romeo? Riley's gang got him.
They got Freddy, too. And Harpo. And Two-bits.
They got Two-bits coming down the steps, right by
the old bookstore."

"That bookstore," Judy said, "certainly sounds
like the ideal place for a good quiet browse!"

"It was a delightful store," Leonidas said. "Run by
a charming man named Peters, who had a penchant
for Stilton cheese. I'm sorry to hear, Frenchy—that *is*
what you're called now? I'm sorry to hear that so many
of your old friends have been—er—liquidated."

"You know, Bill," Frenchy said, "out of all the
boys, there's only me left? And you want to know
why? Because on account I took your advice."

"Er—my advice?"

"Yeah. One day you said to me, 'Easy,' you said,
'if I loved life like you do, I'd give all this up and learn
some safe and useful trade, where if anything hits you,
it's an accident.' And then you said, 'Plumbers usually
die in their beds.' So I got out of the rackets, and went
to work. I'm the hell of a good plumber."

"I am deeply touched," Leonidas said. "Tell me,
what were you doing at Marcus Meredith's this evening, Frenchy?"

"Where?"

"At Marcus Meredith's. On Bald Pate Hill."

"You mean that old place with the stone posts out front? That one? Say, how'd you know I was up there, Bill?"

"You left your pasteboard harp behind."

"For God's sakes, was that where I left that! I been hunting that harp the hell and gone over Carnavon!"

"Why did you go there, Frenchy?"

"Oh, I went there to get the old man."

A little silence followed his casual statement.

"I never heard," Mrs. Beaton said, "of anything so utterly horrible! Did you go all of your own accord, or did someone send you?"

"Some of the boys up to the St. Alphonsus," Frenchy said, "they asked me would I go up and get the old man. So I did. You know me, Bill, always ready to help out a pal. Besides, they gave me a buck."

"I think," Mrs. Beaton said in a shocked voice, "this is the most utterly hideous and cold-blooded thing I ever listened to in my life! Why did they want to get that poor old man?"

"Why, he started the club," Frenchy said. "He always comes. Him and his wife, too."

"His wife? Whose wife? Marcus's wife? He hasn't got a wife!" Mrs. Beaton said.

"Er—I think," Leonidas said, "that Frenchy is referring to William."

"William?"

"Marcus's man. Isn't that so, Frenchy?"

"Sure," Frenchy said. "Him and his wife."

"You knew all the time!" Mrs. Beaton said to Leonidas. "Didn't you? And you just sat there and let me run on!"

"Sure," Frenchy said. "Bill knew. Bill always knows everything. Good old Bill! Say, lady, you didn't think I meant that guy they work for, did you? That old crab?"

"Ah," Leonidas said. "Did you happen to see him, Frenchy, when you were there?"

"Yeah. He came out and pinned up a note for William and his wife, while I was waiting in the front hall. He gives me a dirty look and says what was I doing there, and if I was somebody for William, why wasn't I out back. And I says, 'Out back where, mister?' And he gives me another dirty look, and went off. Kind of crabby guy, I thought."

"What time was that?" Leonidas asked. "By the way, Frenchy, you don't mind my asking you all these things, do you? It's rather important for me to know."

"Bill," Frenchy said earnestly, "you can ask me anything. Anything you want. You can take a census of me. Anything you want to know is perfectly okay by me."

"Thank you," Leonidas said. "What time were you there?"

Frenchy thought for a moment.

"About ten minutes past six, I guess it was. You

see, this supper was for six-thirty, and William and
the woman was steaming around so for fear they
wouldn't be on time, they nearly bust a boiler. I guess
that's why I forgot about the harp, getting them and
their stuff out. They had a real harp."

"I wonder," Leonidas said, "what time they will
return from this party? That's something that's been
rather bothering me."

Frenchy grinned widely.

"I don't think nobody'll get away from that party
for a good long time," he said. "I'm going to take 'em
back, see, so I asked 'em when, and they said three or
four. But if you ask me, it's going to be six or seven
before they start shovelling 'em out of there."

"Fine," Leonidas said. "Now, Frenchy, will you
do something for me?"

"Say the word," Frenchy returned. "Anything
you want done, Bill, just say the word. Anything."

The significance of the slight emphasis of his final
word was missed by Mrs. Beaton, but Judy raised her
eyebrows.

"I told you," she said, "that he was sweet."

"M'yes," Leonidas said. "Take him, Judy, and the
two of you find Link Potter. Go where he lives. Go
to the people he knows—you must know some of his
friends, Frenchy, or have some idea where he might be.
Go to the lane. Go around Marcus's, in a general way.
En route, Judy, you might explain to Frenchy what
this is all about."

Judy shook her head.

"Really, dear child," Mrs. Beaton said, "we *can't* take the time to tell him. Why won't you?"

"I can't, Mrs. B.," Judy said. "I don't know what this is all about. I just vaguely know a few details that take ten years off my life every time I think of 'em. The only thing I really know is that you two are in enough trouble, right now, to join Frenchy's brother in Alcatraz, and God knows what you've got up your sleeves!"

Frenchy's eyes narrowed.

"Come on, kid," he said briefly. "We'll get Potter for Bill."

"Wait. Where'll we find you?" Judy asked.

"Here," Leonidas told her. "At least, we'll be here until we can take our friend the Wimpernel away in safety. We—"

"We can take her any time," Mrs. Beaton interrupted.

"I'm afraid," Leonidas said, "that we can't take any chances with Evelyn. I won't go so far as to state that he has conceived a great passion for her, but she thinks he's like Spencer Tracy, and he thinks she's a dear, trusting child. I fear we've got to wait until Evelyn is safely out of the way. After we leave here, Judy, we'll go—"

"To my house," Mrs. Beaton said. "After we've left with her, we'll take a look at Potter's store, and leave a note for him to come to my house in case you miss him and he returns there. Only for goodness sakes, do manage to find him!"

"We'll try to bring him back," Judy said, "or a reasonable facsimile. I think Frenchy'll add zest to this hunt for the missing Link."

"And don't forget gas," Mrs. Beaton warned. "Remember yesterday. Don't run out of gas again!"

"I'll get it. Come on, Frenchy. You know, I don't think I'll mind going up that lane again if I have a man to dig me out. And if you don't turn up by breakfast, Mrs. B., I shall tell Cabot!"

"She means my son," Mrs. Beaton explained to Leonidas after they left. "Her direst threat is to tell Cabot—d'you think it's quite safe for her to go off with that ex-gangster?"

"M'yes, indeed," Leonidas said. "Frenchy's quite all right. He used to feed all the stray cats in the square, and once he got a man with a ferret to round up the rats in the cellar beneath the bookstore, where I tended the furnace. Sometimes when I think my lot is hard, I reflect on the days when I fed coal into the hungry maw of that furnace."

"I've been dying to ask you," Mrs. Beaton said suddenly, "what *do* you do now that you're retired? D'you tutor, or teach, or write? Or what?"

Leonidas smiled.

"You mean," he asked her, "how did I stop being a janitor? It was quite simple, Mrs. Beaton. A convenient relation left me some money, and I manage to add to that income—yes, Judy is quite safe with Frenchy. He's thoroughly reliable, and the fact that he alone of that group is extant proves his soundness.

Er—the thought occurs to me, do you find Judy exceptionally efficient?"

"She's a dear child," Mrs. Beaton said. "She's very useful. And she keeps me from getting lonely and bored."

"Somehow," Leonidas said, "I can't imagine your ever having time to be either. So she is really a useful secretary?"

"She's very amusing." Mrs. Beaton's voice, Leonidas noticed, had again acquired that defensive note. "She's a dear girl. I'm very fond of her."

"M'yes, I like her, myself," Leonidas said. "But—er—I mean, you send her for Hornblower and pigeons, and she picks up me, so to speak, and ducks. I send her for Link Potter, and she casually brings back a man who had a harp. She's a pleasant child, but is she really the—er—ideal secretary?"

"Well, if you really want to know," Mrs. Beaton said, "she isn't. My son Cabot—he's terribly efficient and just a little monotonous—was going to fire her. She's really not a secretary, you know. So I kept her. Her regular work isn't easy to come by."

"What does she do?"

"Did you ever hear that radio serial about Lieutenant Haseltine? 'HASELTINE to the RESCUE!' That one?"

"Er—often," Leonidas said.

"She had a perfectly magnificent job being the Princess Alicia on that. As she says, being Alicia was practically her life work. Then Haseltine went to

Deepest Africa, and gave up Alicia for a new girl friend named Zora. Well, Judy'd made a name for herself as the Princess Alicia, and it was virtually impossible to find anything else like her to do, and people said she wasn't the type for anything else, anyway."

Leonidas swung his pince-nez in a slow circle.

"She's been promised the Alicia part if Alicia ever gets back into the script, and she has half a dozen irons in the fire. In the meantime, she's here amusing me. Shakespeare, I'm amazed that you should know Haseltine!"

"Er—really?" Not even Cassie, Leonidas reflected, had ever guessed that he was the creator of the excellent lieutenant, or that he mentally referred to his Dalton home as "The House that Haseltine Built."

"Somehow," Mrs. Beaton said, "I can't picture you listening to that blood and thunder."

"Ah, but I do! And d'you know, I have a feeling that Alicia will return? Frankly, I've missed Alicia. She had a certain verve. Er—I've felt, for some time, that Zora was a mistaken effort on the part of the sponsor to inject unnecessary glamour. M'yes, indeed, I know Haseltine well enough to assure you that Alicia is his only true love. Judy will get her job back. I wonder how long," he added hurriedly, "we will have to wait before Evelyn departs? And where is the Wimpernel? You've been so calm about her that I really haven't given her a thought."

"She's perfectly all right. If our janitor couldn't

get out of that place, she can't. Shakespeare, I've forgotten to tell you something important. I've got Ellen. You can cross Ellen off Marcus's list."

"M'yes? Who is she?"

"She's the Ellendorf Oil Company," Mrs. Beaton told him. "I was looking at my tomorrow's list during Hornblower's question period—by the way, people were angelic about questions. They never uttered a word about divorce. Anyway, there was Ellen, right at the head of my list. It meant I had to phone for the oil man to come. And Marcus has the same oil man."

"That leaves us," Leonidas said, "with Myrna. And I begin to entertain a strong suspicion that the Wimpernel is Myrna."

"I know she is," Mrs. Beaton returned. "When I went up to her, I said, 'You're Myrna?' And she said, 'Yes.' And I said, 'Come.' And she came. Of course, if she'd said she wasn't Myrna, I should still have told her to come, and I'm sure she would have. When I got her downstairs, I pointed to the metal door and said, 'That's the ladies' room,' and she said, 'Thanks,' and went in, and closed the door behind her! She's apparently one of those suggestible people, and I'm so glad we got hold of her before she did any fatal damage. She could. My, wasn't it lucky you fell in with Johnny Robbins!"

"M'yes," Leonidas said, "I'm seriously considering buying some cement, out of sheer gratitude. He's going to spend a whole day next week taking pictures of me."

"He's a fat lamb. You know, I thought when I went up to the Wimpernel and Evelyn that he had a gleam in his eye!"

Leonidas told her about his conversation with Evelyn on the subject of the girl.

Mrs. Beaton chuckled.

"You don't know how funny that is! He's had every eligible girl in Carnavon hurled at his head since he's been here, and not one of 'em ever made a dent. Shakespeare, we can't waste any more time here! You'll have to engage Mrs. Spoffard and Evelyn in diverting chatter while I lead that girl out to my sedan. We've got to find out if she's as dumb as she appears to be, or—"

She broke off as Mrs. Spoffard trailed into the office.

"I don't understand Evelyn," she said plaintively. "He's still going around asking everyone in the East Room if they've seen a girl in red!"

"Er—he's lost a girl in red, you know," Leonidas said. "He told me about it. He feels quite strongly about her."

"It's disgraceful," Mrs. Spoffard said. "All these nice girls in town, wholesome and nice and all! Darling," she turned to Mrs. Beaton, "we made four hundred and eighteen dollars and sixteen cents on the rummage alone, and I don't understand that either. We never made more than thirty-five or forty before. What'll I do with the money?"

"Give it to Evelyn to put in the safe."

Mrs. Spoffard sniffed.

"Think of him, hunting that girl! And do you know where she *was?*"

"Er—where?" Leonidas asked with a sinking heart.

"I don't understand what for, but she was in that organ sound thing! I went there to put away the clean tablecloths we didn't use at supper. We've been using that place for the linen, you know, since Evelyn's using the linen closet for his files till he gets new ones. And there was this terrible girl in red!"

"What did you *do?*" Mrs. Beaton demanded.

"Where did she *go?*" Leonidas added.

"Why," Mrs. Spoffard said, "I let her out, and she went."

CHAPTER 6

"ER—WHERE?" Leonidas asked. "Where did the girl go?"

"I'm sure *I* don't know!" Mrs. Spoffard said in her most aggrieved tone. "She just went. And do you know what I think?" she lowered her voice confidentially. "I think she'd been drinking! I truly do. Because do you know what she asked me? She asked me where Spencer Tracy was!"

"Indeed!" Leonidas said. "And—er—what did you tell her?"

Mrs. Spoffard sniffed again.

"I told her," she said, "that Spencer Tracy was in the next block, where he belonged!"

"The next block?" Leonidas said. "Why the next block?"

"Because that's where he is! I forget the name of the picture, but it's at the Bijou. I'm getting pretty tired of people taking this church for a movie theater! I didn't understand when he put them in why Evelyn had to have all those lights out front! I simply don't understand how Evelyn—"

"Darling," Mrs. Beaton rose and buttoned up her coat, "you've done magnificently tonight. I'm terribly pleased and proud of the way you've handled everything, and I'm going to make a point of telling everyone how efficient you've been."

"Really?"

"And I want you to lunch with me a week from Monday. I'll call for you at twelve-thirty. You'll make a note of it, won't you? So you won't forget the way you did last time. And tell Evelyn to take care of the youngsters in the East Room, and shoo them out on time. You'll watch right over him and see that he does, won't you?"

"Where are you going now?" Mrs. Spoffard asked plaintively. "I thought of course you'd stay and settle everything, and I was going home and go to bed!"

Mrs. Beaton sighed. "I had hoped," she said, "to stay and help you clear up, but I must take Mr. Budenny home, darling. I'd offer to settle things here and let *you* take him, but I know you'd hate that long drive this time of night, with the roads in such hideous condition. Wouldn't you? And I must say," she gave Mrs. Spoffard no chance to speak, "you simply look fresh as a daisy, and I don't see *how* you do it. I'm a rag, personally. Who *did* you, Emil or Pierre?"

From his experience with Cassie Price, Leonidas knew that Mrs. Beaton did not insinuate that Mrs. Spoffard had been bilked by either of the gentlemen mentioned. She wanted to know who had dressed Mrs. Spoffard's hair.

"Eugene," Mrs. Spoffard said. "But I didn't like the back."

"Eugene?" Mrs. Beaton wrote "Eugene" on a pocketbook memorandum pad. "I'm going to him next time. That back's wonderful. I love those little curls. Now, darling, thank you a million times for helping me out, and I don't know how I could possibly have got through the evening if it hadn't been for you! Ready, Mr. Budenny? Where are your things?"

"On a chair in the hall," Leonidas said. "Good night, Mrs. Spoffard, I'm—"

"Wait!" Mrs. Spoffard said. "I haven't paid you. Five dollars, wasn't it? Here. You were quite good, Mr. Budenny, although I still don't understand how you could get twenty-one dollars and fifty cents for those moth-eaten old Indian feathers, and only twenty-one cents for Aunt Annie's green cloisonné jardiniere!"

"Thank you, dear lady." Leonidas took the bills she held out, and then gave them back to her with a bow. "Will you accept this as my contribution for such an excellent cause? Er—by the way, what *is* the cause?"

"I never did understand if it was the Day Nursery," Mrs. Spoffard said, "or the Building Fund. Which was it?" she appealed to Mrs. Beaton.

"New furnishings," Mrs. Beaton said briskly. "Come on, Mr. Budenny!"

"Er—furnishings for what?" Leonidas asked.

Mrs. Beaton took his arm. "Come on! Good night, darling! Good night!"

"What furnishings?" Leonidas persisted as they left the office.

"Well," Mrs. Beaton said, "I did know, once. Pick up your things from that chair—is it absolutely necessary for you to carry all those things? A cane, a Transcript, that package—what *is* in that leg-shaped brown paper package? It gives me a horrid start every time I see it!"

"Stocking stretchers. I told you it was a pair of stocking stretchers," Leonidas said gently.

"Yes, I know you did. But what have you got them with you for? It's such a wretchedly untidy package! Did you buy the stretchers in Tilbury?"

"Er—no." Leonidas put on his coat.

"Hm. D'you just always carry stocking stretchers around with you, the way my son Cabot always carries a brief case?"

"Er—no." Leonidas tucked his cane and his paper and his package under one arm, and picked up the green-handled sickle.

"Well," Mrs. Beaton asked impatiently, "what on earth have you got 'em for?"

"I was asked," Leonidas said, "to give them to Professor Davis, another former colleague, in Dalton. My polite protests that I rarely saw the man from one year's end to another were vigorously overruled. To have made an issue of the stocking stretchers would have been rude, and it would have caused me to lose my bus. Therefore, I took the stocking stretchers with me."

"Hm. That's very interesting," Mrs. Beaton said.

"Isn't it? It's just as interesting as that facsimile Shakespeare folio. Hm. Isn't it high time, Bill, that we faced this?"

"We still have got to get hold of the Wimpernel, and settle Myrna," Leonidas said. "I am not allowing myself to jump to any conclusions until I have ruled out every name on that list of Marcus's."

"Perhaps it's the wisest thing," Mrs. Beaton said as they went along to the vestibule. "How *can* we find that girl? We've taken this casually, but you know it's serious, and so do I! She may be only a block away, or she may have thumbed a ride and be miles away! If only we knew which door she might have taken, even! If she went out the side door, she'd head toward Carnavon Falls, but if she came out this one—oh, there's John! Maybe John saw her!"

She hurried down the flagstone path to where Mr. Robbins was busily loading his camera paraphernalia and his rummage purchases into the trunk of an enormously long, shiny black sedan.

"Hi, there, Shakespeare," he said. "Hi, Topsey. Never had a better time than I did at your shindig here tonight! Never laughed so much in my life. My stomach aches, I've laughed so. Take you anywhere, maybe, or drop you off?"

"Thanks, John," Mrs. Beaton said, "but my car's around the corner. Did you happen to catch sight of that girl in the red coat and red hat?"

Mr. Robbins rumbled with laughter.

"Boy, she's a pip, she is! Know what? She came

and stood here watching me for about five minutes, and then she asked me if I was going to Boston. And—"

"Where is she now? Where did she go?" Leonidas interrupted.

"I told her I was waiting for my wife," Mr. Robbins said. "Not that I was, because Mary's still in Florida, but it did the trick. She went."

"John Robbins, where did that girl *go?*" Mrs. Beaton demanded.

"She tripped off to the corner—"

"Which corner?"

He pointed.

"That one. Then she turned around and came back, and asked me which way was the Main Street. I told her she was standing smack on it. Then she said, she meant the main road that went to Boston, where the buses went. So I pointed out the Four Corners, and she tripped off again. She just left, just before you came out. I think you can see her—uh-huh. You can. She's up the line at the corner of Maple. See her?"

Mrs. Beaton flung a hasty word of thanks to him as she grabbed Leonidas's arm.

"Quick, Bill! We'll get my car and pick her up. Hurry. This way. On the side street. We'll pick her up, and keep her! Hurry!"

At the corner, she stopped short.

"Look!"

Leonidas looked.

Two policemen were standing ominously by the sedan parked on the side street.

"That's Harrigan!" Mrs. Beaton said as she and Leonidas simultaneously wheeled around. "And that tall thin cousin of his! I could tell those silhouettes anywhere, after watching 'em up at Marcus's. Bill, what'll we do?"

"Dear me!" Leonidas said. "How very inconvenient of them!"

"Inconvenient! D'you realize that girl's getting away from us? We've got to get that car! We've got to get her! We can't chase after her on foot or take her away without a car! What'll we do?"

Leonidas took her arm and firmly steered her back to Mr. Robbins, who was just heaving himself in behind the wheel of his shiny car.

"Mr. Robbins," he said, "did you happen to see two policemen wandering around here?"

"Ugh!" Mr. Robbins said. "Damn these new cars! I bought the biggest damn car I could find, and I still bang my head on the damn top every time I get into it! What you say?"

Leonidas repeated his question.

"Uh-huh. I saw 'em. They asked me if I knew who owned that sedan on the side street, and I told 'em I didn't. Ha ha! That *your* car, Topsey?"

"Yes, it is! What's wrong? What are they hanging around it for?"

"Want you, Topsey."

"What for, I'd like to know?"

"You parked your car plunk on the bumper light gadget," Mr. Robbins told her. "Light's been red on that corner for hours, I guess, from what they said. Didn't matter till the crowd started coming out of the church, and then they got a traffic jam all the way to Grant Avenue. That's why I'm still here. I got stuck in it. Whyn't you women ever park a car close to the curb, Topsey? Mary does the same thing, parks forty feet out in the middle of the street!"

"That's all those two want me for?" Mrs. Beaton asked. "Just for parking on that thing?"

Mr. Robbins chuckled.

"Something about ducks, too. Little problem of ducks. What you been doing with ducks, Topsey?"

"Ducks!"

"That's what they said. Said when they looked into the car, there was a crate of ducks."

"Merciful heavens!" Mrs. Beaton said. "I know what's happened! I told Judy to put that crate straight back in the car. I meant the beachwagon, but then I took that to go to Marcus's in, and so she put those infernal ducks in my sedan, and forgot all about 'em! That's what happened. I know!"

"What in blazes you stealing crates of ducks for, anyway?" Mr. Robbins asked interestedly.

"*Stealing* ducks? I'm not! I didn't!"

"Cops said so. Said the ducks were stolen from someone up Carnavon Hills way. State cop was around and had a look at 'em, too, but he's gone off now. Honest, Topsey, sometimes I think you do the damnedest things!"

"John, I never stole any ducks! I never did! Oh,

this is awful! Bill, what'll we do? We *can't* get my car!
We can't wait to explain about ducks! Not now! John,
will you lend me your car, just for a few minutes,
please? Will you?"

Mr. Robbins shook his head.

"John, please!"

"Listen, Topsey," he said, "I'd like to oblige you,
but I won't lend you my brand new car! I've seen you
drive. But I'll take you anywhere you want to go. You
want to go somewheres?"

"Yes, but—no, John, you can't—oh, dear! Bill,
what'll we do?"

Leonidas opened the rear door.

"Get in," he said. "Mr. Robbins, thank you. Will
you be good enough to drive along Main Street until
you see that girl in the red hat? Er—quickly?"

He shoved Mrs. Beaton in, got in beside her, and
Mr. Robbins started the car.

"Bill!" Mrs. Beaton whispered. "We can't! We
can't let him—"

"I see your girl friend," Mr. Robbins interrupted.
"She's looking into the Star Store window. Say, did I
have fun with those dummies there tonight, Topsey!
I was telling Shakespeare all about it. I saw this fellow
in a St. Patrick's costume, see, and—"

"Mr. Robbins," Leonidas leaned forward, "how
much milk of human kindness have you?"

Mrs. Beaton noticed with alarm that he was force-
fully gripping the green-handled sickle in his right

hand, and that the sickle point was not very far from
Mr. Robbins's broad shoulders.

"Oh, I got as much as the next man, I guess," Mr.
Robbins said. "What you want?"

"Mr. Robbins, to state the situation with excep-
tional bluntness, it is the intention of Mrs. Beaton and
myself to kidnap that young person in the scarlet
wimple. Do you feel willing to co-operate with us in
this reprehensible albeit imperative process, or do you
feel obligated to uphold and maintain the law?"

"Huh?"

Leonidas repeated his little speech, and waited.
Mr. Robbins, he thought, had been given his choice.
And if the man chose to be a lawful citizen, he was
going to reverse that choice at the point of a sickle.

To his amazement, Mr. Robbins shook with
laughter.

"Boy," he said, "you kill me! You slay me, you do!
You're certainly one of the greatest kidders I ever met
in all my life! I'm going to get you to talk to the Rotary.
Boy, would I like to get a shot of their faces when you
start slinging those syllables around!"

"Mr. Robbins, I am not jesting!" Leonidas said.
"I mean it!"

"Sure!" Mr. Robbins slowed down the car. "All
right, run along and kidnap your girl friend. Going to
hold her for ransom, I suppose?"

"I'll get out," Mrs. Beaton was whispering excited
plans in Leonidas's ear, "and you stay in the car, out of

sight, and then if I can't induce her to get in, you get out and—look!"

At the sight of the car, the girl walked over to it.

"Hi." Mr. Robbins opened the front door and spoke to her genially. "Hiyah, sister. Hop in!"

The girl hopped in.

"Got some friends of yours in back, sister," Mr. Robbins said.

The girl twisted around.

"Well!" she said. "I certainly never thought I was ever going to see you with the beard again! Have I ever hunted you high and wide! Hello!"

"Er—hello," Leonidas said.

"Got my pocketbook, huh?"

"M'yes," Leonidas said. "Not here, but we'll get it. Will you take us, please, to Potter's hardware store, Mr. Robbins?"

"Call me John," Mr. Robbins said. "Everybody calls me John."

"Potter's hardware, John," Leonidas said, and leaned back against the seat.

"Say!" the girl said suddenly to Mrs. Beaton. "Say, that reminds me. You know what? That wasn't no ladies' room. That was a closet!"

"No!" Leonidas wondered how much of the bewilderment in Mrs. Beaton's voice was genuine, and how much was assumed. "No!"

"Yes, it was. They ought to put up a sign."

"I shall certainly see that they do," Mrs. Beaton

said, "at the first opportunity. But you got out all right, didn't you?"

The girl nodded vigorously. "I got out."

Leonidas and Mrs. Beaton nervously awaited further comments on the subject of being locked up in the metal chamber, but none were forthcoming. Apparently the girl had dismissed the incident.

"Say, sister," John said, "what's your name?"

"Myrna. Myrna Reel."

"Myrna what?"

"Riley," the girl said.

"That isn't what you said before," John told her. "You said something like 'Reel.'"

"Reel's my suitor," the girl paused, "him."

"Your suitor? Who's your suitor?"

"My suitor him. Like my stage name," the girl explained.

"On the stage, huh? Now I wonder," John said, "why I didn't guess that. Act, do you?"

"I sing," the girl said.

"Give us a number," John said.

The girl opened her mouth, and at once the car was filled with what Leonidas had previously called banshee noises.

"I sing hot," she said when she got through.

Mr. Robbins opened the car window. "Sister," he said, "you'd make the average furnace look like a cooling system. I got to say you got power, too! Here you are at the hardware store, Shakespeare. Now what?"

"Bill, why don't you and Myrna go in and find that pocketbook," Mrs. Beaton said brightly, "and I'll stay here with John. Are you very busy, John, or can you wait a few minutes and take us all along home?"

"You just going to leave your car sitting there, huh?" John said. "It won't do you any good, Topsey. It's just like I tell Mary when she tears up parking tickets and throws 'em away, it won't do her a speck of good. They'll just track you down tomorrow!"

"Tomorrow," Mrs. Beaton told him with a little sigh, "is another day. Will you drive us home, John?"

"If you take my advice, you'll go straighten it out about those ducks right now, Topsey. The longer you let those sort of things ride, the madder the damn fool cops always get. I'll take you home if you say so. I haven't got anything else to do, but I think you—"

"John, you're a lamb! Go in with Bill, Myrna. And don't be too long hunting that pocketbook, will you, Bill? John, how *is* Mary? I'm ashamed to say I haven't acknowledged her card. It had the loveliest alligators on it, and she said that the weather had been simply frightful! I remember I was there in thirty-two, and it was just the same—"

Leonidas smiled as he and the girl walked across the sidewalk to the door of Link's establishment.

If Mr. Robbins was entertaining any doubts or suspicions about this expedition, it was clear that he was never going to have any opportunity of voicing them.

He finally found the key which Link Potter had given him earlier, and opened the door.

The girl followed him in.

"Ah!" Leonidas said. "There it is!"

He pointed to the scarlet pocketbook sitting under the night light on the rear counter.

"Well!" the girl said. "I certainly am releafed to see that again! Thanks, mister!"

Leonidas scooped it up and held it in front of him so that it would not be visible to Mr. Robbins, outside in the car.

"Er—come into the back room," he said. "We'll turn on the light there and make sure everything in your bag is as you left it. Come!"

The girl followed him without question.

"Say," she said, "you know what? I'm sorry, mister."

Leonidas looked at her. She looked sorry, he thought, and she sounded sorry.

"Honest I am. You know. About the bus."

"I'm glad," Leonidas said, "to hear you say that, and I'm inclined to believe you. But—er—I could wish that this remorseful interlude had occurred before I was forced to leave the bus so hurriedly."

"Honest, I thought it was all a rib!"

"A what?"

"A rib. You know. A joke. I didn't think you'd be somebody like you. I thought it was all a rib, all the time. I thought you knew it was. I thought you was

going to tell the driver so when you got up, that time
he called you."

"Indeed!"

"Yeah. Just you wait till I get my hands on that
big lug! Say, he better watch out when I get my hands
on him! He better keep out of my way, that big lug!"

"Er—what big lug?"

"The big lug that thought it up. He *said* it was a
rib!"

Leonidas looked at her thoughtfully.

"Myrna, could you use fifty dollars?"

"Say, could I! That's what that big lug was supposed to pay! I'm telling you, when I get through with
that big lug," Myrna said, "he's going to be rat food!
I don't care what Rosalie says, neither!"

"Er—who is Rosalie?"

"My girl friend. She and I are like that." Myrna
held up two fingers. "See? It's her fault for thinking
this big lug was a gentleman!"

"Myrna," Leonidas said, "that lady out in the car
is Mrs. Beaton. If you will come to her house, and answer a few questions I should like to put to you, it
will give me great pleasure to present you with fifty
dollars, and to send you back home to Boston in a taxicab. Prepaid, I might add."

"In a taxi? Honest? Gee! Only," her smile suddenly faded, "only—well, it's like this, see. I won't get
that fifty from that big lug. Not now. He's scrammed
by now. He won't be waiting at no bus stop in Park
Square. I don't think that big lug ever meant to pay

it anyway. I did, that is, until this other guy said most likely he didn't—"

"Er—what other guy?"

"This other guy with the moustache, see? The one at the Four Corners. He had a moustache."

"Are you, by any rare chance," Leonidas asked, "referring to that individual who picked up my white rubbers, that the bus driver hurled after me?"

"Yeah. That one. I told him I had to get my pocketbook because I had to get back to Boston because there was this man going to give me fifty bucks at the bus stop, see? And he asked why, and I told him it was a rib, and he said he bet I got ribbed out of my fifty, see? And he said he'd help me get my pocketbook, and if I didn't, he'd give me the loan of ten bucks to get home on, see? But then he scrammed, too. So that's sixty bucks I lost, see, on account of everybody scramming first. So—"

"Say no more." Leonidas drew out his wallet. "Here. Ten, twenty, forty, and two fives make fifty. Put it in your bag. And now, come. At Mrs. Beaton's, we will make an effort to settle all this."

"I wish you would!" Myrna returned. "Honest, what a night I put in! What a night! I feel like the wrath of grapes!"

"To a certain extent," Leonidas told her, "I share that feeling. Come!"

He stopped long enough in the front part of the store to leave in conspicuous places three notes telling Link Potter to join him at Mrs. Beaton's.

Then he and Myrna returned to the car, where Mrs. Beaton was still doggedly discussing Florida.

"Did you leave notes for Potter?" she asked. "Did you tell him where you'd be?"

"M'yes," Leonidas gallantly assisted Myrna in, closed the door, and then got in back with Mrs. Beaton. "I did. Er—home, John."

It was a silent ride.

The girl sat quietly on the front seat, gripping her pocketbook, and Mr. Robbins hummed in a minor key. Mrs. Beaton drummed on the arm rest with her fingers, and Leonidas toyed with his pince-nez.

Finding out about Myrna, he thought, was going to prove easier in one way than he had anticipated. In another way, he was not so sure.

The car swung up the driveway of a long, rambling white house, and pulled up at the front door.

"Well, boys and girls," John said genially, "here we are!"

Mrs. Beaton sat up.

"John," she said, "you've been perfectly wonderful to help us out, and I can't tell you how I appreciate what you've done for us. Tell Mary I said you were a dear lamb. And you must come to dinner the first week she's home, won't you? Tell her to call me just the minute she gets back! Good night, John—and do be careful of that big puddle at the turn going out. It's skiddy. Good night, John!"

Mr. Robbins made no move whatsoever towards starting the car.

"Say, Topsey," he said, "you don't mean after all this toting around I've done for you, you're packing me off without even offering me a cup of coffee, do you?"

"John—"

"I know you're not. You wouldn't do that to a mongrel dog. I'm hungry," John said, "and I'm thirsty. I should think you'd be dry as a bone, yourself, the rate you've been talking."

He extricated himself from behind the wheel, and got out of the car.

"Damn that low top!" he said. "It bangs you going and coming! Come on, sister," he hooked one arm through Myrna's and the other through Leonidas's. "Come on, Shakespeare. Let's go!"

There was more than a trace of grimness to the set of Mrs. Beaton's jaw as she opened the front door.

Leonidas, with narrowed eyes, watched Mr. Robbins's bland, rotund face. It was, he decided, just a little too bland.

"Say, Shakespeare, you seen the colonel lately?" John inquired as they entered the front hall.

"Er—who?"

"The colonel. Colonel Carpenter. The colonel's a great friend of mine."

"Is he," Leonidas said, "indeed."

Mr. Robbins sat down on a ladder back chair in the hall, and practically collapsed with laughter.

"I knew you all the time!" he said. "Ha ha! The

look on your faces, you and Topsey, when I said I was coming in! Boy, if I could have got a shot of you then! Sure, I knew you all the time, but I wasn't going to let on! You're Witherall, aren't you? What's up? What's all this about? What were you playing auctioneer for? And don't tell me you weren't! I know what Budenny looks like. His junk shop's around the corner from the coal yard! What's up?"

"John Robbins," Mrs. Beaton said, "do you want to know the wisest thing you can do? Besides getting yourself off that chair before it breaks? You go right straight home, John Robbins, and forget all about this! Right this minute! I mean it!"

"Home? Not on your life!" John said. "I'm not —ow!"

"I told you so!" Mrs. Beaton said. "I told you that chair would break! It isn't supposed to be sat on."

Mr. Robbins, displaying unusual nimbleness for a man his size, got to his feet and surveyed the prostrate chair.

"What in blazes you keep chairs around for," he inquired, "if they're not supposed to be sat on?"

"For the décor!" Mrs. Beaton told him. "And don't let's waste time going into the whats and why-fores of décor! You go home, John, and forget about this. This is nothing for you to meddle in, and take pictures of!"

"From what the colonel's told me," John said, "about Shakespeare here, he's just the man you want to stand near with a camera, Topsey. The colonel says more damn things happen to this fellow than any ten men he ever knew in his whole life!"

"M'yes," Leonidas said. "Like his sister, the colonel is prone to exaggerate. But may I suggest, John, that your continued presence here might conceivably involve you in distressing circumstances which would not, I feel sure, prove ultimately beneficial to the concrete business? In short, Mrs. Beaton is right. Go home. This is not—where's that girl? Where did Myrna go?"

"Myrna!" Mrs. Beaton raised her voice and called. "Myrna!"

Myrna appeared at a doorway leading from the hall.

"I was just looking around," she said. "You mind if I look around? What a swell house! Orris chairs, and broadtail rugs, and indiscreet lighting—just like a movie! Is it all right if I look around?"

"Look," Mrs. Beaton said weakly, "to your heart's content!"

"Gee, thanks!" Myrna departed.

John Robbins leaned back against the newel post and laughed until the tears rolled down his cheeks.

"Orris chairs!" he said. "Broadtail rugs! Indiscreet lighting! Topsey, you couldn't pay me to leave now!"

Leonidas sighed. He felt that John meant just what he said.

But Mrs. Beaton tried again.

"John, this is terribly amusing for you, but—"

"Boy, I'll say! I never had a better time! Orris chairs!"

"But it's rather grim for us. Won't you be a lamb, and leave?"

"Topsey, I won't! You couldn't drive me away! I never laughed so hard!"

"Bill," Mrs. Beaton said despairingly, "what'll we *do* with him? We can't throw him out!"

"Er—I fear," Leonidas said, "we'll have to let him stay. For a while. Er—John, will you give me your word that under no circumstances will you feel inspired to summon the police?"

"You mean call the cops? About that car of Topsey's, huh, and parking on that bumper gadget?"

"Er—no. Not about the car."

John raised his eyebrows.

"The eccentric parking of that car," Leonidas said, "and the illegal possession of ducks are possibly the smallest of the problems confronting us at the moment, and certainly the least of what the police might want us for, I assure you."

"I know!" John said, waggling a finger at Leonidas. "I know! Carpenter told me about that murder case you solved for him last year. You're mixed up in something like that! Aren't you?"

"M'yes," Leonidas said. "Exactly like that."

"Well, for Pete's sakes!" John said. "What do you know about that! Well, say, I'm sorry I been clowning around so, if that's true. I guess I sort of been in the way, haven't I? Well, I'll go along home if you really want me to—"

"John," Mrs. Beaton said, "you *are* a lamb!"

"Only I think," he continued, "that maybe I better stick around after all. You might need me to cart you somewhere, or take some pictures, or something. You know," he added, "I read a lot of mystery stories, and I always thought if I ever got mixed up in a murder case, myself, I could do just as good as any of those fellows that detect and find out who done it. So I guess I'll stay. I won't be a bit of bother. Not a speck. I'll just listen in, and if I think of anything that might help, why, I'll tell you. And who knows, maybe I might help!"

"Er—who knows," Leonidas said. "Perhaps you might!"

"Just you go right ahead with whatever you're doing, now," John said. "I won't interrupt or anything. A murder! Think of it! What a day I had! A murder, and that shindig of yours at the church, Topsey, and that fellow with the harp, and this morning—what do you suppose happened this morning, Topsey? Marcus Meredith called me up and asked me to be a trustee of that school of his! Can you beat that?"

"No, I can't," Mrs. Beaton said. "Not meaning to detract from your worth in the slightest, why did he ever think of you?"

"He's cagey. He's planning another group of buildings for his school," John said with a grin, "and he thought it'd be nice to have someone in cement on his board of trustees. I made him admit that when I saw him."

"Er—today?" Leonidas asked. "You saw him to-day? When? What time?"

"Around five. I saw Judy there. She came in just as I left. Meredith said he was making a lot of changes at his school, and he expected to be in his grave before he got things straightened out, and he finally got me to say I'd be a trustee for a year. He—but I mustn't get off the track," John said. "I'm sorry. Say, who was killed, anyone I know?"

"Marcus Meredith," Mrs. Beaton told him.

"Meredith!" John sat down on the bottom step of the stairs. "Well, can you beat that! You know what? I'd like to have a shot of my own face right now! If it looks like I feel, it'd be some picture! Well, for Pete's sakes! Say, that's *awful!* Who did it?"

"That," Mrs. Beaton said crisply, "is what we are trying to find out, if you'll ever give us a chance to continue, John! Bill, will you stop dreaming and come back to earth? Let's get hold of Myrna, and let's *do* something about her! If John wants to get mixed up in this, I suppose we can't stop him, but don't let's let him stop us any more! Where is she, in the living room? Well, come along and get started, Bill! Bill, do you hear me?"

"M'yes," Leonidas said.

"What did I say?"

With a smile, Leonidas put on his pince-nez and repeated her words verbatim.

"And now," he said, "let us get to Myrna, by all means!"

"I hate to sound like Mrs. Spoffard," Mrs. Beaton said, "but I don't understand you, Bill Shakespeare! Now that we've got this girl, you don't seem to care a fig! You sound as though getting to her were some sort of chore. Like spring house cleaning."

"From my brief experience with Myrna," Leonidas said, "I fear that what we are about to find out will not compensate us for the labor involved. But we shall try."

Myrna got up from a three-legged stool in front of the fireplace as they entered the living room.

"What a swell house!" she said. "I like this room. It's like a movie I seen last week where Spencer Tracy—"

"M'yes. Let us recapitulate," Leonidas said quickly. "You're Myrna Riley. Your stage name is Myrna, Reel. You have a friend named Rosalie, who knew a big lug, who planned a rib. He was going to give you fifty dollars when the Tilbury bus reached the Park Square bus terminal. Is that right?"

"Not to me. He was going to give Rosalie the fifty bucks."

"I distinctly remember," Leonidas said, "that you told me that you wouldn't get no fifty from that big lug, who had scrammed, and wouldn't be at no bus stop in Park Square."

"If he was there, see," Myrna said, "and if I was on the bus, he'd given it to me, see? But he thought it would be Rosalie. Not me. He don't know me."

Leonidas drew a long breath.

"Myrna," he said gently, "will you think very hard, please, and begin at what you think is the beginning of all this?"

"Well, this big lug—"

"D'you know his name?"

"He told Rosalie it was Jack Smith, but Rosalie didn't think it was his right name," Myrna said. "Shall I call him that anyway?"

"M'yes. Let's call him Smith. Go on."

"Well," Myrna frowned, "well, there was this compact, see? And Rosalie just took it to the light, but this flatfoot grabbed her, see? Then this lug Smith, he came along and bought it. That's how she happened to meet him. See?"

"Frankly, no," Leonidas said.

"I do. I've had so many maids," Mrs. Beaton said, "I understand this sort of thing. Rosalie was about to be arrested by a store detective for pilfering a powder compact, which she had merely taken to the daylight to inspect, and Smith bought the compact for Rosalie, thus saving the day. Is that right, Myrna?"

"That's right," Myrna said. "Then he asked her to have dinner with him, but she couldn't, because she's working at the Gilt Shoe, see? But she went out with him last night after the show, see, and he asked if she'd do him a favor, and she said sure. She's got a heart big as a box, Rosalie has. So Smith gave her ten bucks, see, and asked would she go to Tilbury tomorrow—"

"Meaning today," Leonidas said.

"Yeah. On the bus, see, and wait for this guy that

was taking a bus back to Boston, see? The guy Smith
was going to rib. And then when the bus got into Park
Square, he'd give her fifty bucks, see?"

"M'yes," Leonidas said, "that's reasonably lucid.
Rosalie was given, I assume, a description of the—er—
guy to be ribbed? She was told what he looked like?"

"The guy had a beard—why," Myrna said, "it
was you! You know. A guy with a beard, like you, and
a package shaped like a leg. Like the one you had."

"M'yes. And what was Rosalie to do?"

"Like I did," Myrna said succinctly.

"M'yes. Including putting your pocketbook in
my pocket? Was that a part of the rib?"

"Yeah. But it was much more funnier when Rosalie told me how she was going to do it," Myrna said.
"It wasn't going to be like it happened. She was going
to take it back. So was I. Sure, that was part of the
rib. And when Rosalie got into Park Square, this lug
Smith was going to give her fifty bucks."

"And what happened to Rosalie?" Leonidas inquired. "Why didn't she perform the—er—rib, according to schedule?"

"Well," Myrna said, "this morning when she
waked up, she opened her pocketbook, and there was
the ten bucks Smith give her, and she went out, and
when she come in, was she ever stinko! She's got an
awful weakness for champagne, Rosalie has. It's the
reason for her worst dipsopation."

"In the morning?" John asked.

Myrna laughed.

"Say, any time is good enough for her! Anyway, she couldn't go off on no rib to Tilbury. I put her to bed and told her to sleep it off."

"And took her place," Mrs. Beaton said.

"Sure. I couldn't let my best friend down! Why, we're just like Damon and Runyan! And like I said to her, money might be the loot of all evil, but fifty bucks was fifty bucks. And I could do the rib as good as she."

"I'm sure," Leonidas said, "that you did. Now, you went to Tilbury on the bus, waited till I appeared, and followed me on the bus. I assume that if I had not appeared in time to take that particular bus, you would have waited until I did appear? M'yes, you would have. We will pass over the ensuing painful interlude, and get to the Four Corners, where I alighted."

"You fooled me," Myrna said. "I thought you knew all the time it was a rib, and I thought you was going to tell the driver so, when he called you up to him. But you fooled me! You got off!"

"Er—and what did you think then?" Leonidas asked.

"I just thought *you* was ribbing me," Myrna said. "I thought you'd come back. You'd left your rubbers, see? And when I seen you on the sidewalk, and then rushing off, I grabbed the rubbers and yelled to the driver, and he yelled at you, and then he threw 'em at you. Then I remembered my pocketbook was in your pocket, and so I got off, and then there was this man with the moustache, see? He'd picked your rubbers up.

And I said, 'Say,' I said, 'those are the man with the beard's!' And he said, 'What beards?' So then I said for him to give me the rubbers quick, because I had to rush after the man with the beard, because he had my pocketbook. And then the bus went off."

"And then?" Leonidas prompted.

Myrna honestly admitted that what took place next confused her. The man with the moustache looked at her, and then he examined the rubbers, and then he said that if a man with a beard had made off with her pocketbook, she must tell the cops about it. And Myrna protested that the man with the beard had not stolen her pocketbook at all.

"I kept saying, you just had it! I told him it was a rib. And all the time he held onto the rubbers and kept looking at them," Myrna said. "I told him it was just a rib for a friend, and he said it sounded to him like my pocketbook had got swiped. So I tried to tell him about the rib, but he was the dumbest cluck! I kept explaining and explaining, all about Rosalie and the compact, and Smith, and the fifty bucks, and her getting stinko, and he just kept asking more questions. Then finally he said he'd tell a cop all about it for me, and the cops would find you and get my pocketbook back. So he walked over to the traffic cop, and I waited."

"Waited where?" Leonidas asked.

"On the sidewalk. It was all sludgey, so I stayed there. He said I better. He said I'd get my feet all wet if I didn't, and to stay there."

"M'yes. So you stayed on the sidewalk, while he discussed the matter with the policeman. Did he take the rubbers with him?"

"Oh, no! He put them in his car before he talked to the cop. And then he and this cop, they walked over to a prowl car, and a sergeant got out, and they all talked and talked! Honest, I never seen people talk more about anything. And then the cops walked over to me and asked if it was true, and I said yes."

"Did you know to what they referred? Did you know what they were talking about?" Leonidas demanded.

"Why, my pocketbook."

"M'yes, but did they say so?"

"No, but I knew that!" Myrna said. "Why, I knew that!"

"Hm," Mrs. Beaton said. "I begin to understand how those fake charges landed on you so quickly, Bill! All that man had to do was to point to Myrna on the sidewalk, and make up his own story. He knew perfectly well she wasn't the right girl, but he realized that he was definitely master of the situation, and that it would all work out. She was simply putty in his hands. Myrna, do you know his name?" she pointed to Leonidas.

"Him? Sure. Bill. Gee," Myrna said, "I wished I'd known it then. I didn't know it then, see, and I had to keep calling him the man with the beard, and everybody would say, 'What man with the beard?' And—"

"M'yes," Leonidas said. "Get back to the policeman, if you please. You told them yes, it was true. Then what?"

"They said they was sorry," Myrna said, "and they'd take care of you, and for me not to mind too much, because they'd settle it all, and they patted me on the back, too. Then they started to say I should ought to come along of them, but the man with the moustache said he'd take care of me, so the cops went off. And then the man with the moustache, he drove me to a corner, and told me to stand right there."

"And, of course, you did," Mrs. Beaton said. "I know you did. Didn't you?"

"Sure. He said for me to stand there and see if I could catch sight of the man with the beard, and he'd drive around and see if he could find him, and he said to wait till he come back, because if he couldn't find the man with my pocketbook, he'd give me the loan of ten bucks to get home on. See?"

"Evelyn," Leonidas said, "was not entirely mistaken in his trusting child estimate, after all. M'yes. You stood on the corner, and after a while, the man came back and said he'd seen me, and would drive you to where I was."

Myrna nodded.

"And he did, and I yelled at you, but you run off. Say, did I ever hunt you high and wide! I hunted for you like a needle in a hatrack! But I couldn't find you no place!"

"And what became of this kindly man with the moustache?" Mrs. Beaton asked.

"I guess," Myrna said, "he just scrammed. I went back to that other corner, the first one, but he wasn't there. He'd scrammed. I guess he didn't want to loan me no ten bucks. If I'd of known his name, I'd of tried more to of found him."

"But of course you never asked him," Mrs. Beaton said.

Myrna shook her head.

"I guess," she said with a little sigh, "Rosalie's right. Rosalie always says you should ought to find out their names, and then you got something you can start from. But I keep forgetting to ask."

"M'yes," Leonidas said. "You seem to. Er—Myrna, did this man Smith have a moustache? Did Rosalie happen to say?"

"She didn't say he did, so he couldn't of," Myrna told him. "You see, Rosalie's making like a collection of men with moustaches. I always tell her if she's got a hobby, it's a man with a moustache."

John Robbins began to rumble.

"Shush, John!" Mrs. Beaton said. "Don't you dare start us really laughing, or we'll never get anywhere. Hm. I see what you meant, Bill. We begin to see how things came to happen to you, but it really doesn't advance us any. Hm. Smith and the man with the moustache are the same person, don't you think?"

"Oh, no!" Myrna answered before Leonidas had a chance to speak. "Smith didn't have no moustache. This guy did. You can't grow a moustache over night!"

"M'yes," Leonidas said. "This man has a moustache, Smith has none. But a false moustache can be put on in the twinkling of an eye. And no mere moustache can serve to disguise such a pronounced streak of uncanny opportunism. He laid his plan like a crafty opportunist. The plan went awry, but he carried on like a crafty opportunist. Now I wonder why he didn't realize that Myrna wasn't Rosalie, back in Tilbury—er—Myrna, I wonder if you possibly could be wearing Rosalie's hat and coat?"

"What's Rosalie's is mine," Myrna said, "and what's mine's hers. Whoever gets dressed first gets the best. First come, first serving. She got this coat and hat first yesterday, and this morning, too. But I put it on after she got put to bed. Say, about this moustache."

"What about it?" Mrs. Beaton asked. "You don't happen to remember its falling off, do you?"

"Say, it's just come to me like a flash in the pan. When I was in the car with that guy, going after Bill—only I didn't know it was Bill, then—well, something flittered, and I was going to ask what flittered, and then he told me quick as a blink to look at a puddle, and I did. But you know what? Afterwards that moustache was different. All crooked on one side. Say, what do you know about that! Won't Rosalie howl when she hears that!"

"M'yes," Leonidas said. "Now, how did you go to Meredith's?"

"Up there? I thumbed a ride. I wanted to go to Boston, see," Myrna said, "but nobody ever seems to

be going to Boston, out here. So I got a ride with a
guy in a truck going that way."

"And why did you go to Marcus Meredith's?"

"To get some money," Myrna said. "I work for
him. I know him. I been there twice for him to hear
my fiction."

"Your what?" Mrs. Beaton demanded.

"My fiction. About a month ago, see, I got a call
from the agency, and I went and talked with the lady
there, and she sent me out to Mr. Meredith. He listens
to my fiction. He makes records of my genetics."

John Robbins hurriedly left the room.

"If I don't go," he paused in the doorway, "I'm
going to bust your sofa like I bust your chair, Topsey.
Ha ha! I bet the old boy had some fun!"

"Fiction!" Mrs. Beaton said weakly. "Genetics!
Bill, can you make out what she means?"

"Diction," Leonidas said. "M'yes. He listened to
her diction, and made phonograph records of her speech
for his work on phonetics. M'yes, I understand that.
He often called various types of employment agencies
and had different types of people sent out to him. He
has thousands and thousands of records down in his
cellar—did John go outdoors?"

"I don't think so," Mrs. Beaton said, "and if he
did, he hasn't gone far. I can see his coat and hat in
the hall. Go on, Myrna. You went to Meredith's, and
no one answered the bell."

"That's right." It never seemed to occur to Myrna

to ask how anyone happened to know so much about her movements. "There wasn't no one home. I was supposed to go there at five-thirty today, see, but I forgot all about it, and it was lots later when I got there tonight. But I thought I'd say the bus broke down, see, and then make him a genetics record, and then he'd give me five bucks, and then I could get home. But then—"

"Then what?"

"Well," Myrna frowned. "Well, I don't understand that. Something hit me in the back, and I thought I'd been shot, and then I yelled, and then some cops came, and then they started talking about incest," she hesitated, "about incestuation."

"Initiation!" Mrs. Beaton said.

"Well, it was all about riding goats, anyhow. And then one cop said the man with the beard was phony. I got scared. I beat it. I thumbed a ride to town—honest, there don't never seem to be no cars ever going to Boston," Myrna said. "I never seen such a place anyway. All country, and hills and bales, and nobody never going nowhere, except from one hill to another bale!"

"Then you went to the church. Why," Mrs. Beaton demanded, "a church, of all places?"

"It was bright," Myrna said simply. "Say, Bill."

"M'yes?"

"When I go home in that taxi, I think I'll stop off first about a block beyond that church."

"Er—why?"

"There was a guy looked like Spencer Tracy,"

Myrna said. "He told me he'd take me home. Gee, he was swell, he was! A perfect gentleman. I'd like to find him again."

"If I had a camera in my hand to get that look!" John loomed in the doorway. "She mean the padre asked to take her home, Topsey? Wo-hoo! Ah-wahh! Ha ha! Ha ha!"

"John, stop being lewd, and go away! You distract us—what did you say?"

"Said where's your kitchen?"

"Through the dining room, and follow your nose," Mrs. Beaton said. "There's cold turkey in the ice box, you slave to your stomach! Bill, what are we going to do? This business was all planned, obviously. Whoever Smith is, he had it planned with Rosalie last night. Hm. I suppose you know a lot about Shakespeare folios, don't you?"

"I wrote a book on Shakespeare once," Leonidas said, "a rash action I've regretted ever since. It endowed me, among my former colleagues, with a thoroughly unjustified reputation for being a Shakespeare expert, and, furthermore, a Shakespeare enthusiast."

"In short," Mrs. Beaton said, "if someone—shall we come right out into the open and say his name? If Professor Colfax wished to lure you to Tilbury, he would very likely use a Shakespeare item for bait—how everything hinges on that folio! No folio, no call, no call, no bus ride, no girl planted to annoy you! Myrna, just exactly how far was Rosalie told to go?"

"Smith said the sky was the limit and let her conscious be her guide. He said if there was any trouble, he'd fix it all up."

"There!" Mrs. Beaton said. "You see, Bill, he planted her, he planned every last thing about this murder!"

"Murder?" Myrna said in a voice of pained surprise. "You mean somebody's got bumped off?"

Mrs. Beaton assured her crisply that somebody certainly had, and, after a moment of laborious thought, Myrna nodded.

"You know what I think?" she said. "I think the country's dangerous. The minute you get away from the city, it ain't safe. Gee, what things happen! Murders, even!"

Mrs. Beaton drew a long breath.

"Myrna," she said, "don't you want to look around the house? Find John. Get some turkey. There's a dear. Now, Bill. That man planned everything. You were supposed to be on that bus. That girl was supposed to make a scene. That inviting you to Tilbury was just bait! You know it. And yet you keep shying away from Colfax, and you know perfectly well everything hinges on that folio, and he was the one who persuaded you to come see it!"

"M'yes," Leonidas said. "I've thought of it every time anyone has called me Shakespeare tonight. But—"

"There aren't any buts! He planned everything!"

"Er—no. Not everything. Remember," Leonidas said, "I left the bus at Carnavon. I had not planned to. There were other stops where I might have alighted before reaching Carnavon. The girl was supposed to go on to Boston. No one could have planned *all* of this. No one could have planned to leave my rubbers beside Marcus, or to involve me as they have done. No, there are many things no one could have planned last night, including the murder."

"If a murder wasn't planned," Mrs. Beaton said, "I'd like to know what was!"

Leonidas twirled his pince-nez from their broad black ribbon.

"The original plans misfired when I got off the bus at Carnavon," he said, "but in the light of what steps were instantly taken by the man with the moustache, I think we can make an excellent guess as to what those original plans were. Someone wished to put me in an embarrassing and uncomfortable situation."

"And went to all this work, and threw in a murder for good measure? Don't be silly!"

"The first and most important point," Leonidas said, "was to frame charges against me. Myrna's mental capacity being what it is, I think we can assume that she didn't entirely understand the significance of putting her pocketbook into my pocket. I feel sure that Rosalie's purse, for example, would have been nestling in my pocket when I got off the bus at Dalton, had the original plan gone through. Rosalie would have screamed to the bus driver, the bus driver would have raced after me, the police would have been summoned, and I should have been held for stealing her pocketbook.

I feel convinced that some charge about my annoying her would have been added."

"But you could have proved it was all a mistake, and a frame-up!"

"M'yes," Leonidas said. "Tomorrow I could have. Doubtless Rosalie, after giving a false name, would never have appeared against me. But by then, Topsey, there would be headlines in the local papers, and a great stir and to-do among people who knew me. Remember that Myrna, who got her instructions second-hand, nevertheless played her part well enough to convince both the passengers and the driver of that bus that I was a lecherous old man. I shudder to think what Rosalie might have done!"

"Hm!" Mrs. Beaton got up and went to the hall. "Myrna! Oh, Myrna! I want you. Will you come here, please? Now," she said when the girl came, "listen, Myrna. Bill is going to tell you what the man with the moustache looked like. Listen hard, now. Bill, you describe Professor Colfax! No, go on!"

"Carl Colfax has no motive in the world to engineer such an episode, Topsey! He has nothing to gain by discrediting me, and he has everything to lose by killing Marcus. That is the trouble!"

"You go ahead and tell Myrna what he looks like!"

"Very well," Leonidas said. "He is fifty-two. He has a red face. He is bald. He is not as tall as I am, but taller than Mr. Robbins. His voice rasps. He smokes cigars. His face is full. He has a fattish stomach—wait.

There's a picture of him in tonight's Transcript, award-
ing prizes at yesterday's track meet in the gymnasium.
I'll show you what he looks like."

"I'm glad," Mrs. Beaton said, "that that paper is
eventually serving some purpose, after you've lugged
it all over town. Spread it out on the table. There,
Myrna. See that man? Isn't that the man with a moustache? Draw in a moustache, and see if it isn't!"

Myrna giggled.

"That ain't him! Nothing like him!"

CHAPTER 7

"HE was young," Myrna went on. "And tall, and dark, and he. had a swell voice. Rosalie said Smith had a swell voice too."

"Myrna, think!" Mrs. Beaton said. "Are you sure this isn't the man with the moustache? Are you positive?"

"That pongee thing in the picture there? No! The guy with the moustache, he was tall, and young, and dark!"

Mrs. Beaton thrust a pencil and a piece of paper into Myrna's hand.

"Here. Draw a sketch of him!"

"Say, I can't draw! I can't even draw a stray lion!"

"Try."

"But—"

"Try!"

Even Mrs. Beaton was forced to admit that the resulting sketch was not a complete success.

"It might be Hitler," Leonidas looked at it critically. "Or District Attorney Dewey. M'yes, there's a touch of Dewey at Manila Bay. But it bears out her point that the fellow was tall, dark, and had a moustache."

"Bill, what'll we *do?*" Mrs. Beaton demanded. "I was sure he'd be Colfax! And now we don't even know his name, or who he is, or what he looks like!"

"You wait about two shakes," John Robbins, in shirt sleeves, stood at the door. "About two shakes, I'll show you a nice picture of him."

"What?"

John's shoulders shook.

"Ha ha! Thought I was stuffing myself with turkey, didn't you? Joke's on you. I told you if I thought of something, I might be a help to you. Come along to the kitchen. I'm afraid I kind of messed things up, and I tipped over a pudding when I was using your pantry for a dark room, but I didn't think you'd mind."

The kitchen reminded Leonidas vividly of the rummage auction, and he said so.

"And—er—where did it all come from, all equipment? You've got everything! You've even got an enlarging machine!"

"I keep a couple suitcases of stuff in the trunk of the car," John said casually. "Like to have it handy. That's why I bought such a damn big car. Needed the trunk room. Here."

He produced, with justifiable pride, an enlarged print of a man.

He was undeniably young, tall, and dark. He wore

a dark overcoat, an odd looking moustache, and in his hands, he held a pair of white rubbers.

"He'd just picked 'em up when I got this shot of him, see?" John said.

"You lamb!" Mrs. Beaton hugged him. "You dear, fat lamb! Who is the man, Bill? John, how did you ever happen to *get* that picture?"

"Oh, I was at the Four Corners, waiting for that damn red light—you were in line a couple cars ahead of me, Topsey. And say, about two minutes later, I got a shot of you, up the street, with a cop bawling hell out of you for sloughing into the safety island. You see," John said, "I got this new F 1.9 lens today, and I was sort of taking shots at everything, trying it out. Fellow sold it to me said I could take pictures in the dark, and it looks like I can take 'em at dusk, anyways. Course it helped, his being by the corner light. Who is the fellow with the rubbers? You know him, Shakespeare?"

"To the best of my knowledge and belief," Leonidas said, "I never saw the man before in all my life."

"Say, gimme it a sec," John said. "I'll take off his moustache. Look out, sister, don't get your sleeve in that pan! I'll paint out his moustache, and then you see if he seems to look like somebody you know."

But even without the moustache, Leonidas still was unable to identify the man.

"In fact," he said, "without that hirsute adornment, he looks even more strange to me."

"Funny how things work out," John said. "Now it seems to me he's somebody *I* know, without that brush. Makes me think of a barber shop. Now why in hell should he make me think of a barber shop? That's crazy. I've been to the same barber for fifteen years, and he's a wizened up little guy about a thousand years old, and he don't look anything like this picture."

"But that's the man, all right," Myrna said. "That is, he was the man with the moustache until you razed the moustache. Now he looks like Smith when Rosalie told me about him."

"Anyway," Mrs. Beaton said, "we know he's the man who picked up the rubbers, and manipulated Myrna around—what did you say, Myrna?"

"You got him wrong," Myrna said. "He never laid a hand on me!"

"Hm. Well, he was the one who cooked up those fake charges with his cock-and-bull story to the police. He killed Marcus. The picture proves everything. We've only got to find out who he is."

"I fear," Leonidas told her, "that it is not as simple as all that. We merely have proof that this man picked up the rubbers. We don't know through how many hands the rubbers may have passed from the time they were picked up by this man at the Four Corners until they were finally placed beside Marcus on the floor of his study. The possibilities are boundless."

"You sound," Mrs. Beaton said, "as though the forty-two thousand inhabitants of the incorporated town of Carnavon all lined up like a bucket brigade, and passed the rubbers from hand to hand, and the last man tossed them in Marcus's study! Bill, be sensible!

Those rubbers aren't like flotsam or jetsam. They're not like a bottle tossed in Boston Harbor that bobbles up in Alaska the next year! Those rubbers were taken for a purpose, and put beside Marcus for a purpose, and if ever there was a man of purpose, it seems to be the man in this picture!"

"Taken for a purpose, possibly," Leonidas said, "but not for the purpose of involving me in a murder. This murder wasn't planned, Topsey!"

"How can you keep saying things like that?" Mrs. Beaton demanded. "I've run enough things in my day to recognize plans when I see 'em!"

"M'yes," Leonidas said gently, "I've no doubt you have. But if this murder had been planned, the murderer would not have used as a weapon a loving cup hastily snatched from a mantel. To judge from the way the mind of this man with the moustache works, he would plan a murder with intricate arrangements of firearms and string and wire and belts and pulleys, like a Rube Goldberg cartoon. He never could have stooped to the simple bash! Never! So—"

"Hey!" Myrna nudged him. "Somebody's at the front door."

"Link!" Leonidas said. "At long last, Link!"

But it was Judy Brett with whom Leonidas collided in his headlong rush to the door.

"Don't you," she said wearily, "ever do anything but bump into defenseless girls in halls? No, I haven't found him. But I brought you back this. Here!"

She thrust into his hands Marcus Meredith's miss-

ing leg, adorned with a black silk sock, and an elastic-
sided black slipper.

Leonidas, carrying the leg, followed her into the
living room, where she threw herself down on the
couch and lighted a cigarette.

"Where," he said blandly, "did you—er—acquire
this?"

"In a convertible coupe that Frenchy says belongs
to Link Potter. It's over on Rockledge Road."

"And where is Link Potter?"

Judy shrugged.

"I expect to locate him," she said, "about the same
time some archaeologist digs up the real missing link.
Hello, darling," she got up as Mrs. Beaton came into
the room, "are you sound and whole? Well, well,
added to your little party, haven't you? Hello, Mr.
Robbins. What's that behind you?"

"That," Leonidas said, "is Myrna. Myrna, this is
Judy."

"I'm pleased," Myrna said, "to meet your acquaintance."

"How do you do?" Judy said. "You know, I
thought for a second you might be Zora. I feel Hasel-
tiney, Mrs. B. I've found myself talking like the Princess Alicia for the last hour."

"Where's Frenchy?" Leonidas asked.

"I was almost hoping you wouldn't ask me that,"
Judy said. "He's over on Rockledge Road."

"What's he doing there?"

"Frenchy," Judy said, "is really a sweet thing. But

I've got to break down and admit he's pretty amazing, Shakespeare. I don't think I could have swallowed him if it hadn't been for my Alicia training. After we left you at the church, we drove to his boarding house so he could take off that green satin model. And he came out in a workaday number—two piece, very chic. Dungerees and a sweat shirt with Mickey Mouse on it. He also bore out a bag of assorted tools that clanked, and a blackjack, and at least two guns, which he carefully concealed from me. Then, we drove."

"Where?" Mrs. Beaton asked.

"Where," Judy said, "is entirely beside the point. His driving is the important thing. You know, I don't think I ever saw anyone drive like that outside of the movies. I didn't know anyone could. You know those sound effects of Haseltine's Zeppelin roadster? Well, even those noises don't suggest the way Frenchy drives. It's beyond Haseltine."

"I like Haseltine," Myrna said. "I think he's swell. I think Zora's swell, too. Rosalie and me, we listen to Haseltine every day. He's our favorite pogrom."

"Er—indeed!" Leonidas said. "Judy, where is Frenchy? What is he doing?"

"It pains me to tell you, Shakespeare, and I think he's doing it with the best intentions in the world of helping you. But when I left him to bring the leg back to you, he was burglarizing the house at Ninety Rockledge Road."

A chair groaned as John Robbins sat down on it suddenly.

"That's my house!"

"Is it, really?" Judy said. "I thought the place looked familiar, but all the houses out in that section look familiar. They're so damned Colonial you can't tell one from the other. Besides, I had the impression you lived at Ninety Crestvale, not Rockledge."

"I live at Ninety Rockledge!" John said. "And I won't—"

"You certainly won't have the concert notice I mailed you yesterday to Ninety Crestvale," Judy said. "Well, Mr. Robbins, your house is just being burgled, that's all. Virtually nothing can stop Frenchy when his mind is made up. I couldn't move him. But don't get upset. He promised me he'd be terribly careful, and not break a single thing. He's just hunting Link Potter, anyway. He isn't going to steal anything. Do you know Link Potter?"

"I've been in his store," John said, "but that isn't any reason for anyone to think he'd be in my house!"

"I didn't see why he should be, either," Judy said, "but Frenchy thought he might be there, because his convertible's parked right outside."

"John," Mrs. Beaton said, "where were you at seven this evening?"

"Eating chicken pie at your damn shindig! Topsey, this is going too far! I won't be burgled!"

"Frenchy won't hurt anything," Judy said soothingly. "Really, he won't!"

"But suppose he gets into my dark room! If he gets—huh. I guess I *did* lock that door, though."

Leonidas did not feel it necessary to point out that a locked door meant nothing to Frenchy.

"Er—tell me, John," he said, "who lives near you?"

"Who lives near me? You gone bats? What you mean, who lives near me?"

"Just that. You see, when Link went to Marcus's tonight to hunt me, he parked his car in the lane beyond. So it occurs to me—"

"He went to Meredith's to hunt you?" John said. "I thought you were hunting him!"

"M'yes," Leonidas said. "We are, but he was. Let's not go into all that. It occurs to me that very possibly Link might have parked his car in front of your house, but that his destination was some other spot in the neighborhood. That is why I wish to know who lives near you. Er—Topsey, give him the pencil and paper, will you? Now, John, will you draw a rough map of your street and the surrounding streets, and indicate the houses reasonably near yours, and tell me who lives in them?"

"Gimme a book," John said. "Gimme something to sit this paper on. You know what I ought to have done? I ought to gone right home from church. I ought to minded my own business. Look here, Shakespeare. Here's Rockledge. Here's Crestvale on this side. Here's Oakdale on the other. All parallel, but they kind of wind, and they all run into Rock Park over here, and up to the Golf Club over here. Got it? Now, here's my house. Here's Mac Arthur's. Here's Floyd's. Here's Kennedy's. Here's Chipman's. Here's Rugg's. Here's—"

"Wait," Leonidas said. "Rugg. Madison Rugg? Madison Rugg is the president of the board of trustees of Meredith's Academy."

John nodded. "I talked with him today over the phone about this proposition Meredith made me about being a trustee. Know what I been thinking, Shakespeare? I been thinking, all this business must have something to do with that damn school of his. Remember I said Meredith told me he was making changes?"

"M'yes," Leonidas said. "I've been remembering it for some time. M'yes, indeed. Judy, what were Frenchy's plans after burglarizing John's house? Was he going to stay over there?"

"He didn't confide his plans to me," Judy said. "For all I know, he's going to burgle every house on Rockledge Road. We only found the car a little while ago, after streaking around all over Carnavon. As a matter of fact, we were going so fast, I didn't even notice it, but Frenchy did, and stopped. And then we looked inside, and found the leg, and Frenchy told me to take it to you, while he dropped in—I quote him—to see if Link was at number ninety. Shakespeare, I think you'd better restrain the lad before he drops in on the Kennedys. He's the police commissioner, and he knows Cabot—" she broke off. "I hear a car. That'll be Frenchy. I'll go let him in."

But it was Link Potter whom she led into the living room.

"Link!" Leonidas said. "Link!"

Link surveyed the group, and bowed formally to Leonidas.

"Dr. Livingston, I presume? What a jolly spot you have here! Such a dandy crowd. Now can I have a table with a really *good* view of the floor show? Only not too near the trombone—hey, there's my leg! Who got my leg?"

"I did," Judy said. "And did you see Frenchy?"

"Frenchy? Frenchy, as the fellow who works for me? Or some other fellow named Frenchy?"

"Link," Leonidas said, "I'm delighted to see you! I felt sure you'd be able to cope with any situation that might arise, but I confess that I've been worried about you. Sit down. Tell us where you've been, what's happened! I'm sure you have something of vital importance to impart."

"The only vital thing I had to impart was the leg," Link said, "and that was filched from me by this bright-eyed child. Shakespeare, I know Mr. Robbins, and I've seen the Wimpernel, but—"

"Mrs. Beaton," Leonidas said, "and Miss Brett. Topsey, in other words, and Judy. The Wimpernel is Myrna. Ellen is an oil company. Evelyn is the rector."

"Does he have a moustache?" Link inquired.

"Er—no," Leonidas said. "Do I gather that you have had some experience with a man with a moustache, Link?"

"I've practically spent the night with one," Link said.

"D'you know who he is?" Mrs. Beaton demanded. "Who is he? What's his name?"

Link smiled.

"I just call him X," he said. "Shakespeare, do you want my contribution as a straight narrative, or do you want to ask me things?"

"Begin with your leaving Marcus's," Leonidas suggested. "We'll ask questions as we go along. What happened to you? Where did you go?"

"Well, I cut across the fields to get to the lane," Link said, "instead of following the county road along to it, as I came. In my fanciful way, I thought that would save time. But I guess I'm no woodsman. I got twisted. I couldn't even find the lane! You'd never believe how one patch of snow and birch trees looks like another patch of snow and birch trees."

"Er—the North Star," Leonidas began, "is helpful—"

"I could find the North Star, Shakespeare, but I wasn't sure what direction I wanted to go! I'd probably be wandering around Bald Pate woods yet, trying to find that damn lane, if I hadn't finally seen the headlights of a car coming along it. The car was creeping along, and then it stopped, and a man got out."

"Did he have a moustache?" Myrna asked.

"I couldn't tell at that distance, but he did, I discovered later. Being a friendly soul," Link said, "I started to go up and hail this fellow, and then some inner voice told me not to. You know, Shakespeare. Like one of Haseltine's inner voices. So I crept up on the lad, and eavesdropped. And he started to paw around in the snow under some bushes, and after scratching around a while, he brought out Marcus's leg."

"What? There in the woods?"

"Uh-huh. And then I realized that the bushes were marked with a handkerchief fluttering from a branch, though I didn't catch on to that till he untied the handkerchief and tucked it in his pocket. So then he took the leg back to his car, and started, and began to back around—"

"Why didn't you jump on him?" Mrs. Beaton demanded. "Oh, why didn't you get him, right then and there?"

"Because," Link said, "I didn't think he was the man who put the leg there in the first place."

"Indeed!" Leonidas said. "What prompted that conclusion?"

"His hesitancy. He came there for the leg, all right. He knew where it should be. He had the handkerchief to guide him. But no one who'd put the leg there in the first pace would've fumbled so. So I decided to trail him and look into things."

"You should have jumped him!" Judy said. "Haseltine would have! Oh, why didn't you jump him anyway!"

Link pointed out that Haseltine made a habit of carrying a gun.

"And I don't. It's one of those things you think of, under circumstances like that. After all, there'd been one murder on the hill, and I had no intention of popping up in a morgue with a tag on me saying, 'Unknown Young Man Neatly Drilled in Left Temple.' Should I have jumped him, Bill?"

"Er—I shouldn't," Leonidas said. "Do I gather that this car entered the lane from the far side, and not the county road?"

"Yes, from Mountain Avenue. I'd got my bearings by then, so I sneaked off to my car—"

"Er—just a moment. It's a small point, but a car going past Marcus's on the county road could go past this lane to still another road which would lead to Mountain Avenue? In short, can you circle that hill so easily?"

"Sure," Link said, "on two or three roads. Why? Do you think you saw this fellow going by while you were waiting for me at Marcus's?"

"I'm sure of it," Leonidas said. "M'yes. He was checking up to see if the police had come in answer to his call. Then, when he found the place apparently deserted, he felt safe to get the leg. M'yes. Go on. You returned to your car."

"Which this fellow mercifully couldn't see, because of a divinely inspired curve in the road. It was a swell place, because I could watch his lights and see which way he turned on Mountain Avenue without having him catch on to me. He took the long way down the hill, so I took one of the short cuts across the water reservation, and followed him without his knowing anything at all."

"Didn't the cops chase you at the reservoir?" Judy inquired.

Link grinned.

"Uh-huh. But after the dose of cops Shakespeare and I took, just being chased by a couple in a car was a minor incident. I foxed 'em, and picked up my man again in the valley, and followed him at a discreet distance all the way to the garden city of Dalton!"

"M'yes," Leonidas said. "M'yes, indeed!"

Link misunderstood his bland tones.

"I hated like hell to leave you cooling your heels by Marcus's drive posts, Bill, but I figured you could get back to the store somehow, and following this fellow seemed more imperative. Well, after a lot of circling around Dalton, he finally parked his car, and I pulled mine into someone's drive further up the street, and pretended I lived there and was going in. Then, when he went off, I followed. And he cut across lots to—"

"To a modern house with glass brick and a sun deck," Leonidas said. "M'yes."

"Uh-huh. Yours? Well, well! I decided that. I'm getting sort of psychic," Link said. "The fellow rang your doorbells, front and back, and then he slid around and shinnied up your drain pipe to the sun deck—you oughtn't to leave your casement windows open like that. It isn't safe. He flipped the leg in—he had it wrapped in a sweater or something, by the way. Then he shinnied down, and set off for his car. Was I torn in two! I wanted to get that leg, and I wanted to follow him, and finally I decided that the leg would stay put, and he wouldn't. So I trailed along back to my car. And that's really about all there is to *that*."

"But you followed him back to Rockledge Road, and all!" Mrs. Beaton said.

"No," Link said. "No. My car wouldn't start. His did. By the time I got mine going, a woman came out of the house I was parked beside, and asked what I was cluttering up her driveway for. I said very politely that I'd made a mistake, and the woman said she thought I was very suspicious, and she'd call the police if I didn't go away at once."

"Mrs. Glendenning," Leonidas said. "She was the bane of Colonel Carpenter's life when he was head of the Dalton police. M'yes. Then what?"

"I drove around the block to your house, and shinnied up and got the leg—and what do you know? Mrs. Pennyfeather *had* called the cops, and there they were! We had a very pleasant chase," Link said, "and at last I got out of Dalton—it's nice to think that if anyone gets arrested in connection with leg-leaving at your house, it will be me. I was the one who got seen. Well, I went on my way, sadly reflecting about that item, and then—pulling out of a gas station ahead—there was that sedan!"

"You knew the number plates!" Mrs. Beaton said.

"The number plates," Link said, "were a lovely smudge of mud. Anyway, I followed this Ford sedan to Crestvale Road, and it pulled up in front of Madison

Rugg's house—we put in a new water heater with a
Monel tank for him about a month ago. I know him.
And then the fellow got out of the car. Shakespeare,
my face is definitely red."

"Er—why?"

"Fellow had on a light coat, wore shell-rimmed
glasses, had no hat and no moustache. My man had on
a dark coat, a felt hat, and a moustache, and no glasses.
In brief, it was two other guys. I followed the wrong
car."

"Did it occur to you," Leonidas said, "that hats,
glasses and false moustaches can be put on and taken
off at will, and that coats can be reversed—your own
coat is reversible, is it not?"

"It came to me, but not all at once," Link said. "I
sat in my car—I'd pulled up in another driveway—and
watched him to the door, and the maid let him in. And
I said a number of harsh things to myself, the least of
which was that I was a dolt. Then I got to thinking.
This fellow seemed taller and heavier, but not having
any hat, and wearing that light coat would account
for that. And his walk was the same. Then I thought
about hats and glasses. Then I said the hell with it
and left. And then I cut back to Rockledge Road and
left the car, and walked over to Crestvale to investigate. You know, you feel silly as hell and twice as
guilty, peering into people's houses like that!"

"And—er—what did you see?" Leonidas asked.

"Well, there was this fellow, without the moustache and with the glasses, tinkering with Rugg's fancy

radio. Putting in a new tube, apparently, that he'd just brought back with him. And there was Rugg and his wife and her sister and an older man playing bridge. Nothing peculiar. Nothing suspicious. Just a happy little group having fun in a nice quiet way."

Leonidas picked up his evening paper.

"Is it possible," he said, "that the older man playing bridge resembled this man here?"

Link glanced at the picture of Colfax at the track meet.

"Yes, that's the one. They finished a rubber while I was watching, and started to go. I ducked down in the bushes and waited till they left—that was about fifteen or twenty minutes ago. And by the time they got down the front steps, I knew for sure I was a million miles off the track."

"Indeed," Leonidas said. "Er—why?"

"Why? Because the Ruggs came to the door with 'em, and I could hear every word they said. Said the two must come again, and they'd been delighted to meet the nephew they'd heard so much about, and what's his name—Colfax, is it? Well, Colfax said it had been a superb dinner, and he'd enjoyed the evening so much, and the nephew said that went for him—oh, you know the sort of things people say while they hold the front door open! The Ruggs said they hoped to see a lot of them both in the future, and so on and so forth. And they said it was nice of the nephew to get the tube, and fix the radio, and they did wish he'd let them pay him for the tube anyway, and then they all said good night about a dozen times. Well, the upshot of it all is, I got the wrong man. My man and I parted company back in Dalton when my car wouldn't start. The rest was pure waste effort."

"Indeed!" Leonidas said. "Indeed!"

"Certainly!" Link said impatiently. "If those two men were at the Ruggs' for dinner, they certainly weren't at Marcus Meredith's at seven o'clock! I just picked up the wrong car, that's all. One muddy Ford with muddy plates is just like another. The best you can say of my night's work is that I tried hard, and I got that leg. But the man with the moustache is still careening around, somewhere. Say," he turned to Judy, "how did *you* happen to get that leg? In fact, what have *you* been doing, Shakespeare? Where did you pick up your supporting cast? What've you found out, if anything?"

Leonidas twirled his pince-nez.

"I'll summarize in just a moment, Link. So the young man is Colfax's nephew. I wonder if that could be the youngster I once—I wonder! Link, can you recall what the Ruggs called him? Did you hear his name?"

"They didn't use names," Link said. "I mean, Colfax and the fellow said 'Mr. Rugg' and 'Mrs. Rugg,' and I think Colfax called him 'Madison,' but the Ruggs didn't use any given names to them. They just called them 'Professor' and 'Doctor.'"

"Whoopee!" John Robbins said. "I got it! I got it! Doctor! That's it. He had on a white coat. That's what made me think of barbers! He's a doctor. He's one of the damn doctors in that damn clinic. One of those fools said I ought to stop smoking and eat a lot of damn rabbit food and retire with a hobby! Yes, sir. He's at that damn clinic. But I don't think he's much of anybody. He's kind of a fourth or fifth assistant. Kind of fellow that holds pans and writes things down for some other doctor. Wait a minute now, I'll remember his name. Something short. Like Blotch. Schlitz. Stumpf. Something like that."

"Schultz," Leonidas said. "Victor Schultz."

"That's it! How the hell'd you know that, Shakespeare?"

"Some twenty years ago," Leonidas said, "Master Schultz attended Meredith's Academy. For two days. During the course of those two days, he distinguished himself. He was the only child I ever asked Marcus to expel. I will not go into the harrowing and somewhat repulsive details, but the dormitory house mother, and such members of the faculty as had come in contact with him agreed with me most emphatically that he was the most unpleasant and most perverted child they'd ever seen. Colfax was terribly upset, and said that his sister had sent the child to him to attend the Academy, and that he had no knowledge of him at all. Apparently he couldn't get the child on a train back to Chicago quickly enough. I had forgotten about Colfax's nephew, Master Schultz. M'yes."

"I got something else," John said. "Shakespeare, I think we're going to get somewheres. I didn't see how the hell you could do it, but I think we're getting warm. Look. Meredith told me today he was making a lot of changes at the school—and you know what? He said getting a doctor who could direct athletics was an awful job, and he'd turned down more people. He said he couldn't find any intelligent coach who wasn't a damn poor doctor, or an intelligent doctor who could coach. He said that every star athlete ever graduated had a favorite coach up his sleeve, and all the teachers had relations that was doctors they wanted the job for. Say, maybe this guy Schlitz was one of the doctors he turned down, huh? What you think, Shakespeare?"

"*I* think," Mrs. Beaton said, "that this is the most mixed up mess I ever heard of in all the days of my life. That's what I think. You're way off, John. You're just clutching at straws. It can't possibly be Colfax or his nephew. They can't have anything to do with this. The Ruggs have dinner at seven. I know. I went there several times when I was chairman of the Sailors' Book Drive. Shakespeare, even if you did expel a boy twenty years ago, there's certainly no reason for him to pick tonight to take revenge on you! Certainly if he was one of the men trying for the doctor and coach job, he'd hardly get it by killing Marcus! Colfax and his nephew are out—Bill, are you listening to me?"

"M'yes," Leonidas swung his pince-nez. "M'yes, indeed. I hear every word."

"Say, Witherall," John said. "I got another idea. This nephew that's the doctor gets turned down for

the coach job—and it pays a lot, too. I was surprised
when Meredith told me. Pays as much as any college
head coach'd get. Then you know what I bet? I bet
that Colfax got turned down for headmaster!"

"M'yes," Leonidas said, "but he happens to *be*
headmaster. He has been acting headmaster since
Foster died at Christmas."

"Maybe so," John said. "But Meredith was going
to have a new headmaster. He told me so. He said
usually he made the oldest teacher the headmaster—"

"Er—the senior member of the faculty in length
of service," Leonidas said. "Not necessarily the oldest
professor, but the one who had been there longest."

"That's what I meant. But Meredith said that
right now that wasn't working out at all well. He said
he'd finally solved the problem to his own satisfaction, and he was going to settle it at the meeting of
the trustees tomorrow. He said he knew I'd be there,
and uphold him, because some of the trustees liked
things to keep going on like they always had, but he
was determined to break precedent. I didn't know
what he was talking about, exactly, but now I see.
He meant that instead of making this Colfax headmaster from acting headmaster, like everyone expected, he was going to put in a new one. Witherall,
I kind of think we got this going!"

"Witherall?" Judy asked in a perplexed voice.
"Witherall? Shakespeare, what *is* your name? First
you let me think you're Hornblower, and then you're

Budenny, and now he calls you Witherall! Is your name Witherall, Xenophon Witherall?"

"Er—Leonidas. I'm sorry no one thought to tell you."

"Wait!" Judy said. "Just you wait. Where's my pocketbook? Potter, toss me that pocketbook! It's right in there, in the zipper part, where I put it!"

"Er—what is?" Leonidas inquired.

"This. Here." She produced from the pocketbook Link gave her a special delivery letter addressed in Marcus's small precise handwriting to Leonidas Witherall, Esquire. "He gave me that to mail when I was there to get Mrs. B.'s last note about the forsythia. He said I was to be sure to mail it right away, because it was a very important message to his new headmaster, Leonidas Witherall."

CHAPTER 8

"I MEANT to mail it right away," Judy continued, "but I simply didn't have a minute to think of it afterwards—oh, dear, Mr. Robbins! Here's your notice about that concert. There, I knew I sent it to Crestvale instead of Rockledge. Here. You might as well have it now. And—oh, dear!"

"Judy," Mrs. Beaton said, "is that the check for the bank!"

"Dear me, I'm afraid it is. The one I was supposed to send the day before yesterday! How could that have slipped my mind!"

"You may explain that to Cabot, yourself, when Harry calls him from the bank and says I'm overdrawn," Mrs. Beaton informed her.

"I'll crawl every inch of the way on my hands and knees," Judy said penitently. "Smeared with ashes. Isn't the letter all about being the new headmaster, Shakespeare?"

Leonidas put the letter on the table and looked

thoughtfully at the flames flickering over the logs in the fireplace.

"M'yes," he said. "M'yes. Marcus had decided that I should be headmaster of the Academy until, as he said, I chose to retire, or until a happier and more fitting seniority might occur. I suppose he meant until Colfax retired, and Harriman could take over. M'yes. It never seems to have occurred to Marcus that I might not wish to be headmaster. Er—he seemed to think I would welcome the position from a financial standpoint."

"Well for Pete's sakes, wouldn't you?" John demanded. "He told me today that a headmaster gets a flat sum outright—wasn't it twenty thousand?—from some fund or other, and then ten thousand a year and a house, and a good fat pension!"

"Meredith's Academy," Leonidas said, "has always been a—er—paying proposition. The estimable Elihu, who founded the institution, was not a poor man, and he rushed around setting up funds for this and that and the other thing. It may interest you to know that the school is even endowed with oysters in season, and that every graduate receives a leather purse containing the equivalent of ten shillings. I know of no other school whose students, over a long period of years, have possessed such a fiery zeal for endowing their alma mater. M'yes. But the fact remains, I should not have accepted this position as headmaster—"

He was interrupted by a snore.

"It's only the Wimpernel," Link said. "She's

been asleep for ten minutes. I bored her with my little narrative, I guess. Bill, catch me up on things, will you?"

Mrs. Beaton shook her head.

"Have we really got the *time,* do you think, to go into *every*thing?"

"We can spare three minutes," Leonidas said, "which is all I shall require. Then we must take steps to—er—corral Frenchy. No interruptions, please. Are you ready?"

Exactly three minutes later, he stopped.

"Er—are you caught up now?" he asked.

"Well, you can take a few stitches here and there," Link said, "but I get the jist of it. And I must say I'm relieved to know my envelope of money's safe! Frenchy did ask me for his pay, and I forgot all about it. And you even suggested that angle, yourself! I'm clear on the issue of my money, but my God, how can you ever make sense of the rest?"

"Plain as the nose on your face," John said. "Now I got the holes filled in, I begin to get this. Shakespeare, this Colfax must have got wind of your appointment somehow. Maybe Meredith told him. Maybe, like a fellow I know in Boston, he caught on he was on the skids when they started erasing his name off his door and putting on somebody else's. Anyway, he caught on. That's why there was all this planning to get you in Dutch. If your name got into the papers tomorrow morning about the girl and the pocketbook and all, those old fogy trustees of Meredith's'd be sure to question your appointment at that meeting tomorrow afternoon. Meredith could have overridden 'em, but with a paying proposition like you say this school is, he couldn't afford any bad publicity about his headmaster. Colfax had a lot to gain by putting you in a hole like that."

"Granted," Mrs. Beaton said. "But, why on earth should he have killed Marcus?"

"It begins to filter through my mind," Link said, "that if this Colfax had planned on being upped from acting headmaster to real headmaster, he might have anticipated it. I bring up that crassly material angle, because I know that for my part, my loan was as good as wiped out of my mind forever the minute that envelope of cash went into my cash register this afternoon. The formalities of paying the money back were just an item. Now, take Colfax. He has every reason to believe he's going to be headmaster of Meredith's, and that twenty thousand grant is as good as his. The formality of being presented with it is just an item. He's as good as got it. You were at his house today, Bill. Didn't you spot some signs of his letting out and spending money? Maybe he had a new car."

"M'yes," Leonidas said. "One like John's. Long and black and shiny. He also had a new radio—one of those incredible things which is a phonograph, and makes records, and has television for good measure. He had many new and expensive books, and he was wearing the first really well-cut suit I ever saw him wear."

"There you are," John said. "That's the real answer. The money. He's probably spent a lot—say, I wonder if he's done a little borrowing and run himself in debt? I bet you he has! Where's he live, Tilbury? Well, I'll find out about that. I'll phone old Charley Cooper. He runs the bank there. He runs the whole damn town, really. He knows everything. He'll tell me. I know him."

Mrs. Beaton pointed out that it was well past one o'clock in the morning.

"Won't matter to old Charley," John said. "Where's your phone, Topsey? Got one in this room? Oh, I see it. Why do you women always hide telephones inside of a damn tin box? Mary does, too. Say, Shakespeare, this is kind of fun! I kind of thought I might be able to help you out!"

His telephone conversation with his friend Charley, who didn't appear to be annoyed at being routed out of bed, was in a language almost incomprehensible to Leonidas. But John was beaming when he replaced the phone in its decorated green tin hiding place.

"Old Charley," he reported, "says if he was me, he wouldn't sell Colfax any cement except for spot cash. In other words, brother Colfax has borrowed up to his ears. Brother Colfax is in a jam. Well, Shakespeare, there's your motive all right. He's *got* to be headmaster to get the money to pull himself out with. He finds you're being shoved in over his head, so he moves to see you don't get there. Gets his nephew to help—hey, I wonder if Colfax didn't plan to get him the doctor-coach job when he got to be real headmaster? I bet he did. Or else he promised him the job if he'd help smear you. Yup, that's the story. Colfax wants the money, nephew wants the job. Got to get you in wrong to get you out of the way."

"I still," Mrs. Beaton said firmly, "don't understand why Marcus was killed! And I think it's simply incredible, the way you men talk! Just as if you were everything! Just as if you were talking about facts, instead of—well, I don't know what to call it! I never heard such flights of fancy! It's all guesswork! Pure, sheer, unadulterated speculation!"

"Trouble with you, Topsey," John said, "you're like all women. Want everything to be like a recipe for a sponge cake. Want a neat little list, with everything in order. Eggs. Sugar. Flour. Salt. Baking Powder. All like that. We got the list, right here. Shakespeare's dug out all the ingredients. All we got to do is straighten 'em out and put 'em in order. This is just a simple murder, like in a book."

"Simple! You didn't flop into snow with a wet sheet over you! You didn't—is she asleep still? You didn't have to maneuver people into metal closets! You—"

"All right, all right," John said. "It's still a simple murder. Somebody killed someone for something."

"I'm going to scream!" Mrs. Beaton said. "I tell you, I still can't see any reason for Colfax or his

nephew to kill Marcus! I can understand why they
might want to get Bill in trouble, but why did they
kill Marcus? You can't figure that out!"

"I think so," Link said. "I think I begin to get it.
You've already got it, haven't you, Bill? You see,
Mrs. Beaton, when the man with the moustache told
that cop at the Four Corners that Bill had stolen the
Wimpernel's pocketbook and made improper advances
to boot, that was all that was needed. That would do
what they wanted. Then they cruised around to find
Bill, set the Wimpernel on his trail, and then they beat
it up to the hill and told Marcus they'd just heard
over the car radio that Witherall was wanted by the
cops. Girl charges, and theft. They had your rubbers
to add weight to the story. That right, Bill?"

"M'yes," Leonidas was still staring at the burning
logs. "M'yes. I think so."

"Well, you're all wrong right there!" Mrs. Beaton said. "There wasn't any 'they' in the car! There
was just the man with the moustache. Wake up
Myrna, Judy. Poke her. Myrna! Listen to me. Was
there anyone but the man with the moustache in the
car when he took you to find Bill and your pocketbook?"

Myrna yawned.

"No. Gee, I'm sleepy! There's something about
this room makes me relapse."

"Er—did you happen to look in the back seat
of the sedan?" Leonidas inquired.

"Let me think," Myrna said. "Yeah, I did."

"Was there a bundle on the floor of the car?"

"Myrna nodded.

"Swaddled in a blanket," she said. "Gee, yes. I forgot all about that!"

"It's a cinch," John said. "Nephew put on a fake moustache, and a hat, and took off his glasses, and wore his coat with the dark side out, so if anything went wrong, he could take off the moustache and the hat, slip on his specs, and turn his coat to the light side. Be two other people. Fool everyone, like he fooled Link. Colfax just sat on the floor and put a blanket over himself. Wasn't taking any chances of having Shakespeare see him. It's a cinch. They meant to follow the bus to Dalton, watch the start of Bill walking into trouble, and then come back here and have dinner with the Ruggs. Way things turned out, they got him into trouble here in Carnavon, and then went on to Marcus's. Sure."

"I never," Mrs. Beaton said, "heard—"

"Darling," Judy interrupted her, "you should read Haseltine. I've often told you so. Even I begin to understand. They rush to Marcus and tell him about these charges, and say, in effect, 'Neyeh, neyeh! See the foul thing Witherall is!' And if I know Marcus, he promptly told them it was a silly mistake. Don't you think so, Shakespeare? After all, Marcus *knew* you!"

"M'yes," Leonidas said, "it's so definitely the sort of charge which would move both of them that they expected it to move Marcus. I very greatly doubt if it moved him one whit."

"I suppose," Mrs. Beaton said with elaborate irony, "you even know just what Marcus did then, and what he said to them!"

Leonidas smiled.

"Er—you have had some brief experience with what happens when Marcus has his mind set on a point, have you not? I can tell you what happened as accurately as if I had been there. Colfax showed Marcus my rubbers, and repeated his assertion that I *had* been on the bus, that I *was* the man for whom the police were hunting. And Marcus became suddenly very deaf, and refused to discuss the situation. I've no doubt he said coldly that he would take the matter up in writing, if Professor Colfax so desired. That should have made Colfax hesitate. But, having gone that far, he and his nephew probably persisted, and yelled at him—you recall, Topsey, the sort of mood Marcus was in when you left?"

"He was simply furious."

"M'yes. You had yelled at him and annoyed him. Then these two came. They yelled at him and annoyed him. Marcus was not accustomed to being yelled at. Marcus has always been accorded the greatest deference, particularly from the members of his faculty. M'yes, I can hear Marcus, in his coldest voice, informing Professor Colfax that his contract will not be renewed."

"H'm."

"I have known Marcus for so many years!"

Leonidas said. "If he considered Colfax so inadequate as an acting headmaster that he was willing to break an Academy precedent by making me headmaster in his stead, I can assure you that his annoyance with Colfax was not of recent origin. It began long before tonight. I should say that Marcus was waiting for the opportunity to get rid of Colfax with justification. And Colfax gave him that opportunity tonight."

"Wow!" John said. "Zowie! Smack between the eyes for Brother Colfax. All his pretty plans to smear you bounce back in his face. No getting to be head man. No getting the twenty thousand. Loans coming due. House mortgaged. No job for Blotch. That's all bad enough! Then Meredith cracks the whip—and oh, boy! No job!"

"I'm sitting," Judy said, "on the edge of my seat! Isn't this exciting, Myrna?"

"Yeah," Myrna said. "Wasn't it at Keith's last week?"

"Go on, Bill!" Judy said. "Then what?"

"Then," Leonidas said, "they leave."

"They what?" Topsey demanded.

"They leave," Leonidas said.

"And sent their astral bodies back to kill Marcus?" Link inquired. "Sorry, Shakespeare, but this is where I'm stuck."

Leonidas didn't seem to hear him.

"Topsey," he said, "came at six-thirty, and stayed only a few minutes. They came, say, between twenty-

five and twenty minutes to seven, and probably burst
out with their news at once. I should say that they left
at quarter to seven."

"You mean," John said, "they pretended to leave.
Only they didn't. They decided they were so far in
the soup that only killing him would do."

"Not they," Leonidas said. "Colfax decided that.
Colfax thought very quickly. M'yes, very quickly indeed. They took their leave of Marcus at quarter to
seven, and during his passage from the study to the
front door, Carl Colfax thought very quickly, and
formulated his plans. You see, this is too simple for
the nephew. Besides, the nephew hasn't a sufficiently
strong motive for murder. He probably enjoyed—er—
taking a crack at me through Rosalie. But the nephew
did not kill Marcus. I doubt if he ever contemplated
such an action. Colfax did it all. M'yes. And what
irony is involved with the use of that loving cup as a
weapon! That has been haunting me!"

"It's diabolical!" Judy said. "He remembered the
loving cup on the mantel, and he thought what a fine
blunt instrument it would be—oh, it's hideous! Go on!"

"M'yes." Leonidas fingered his pince-nez. "They
take their leave of Marcus. They go to the front hall.
There, I think, is where they separate. It's obvious
from Link's story that they must have separated, if the
boy didn't know where the leg was. The boy must
leave the house in the car—m'yes, I see. I see. The car
must leave to clinch the time of their departure. But
Colfax remains. Colfax returns to the study. Colfax

has made his diabolical plan, and he knows what he is going to do. He is going to kill Marcus—"

"Because," Link said, "it's his chance to save everything. I'm back on the track, now. Marcus won't believe in any trumped-up charges against you, Shakespeare, but the trustees will read them in their morning papers tomorrow. And if your name ever comes up at a board meeting as Marcus's deathbed choice, so to speak, the trustees will remember the headlines. They'll decide that this is no time to break precedent, or change horses in the middle of the stream, or whatever you want to call it. Without Marcus standing over them, the trustees'll do what they think is proper according to Meredith tradition. They'll keep Colfax on as acting headmaster, and then make him head."

"I think so," Leonidas said. "M'yes. Now, Colfax knows what he is going to do. He makes up his mind very quickly. Too quickly, I have always thought. Perhaps we may hazard a guess that his tendency to pounce too quickly on an idea is the reason why he was not entirely successful, in Marcus's mind, as acting headmaster. The head of the Academy must not jump to conclusions. Anyway, Colfax gives his nephew certain instructions, but I doubt if the boy knows what his uncle is planning to do. We will now pause to find out exactly how this alibi goes. I have a feeling that it will be exquisitely simple, and practically without flaws."

"Huh!" John said. "How the hell you expect to find out about that?"

"Er—Judy," Leonidas said, "d'you remember Princess Alicia's practice of telephoning to the villainous Count Casimir in order to find out tidbits which the excellent Lieutenant Haseltine needed to know?"

"You mean the fake telephone operator and long distance routine? I've made so many of those fake calls," Judy said, "I could do 'em in my sleep! Who do I call? What do you want in the line of tidbits, Bill?"

"You call the Ruggs. You wish Professor Carl Colfax. They will tell you he has gone. Then you go into your classic speech, 'Ca-yun you in-form me if he happened to re-seeyuv a long dis-tance coll at se-ven this e-vening?' They will assure you that he did not. You ask if he was there at seven, because you are checking on a complaint from the potty calling. Bully them into telling you exactly what time the professor arrived, and how long he was there, and if he left at any time during the evening. You know how to do that."

"The Ruggs," Mrs. Beaton said, "will be in bed, soundly sleeping!"

"M'yes, all the better," Leonidas told her. "Let us hope that in their somnolent state they will be more inclined to tell us all than they might, say, when thoroughly awake and alert."

"They'll never tell you a thing!"

"Possibly not," Leonidas said, "but you would be surprised to know how well this sort of thing

works out for the heroic Lieutenant. And Madison
Rugg delights in dispensing information. I once saw
him buttonhole a complete stranger at the Meredith
Club and tell him the best method of ridding a garden
of moles. Judy, perhaps you should be the San Francisco operator. Distance always lends enchantment.
Mind, Judy, you must have a full report, and because
of the imperative nature of the call, you will greatly
appreciate Mr. Rugg's furnishing you with all possible helpful details—"

"Data," Judy corrected him. "Alicia always asks
for data."

"M'yes. And at the conclusion of your little chat,
inquire where the professor may now be found. Er—
much depends on this call, Judy!"

Judy smiled.

"I can do it," she said, "with my hands tied behind me and a cracker in my mouth."

Clearing her throat, she picked up the telephone.

Ten minutes later, when she set it back in its
box, Mrs. Beaton looked dazed.

"If you could only be one-tenth that efficient as
a real secretary!" she said. "Merciful heavens, Judy,
I'm stunned!"

"I knew I could do it," Judy said. "Listen, Bill.
Professor Colfax arrived at the Ruggs' at quarter to
seven. Was he on the premises at that time? No, he
was not. He was out front in his car, and the phone
did not ring for him either then or at seven. There was
only one phone call all evening, and that was a survey

call about what radio program they were listening to. He explained about Colfax's being outside with great care, enunciating very distinctly, as if English wasn't understood very well in San Francisco. The professor was there, you see, but he wasn't there. Not inside. Seems he came in his car at quarter to seven, but when he stopped, he smelled a very peculiar smell, like something burning, in his car—"

"Judy, Madison Rugg never told you all this!" Mrs. Beaton said unbelievingly. "You're simply making this up as you go along!"

"I'm not making it up! He told me. I asked him to explain fully how Professor Colfax could be there and yet not there, and he did. Colfax came, and smelled this funny smell in his car, and his nephew smelled a funny smell, and the nephew got out and looked around, and lifted the hood, and then they started to drive to the nearest gas station to find out what the matter was, but on the way the funny smell stopped, so Professor Colfax and his nephew turned around and returned to the Ruggs' house for dinner at seven. They were right there in the house at seven, Rugg said, and the phone didn't ring. He doesn't understand it."

"What you make of that, Shakespeare?" John wanted to know.

"The Ruggs did not go out into the slush to investigate all of this," Leonidas said. "They were told about it. Doubtless one or another peered out the window, saw the car, and saw the boy get out. They'd hardly go rushing out to the car. They'd simply sit and wait for the pair to come in. If they did decide that something was wrong with the car, they would probably stand in their doorway, and call out, and ask if anything were the matter. Then the boy had only to call back reassuringly and say that they'd be right in, but first they had to go to a gas station. Then he would drive away—"

"Probably racing the engine a bit, to add color to it all," Link said. "No matter how you look at it, Colfax and the boy are both in the car, to the best of the Ruggs' knowledge and belief. Judy, I think you did a swell job!"

"I think so, too," Judy said. "Remember the man who discovered the lever, and said if he only had a place to stand, he could move the world? Well, you give me lines, and I can move it, too. Bill, Rugg said he *saw* Colfax in the car."

"Of course he said so. Colfax told him later that he *was* in the car," Leonidas said. "M'yes. Rugg believes he was in the car with the nephew and the funny smell. He has no reason to think otherwise. He will never think otherwise. He will face a crowded courtroom and assert that Colfax was in that car."

"Huh," John said, "that *is* simple, ain't it? That's a good alibi. Nothing complicated. Just natural and simple. Car heaters are always making funny smells. Mine did this morning. Why, *I* started to the garage to see if something was burning! And then it stopped smelling, and I went on down to the office. Yes, sir. Colfax'll just say he was in the car, the nephew'll say so, too, and Rugg'll back 'em up. You're going to have lots of fun proving he wasn't in that car, Shakespeare! Want to know what I think, you got a hell of a job to prove Colfax stayed up there at Meredith's!"

"But he was there," Leonidas said. "He stayed there. He struck Marcus with the cup, and Marcus pitched out of his chair, never knowing, I should say, what hit him. Now I wonder if, after Marcus fell, Colfax did not lean down, look at him, and discover for the first time the fact that Marcus wore an artificial leg. M'yes, I think so. With one of those quick flashes of inspiration, he removed the leg, and took it with him when he left the house and cut across the fields to the lane. Very likely, Link, you arrived at the house only a few minutes after he left."

"Why'd he takes the leg? Why on earth did he leave it in the lane?" Mrs. Beaton said.

"He took the leg for the same reason that he left my rubbers behind," Leonidas told her. "When the police finally arrived on the scene, they would find my name inside the rubbers, and at once request me to explain their presence there in the study. Er—I feel very sure that my explanations would result in further headlines about me for the trustees to read. My discovery of the leg in my own house would doubtless bring forth the sort of type that newspapers save for the bombing of London."

"How'd you manage to whisk that leg to your house?" John inquired.

"Colfax had no reason," Leonidas said, "to assume that I would go to Marcus's. He well knew that I had my hands full with the Wimpernel, and he expected that the Carnavon police would be taking care of me, anyway. He realized that if he could cause that leg to be placed in my house before I got home, it would create a really sensational situation. He figured that when I found the leg, I would either call the Dalton police, or tell my friend Colonel Carpenter about it, which amounts to the same thing. He figured, and correctly, that if he had not known about Marcus's leg, I would not know, either. M'yes, think of the headlines. 'Scholar Murdered in Carnavon. Leg Missing.' 'Dalton Man Finds Missing Leg of Murdered Savant in Own Bedroom.' M'yes."

" 'Explanations of Ex-Meredith Professor—insert, with beard—Arouse Police Suspicions,' " Link said. " 'His Arrest Anticipated.' "

"Exactly," Leonidas said.

"Why should he leave the leg in the lane?" John asked.

"It would be embarrassing to be found with it," Leonidas said. "Colfax could hardly take it in to dinner with him, at the Ruggs'. And he didn't wish to take any chances by leaving it out in his car. See what happened when Link left it in his! The nephew has been told to pick him up at the foot of the lane, and he does. They go to the Ruggs', and tell everybody about the funny smell."

"Do you suppose he told the nephew about what had happened?" Link asked.

"If he did, I'm sure he pretended that it was an accident," Leonidas said, "and I've no doubt he put the fear of possible consequences into the boy, if the boy didn't continue to do just what he told him."

"Maybe with a touch of blackmail," Link suggested. "He could threaten to show up the part the boy played in getting you into your mess with the Wimpernel. Then he could point out that if everything went off all right, the boy had his job."

"The Ruggs," Mrs. Beaton said, "still had dinner at seven. He told Judy Colfax was there at seven."

"M'yes," Leonidas said. "When you ask people to dinner at seven, seven is what you mean. But from my own experience, I know that seven turns out to be either a few minutes before or a few minutes after, and I doubt if the Ruggs stood by their dining room door with a stopwatch in their hands. I doubt if the Ruggs know if their guests arrived at two, four or six minutes past seven. And I dare say that if Colfax said he was so glad that they got there on time, everyone would accept the fact that they arrived on the stroke of seven, despite obstacles like funny smells. I dare say that Colfax and his nephew are mentally listed by both Ruggs as very prompt people indeed."

"What you mean in a nutshell," John said, "is if you say you come at seven, nobody's going to check you with every clock in the house. Always makes me mad as a hatter in mystery stories when everybody always knows what time it is, and what time he opened the door, and what time he heard the shots, and all like that. Now you take our house. Wouldn't do a damn bit of good to check what time people said they came. Not one damn clock in the house ever agrees with any other. You tell me you come at seven, okay. You did. That's what it amounts to, in a nutshell."

Mrs. Beaton said crisply she thought it was the biggest nutshell she ever heard of in her life.

"You mean," she continued, "that those two men actually went there and ate dinner!"

"Sure," John said. "After all that, they ought to been pretty hungry. Then the boy says he has to go. That's easy enough, because he's a doctor, and they're always flipping in and out. Always got damn calls to make. Hey, he's the one makes the fake calls to the cops to go to Marcus's, huh?"

Leonidas nodded.

"It's definitely to the advantage of Colfax to have the murder discovered while he is safely engaged in playing bridge with the Ruggs," he said. "M'yes, indeed. And the radio tube was a pleasant touch. When the nephew finally returns, he says engagingly that he bought a new tube, because he noticed a squeak in their radio. It's not a usual gesture, but it's a thoughtful gesture, and it doubtless filled the Ruggs with pleasure and convinced them that here was a young man of charm and manners."

"And the beauty of it all is," Link said, "that

when you come to a showdown, Mrs. Beaton left
Marcus alive, they'll claim that *they* did, and if anyone is on the spot, Shakespeare, it's you and me."

"M'yes," Leonidas said. "Well, we have this reasonably clear, now. Now we shall have to set to
work."

"D'you expect to prove any of this fantastic
guessing?" Mrs. Beaton demanded.

"M'yes."

"How? How!" Mrs. Beaton said. "*How!*"

Judy giggled. "Darling," she said, "if you keep
that up, I'm going to start in making cracks about
heap big Injun. I bet I know how. Cannae. Am I right,
Shakespeare?"

"M'yes," Leonidas said. "I have been considering
Cannae for some time."

"Cannae?" John said. "Can you what?"

"Cannae, the battle," Judy explained, and spelled
it for him. "That's out of Haseltine's bag of tricks.
Cannae's the way Haseltine solves things and rescues
things. He's just always being buffeted around by
fate, you know. More buffets and more fate than
you'd ever believe possible. Then after he's been buffeted just so long—it's about once a month on the
radio, and around page two hundred and twenty in
the books, Haseltine thinks of Cannae."

"What of it?" John returned. "What good's
thinking of Cannae?"

"Cannae," Leonidas said, "was the historic battle
between the Romans and the Carthaginians, fought in

Apulia in the year 216 B. C., in which the small, weak army of Hannibal cut the incomparable forces of eighty-five thousand proud Roman legionnaries to pieces—"

"Shreds," Judy said. "Shreds. Not just pieces."

"To shreds. M'yes. In that," Leonidas continued, "by means of an ingenious strategical concentration, it caught the enemy from the flank with cavalry, and surrounded him. Clausewitz and Schlieffen, of the Prussian General Staff, elaborated the idea of Cannae into a general theoretical doctrine, and then compressed the doctrine into an exact strategical system. That, in brief, is Cannae."

Judy applauded.

"You certainly know your Haseltine!" she said. "That's word for word. It just takes me back to the good old days, Shakespeare, when I fought Cannae after Cannae at the side of the gallant young officer. I certainly was more of a help to him than this wench with the sarong he's trailing around with now! You know, Topsey, I'm going to swallow my pride and write that author and ask him what about bringing the Princess Alicia back into the story."

A peculiar little look crossed Mrs. Beaton's face.

"Something has just dawned on me," she said in a choked voice. "I've just had a blinding flash of enlightenment. Bill, you—"

"We're going to try Cannae," Leonidas said swiftly. "I know what you are thinking, and you are correct. Need I say more? We are going to try Cannae.

M'yes. First, however, we must get hold of Frenchy. I think he's entirely capable of taking care of himself, but I require him. We must get Frenchy."

"He said for you not to worry about him," Judy said. "I told him how to get here. He knows. By the way, Link, how did you manage to land here? Did you just like the looks of the place?"

"After Colfax and his nephew left the Ruggs'," Link said, "I went back to my car and found the leg gone. I thought someone passing by had seen it, and swiped it. Which, at that stage, discouraged me entirely. I couldn't think of any way of trying to get it back—"

"You might have opened your mouth and tried," Judy said. "I don't think you're very resourceful. You should have called out, like a junk man. You know. 'Any old rags and bots? Any old artificial legs? Any old papers?'"

"What I did," Link said, "was to go back to the store, very downcast. Then I found Bill's notes saying I'd find him at Mrs. Topsey Beaton's, and since there's only one Beaton in the phone book, that was comparatively easy. I'll go pick up Frenchy, Bill. What are you going to do with the Wimpernel?" he added as he got up from his chair. "Keep her, or pack her off, or what?"

Leonidas smiled faintly as he walked over and looked down at Myrna, curled up asleep in a cushioned arm chair by the fire.

"One would never suspect, to look at that quiescent form," he said, "what anguish she caused me, or what drama she is capable of, or what a—er—er—"

"Stink," Judy said. "Isn't that the word you're really hunting for? You mean what a stink she can make. I'll bet she can! I recognized her when I came in as the Zora type. All she needs is a sarong and a snippet of hibiscus over one ear. Shakespeare, d'you think she has any idea of what's going on?"

"Vaguely," Leonidas said. "She finally grasped the fact that there had been a murder, but it moved her only to comment on the dangers of life in what she likes to think of as the country. Apparently she's put the whole matter squarely out of her thoughts. Er—I'm sure I don't know what she thinks, now."

"I don't think we need to worry about her, anyway," Mrs. Beaton said. "What was her last remark? Something about our describing a picture that had been at Keith's last week?"

"M'yes," Leonidas said. "Er—I see no reason to disillusion her. And unless she makes some extraordinarily violent protest, I think she had best stay with us. M'yes." He stood for a moment by the French windows. "M'yes. I think we should definitely encourage her to believe that we are discussing one movie after another. Possibly even a play. M'yes. M'yes, indeed!"

He twirled his pince-nez as the front door knocker sounded.

"Frenchy!" Judy said. "I'll go!"

"I will," Link said. "I'm up."

He rushed into the hall.

A minute later, he was backing into the living room.

A state cop, with arms folded, advanced in his wake.

"Mrs. Beaton?" he said.

Leonidas, with great gallantry, assisted her to arise from the couch.

"Stall him," he said firmly in her ear.

"You Mrs. Beaton?" the cop asked.

"Which Mrs. Beaton?" Topsey asked promptly, as though there were Beatons in every third house in Carnavon. "*Which* Mrs. Beaton?"

Like Cassie Price, Leonidas thought, this woman was most successful in action. She really needed, as John suggested, a recipe. But once a recipe was given her, she fairly plunged to work on it.

The state cop looked at a piece of paper.

"Mrs. Sebastian Beaton. You her?"

"Yes. What," Topsey asked brightly, "can I do for you, officer?"

"You own a black, five-passenger Porter sedan, model forty-one, de luxe, license number 68807?"

"Dear me," Topsey said, "I'm sure *I* don't know the license number of the sedan. Do you, darling?" she appealed to Judy. "Could you tell the officer if that was the number? It seems to me there are a lot of fives in it."

"Fives?" Judy played up. "Oh, I don't think so. I think it's nines. I don't think I ever noticed, to tell you the truth, Mrs. B., I usually use the beachwagon, anyway."

"Well, dear, we'll simply have to find that registration and see. Where's my pocketbook? That's yours, isn't it?"

She pointed directly at her own.

"Yes," Judy said. "Pocketbook, pocketbook! Now where can that pocketbook be! Just you wait, officer, and we'll find it right away!"

The hunt for the pocketbook was carried on with intense vigor by everyone except Myrna. John heaved himself down on the floor and peered under the baby grand, Link hunted along the tops of books, and Judy and Mrs. Beaton bustled around, getting in everyone's way, and making excited, urgent little noises as they peeked behind couch pillows and under chair cushions.

Myrna slept throughout it all.

"My, my!" Leonidas said gently at last, "I do believe that *is* your pocketbook after all, Topsey! Why, it is!"

"How stupid of me!" Topsey said. "It's the one without the initials, isn't it? Give it to me, and let me find out about that old number before this poor officer loses patience entirely! You've been so patient, officer!"

Her face was a picture of well-bred surprise when, after much pawing around in her pocketbook, she at last unearthed the car registration blank and announced that the license was 68807.

"Okay, Mrs. Beaton. It's your car then. Now—"

"Now don't tell me I'm in some sort of trouble!"

"You left that car parked on the bumper light connection, up by St. Anselm's church. And—"

"Oh," Topsey said in a relieved voice. "That's too bad, I'm sure, but it's nothing really *bad*, is it? It's Evelyn's fault, of course. I lent the car to Evelyn for the evening. But of course I suppose since it's my car, it's my responsibility and not his."

"His?"

"Evelyn is the rector," Topsey said. "The Reverend Evelyn Leicester. I'm sure you must know him. He's Honorary Chaplain of the Carnavon police."

"Oh. He had it, huh? Well, what about them ducks?"

"Ducks?" Topsey said.

"Ducks."

"I'm afraid I don't understand what you mean by ducks!" There was a touch of Mrs. Spoffard in Topsey's plaintive tones. "I can't imagine what you mean, officer! Evelyn doesn't wear ducks!"

"Ducks. Live ducks. Birds. A crate of live ducks. Stolen ducks."

"Stolen! Merciful heavens, officer, there's some mistake! The rector of St. Anselm's doesn't go around stealing ducks! Oh, no! Never in the world! Bill, can you imagine Evelyn stealing *ducks?* Ducks, of all things!"

"Er—frankly, no," Leonidas said. "Perhaps if the

officer will come out to the hall and telephone Evelyn, he will satisfy himself that this is all an absurd and incredible error. Will you come out to the hall, officer?" He took the officer's elbow. "I'm sure you'll find—and do mind the floor. It's just been waxed, and it's very slippery. Do be careful not to fall, won't you?"

"But—" the officer said.

"Evelyn will be glad to set your mind at rest, if you'll just step this way and telephone him. He is always eager and willing to assist the forces of law and —look out!"

As Leonidas steered him from the living room into the hall, something wielded by a hand behind the curtains thudded against the officer's head.

He crumpled into a little heap on the floor.

"Well," Frenchy, swinging a blackjack, stepped out into sight. "Well, that's that! What you want me to do with him, Bill? Say, this is just like old times, this is!"

"M'yes," Leonidas said. "Thank you so much, Frenchy. It was the work of a benign providence that I saw you from the window, and it was sheer genius on your part to understand the situation."

"Aw, I got it right away when you give me Bat's old signal from the window, Bill. I'd have spotted the copper's car, anyway. The dope left it right out front. What you want me to do with him, Bill? I'll dump him anywhere you say. Reservoir's up the line."

"Of course," Link found his voice, "you realize this

is the third, don't you? You're bearing in mind that there are two others laid out? And this is the third? Frenchy, I—"

"Hi, Boss,". Frenchy said. "You okay, huh? I been hunting you. I seen you get into the car and drive off, but by the time I got out and could yell, you was gone. I had to take a bus here. Nobody wouldn't give me a lift."

"I hate to tell you," Judy said, "but I think it's your outfit. There's something awfully sinister about that Mickey Mouse sweatshirt. And that cap. You should have kept on your green satin. I said so."

"Hi, kid," Frenchy said. "Always kidding! The money's okay, Boss. I'm sorry about that. Bill, where you want I should dump this mug? You better decide before I have to tap him again for luck."

"M'yes," Leonidas said briskly. "You're about his size, aren't you, Frenchy? Remove his uniform, and put it on—"

"Say, remember when I used to have six cops' suits, and a bag of badges, huh?"

Leonidas nodded.

"Er—vividly. Then put this fellow away somewhere in this house. In the cellar, I think, and—er—arrange it so that his mind will be reasonably confused when he awakes some six or seven hours from now. Can you do that?"

Frenchy grinned.

"Give me a lift with this mug, Boss," he said. "I feex, Bill. I feex!"

"Hm. What's he mean, he's going to feex? What's he going to do?" Topsey demanded as Link and Frenchy bore off the officer's limp form.

"Perhaps," Leonidas said, "it will be wiser if we do not inquire too closely into Frenchy's methods. Let it suffice to say that his experience with this sort of thing is infinite. Topsey, you were excellent. And now, will you get your pad and pencil? We have a list to make."

"I suppose," John said, "you know what you're up to, Shakespeare. But it's one thing to tamper with the local cops, and it's something else to knock out one of these boys. This is bad."

"Really," Leonidas said blandly, "I can assure you that this is not bad, John. It is good. M'yes, most fortunate. If he hadn't happened in, we should have been forced to wander abroad and seek a state cop, and state cops are not always easy to come by. Now, as soon as Frenchy attires himself in that uniform, we are all ready."

"For Cannae?" Judy asked.

"M'yes. We shall concentrate our forces, and attack on the flank."

"Forces?" John said. "You mean us? Us, here?"

Leonidas nodded.

"We going to attack a flank? Whose flank?" John demanded. "Colfax's?"

Leonidas nodded again.

"Well," John said, "I'd like to know how in hell *how!*"

"I have a plan," Leonidas said, "a simple plan, based on a simple fact."

"Like what?"

"Er—like," Leonidas said, "the lack of obstacles. While Colfax's mind works very quickly, he has not had any real obstacles inserted in his path at any time tonight. He has not had one single agonized moment of wondering if he's really succeeded, or if failure is about to engulf him. No one has chased him. No one has followed him. Or challenged him. Or forced him to alter one single plan. He has felt no pressure of any sort. He has thought things out quickly, and without exception, those things have all come to pass. He has been entirely successful. He knows it. Back at his home in Tilbury—by the way, Judy, he is home there, of course?"

"Rugg said that 'they' were at Professor Colfax's home in Tilbury, Shakespeare. I jotted down the address and phone number. The Birches, Hilltop Road. Tilbury. Phone is Framingham something or other. Four-eight-six—three, I think. Rugg said I'd be sure to find the professor there, as he was going straight home. Do you suppose he and the nephew really did go right home?"

"M'yes," Leonidas said. "Why not? They have nothing to gain by doing otherwise. Their job is done. Their purpose is accomplished. Their trail, if you choose to call it that, is sufficiently obscured. They have their alibi. They have the Ruggs as unimpeachable witnesses to their complete innocence, and indeed to their complete and utter lack of connection with any part of this ugly matter. I've no doubt that Colfax and his nephew are both sleeping soundly in Tilbury this minute."

"Does the nephew live with him?" John asked.

"I don't know," Leonidas said. "His name was not brought up during my visit there today. But I feel quite sure he will spend the night there tonight, doubtless sharing his uncle's glow of confidence."

"I still don't get what you're going to do," John said. "I see what you mean it's been a cinch for him, and he's sure he's safe, but what can we do about it?"

"We have found out," Leonidas said, "enough to piece things together. We have found out as much as any group could possibly find out, working without any elaborate paraphernalia, or without—"

"Without practically anything," Topsey said, "including without the law!"

"M'yes. But we still have managed to put our hands on and extricate the story from the people who can piece this and put it together. Now we are going to attack. We are going to insert obstacles, and apply pressure, and—er—see if Colfax's mind works quickly under adverse circumstances. We are ready. We shall start at once. Now—"

Judy clutched at Leonidas's sleeve.

With an audible gulp, she pointed toward the living room.

"Look! Look who's come in the French door!"

CHAPTER 9

"EVELYN!" Topsey said. "Evelyn, of all people! Merciful heavens above! Evelyn, of *all* people! Here! *Now!*"

"Send him packing," Judy said. "Tell him Cabot's sick and you're rushing to the hospital! Quick, Mrs. B.! Get rid of him before he spots Myrna!"

Topsey started from the hall with a look of dogged determination on her face, but Evelyn was already inside the living room.

And, furthermore, he had caught sight of Myrna, still slumbering in the big chair by the fire.

Topsey drew a long breath.

"Well, really, Evelyn!" she said. "Really, I hardly expected *you*, at *this* time of night, popping in my house like this! Really!"

"Ah, Topsey, I saw your lights were all on," Evelyn said hurriedly, "and I thought I'd come and see if you possibly might have caught sight of this girl—I've been hunting for her everywhere, ever since I left the church! And I peeked in your window, and here she is!"

"Yes," Topsey said, "here she is, and you needn't give her another thought. We'll take care of her. No, I wouldn't disturb her, Evelyn! Just let her sleep. She's had a very trying night. Very. The poor thing's exhausted. Good night, Evelyn," she took him by the elbow and led him toward the French door through which he had just entered, "good night! Tomorrow morning I'll call you, and we'll settle everything. She'll just spend the night here safely with me. Good night!"

"But—"

"My dear boy, there's nothing *you* can do about her now!" Topsey said. "Not tonight! Tomorrow we'll settle everything. Run along, now, and don't give her another thought!"

Evelyn was half way through the door when Myrna awoke.

"Spencer Tracy!" she said. "Spencer Tracy!"

Evelyn beamed as he swung around and re-entered the living room.

Out in the hall, John looked at Leonidas and Judy, and started to rumble.

"Well," he said, "there goes the old ball game, Shakespeare! Attack! Ha ha! Let's see you attack any flanks now! Honest, I hate to laugh, but this is as good as a play! Yes, sir, Shakespeare. You're licked now. You can't get rid of the padre. And if that girl starts spilling any beans about Meredith!"

"Play," Leonidas said. "M'yes. M'yes, indeed.

John, this is a play. You go tell Link and Frenchy that this is a play. Judy, this is a play. Go in there and tell Topsey. This is a play!"

"Listen," John said, "you can go just so far, but there's limits, Shakespeare! The padre ain't stupid!"

"Er—no. But he has a pliant streak," Leonidas said. "M'yes. I think we can manage."

"What'll you do with him?" John demanded. "You can't leave him! You can't go off and leave him here! And you can't pry him away from that girl! She's already clinging to him like a barnacle! You can't leave the both of 'em here! What you going to do?"

Leonidas twirled his pince-nez.

"Insert him," he said briefly. "John, go tell Link and Frenchy this is a play, and get some of your cameras, and make a press card to wear in your hat band."

"I got a press card."

"Get it," Leonidas said. "Get some cameras. Tell Link to spruce himself up. Tell Frenchy he's playing the part of a cop again."

Judy came back into the hall as John left, shaking his head.

"Topsey's got the idea, Bill, but she can't get a word in edgewise. Evelyn's too busy telling the Wimp how he's been hunting her, street by street."

"M'yes. Judy, do you possess a more glamorous outfit than—er—that which you have on?"

"What's the matter with my neat sheer wool?" Judy said indignantly. "It's supposed to be the ideal costume for the personal secretary! Inconspicuous—"

"M'yes. But have you an evening dress, something glittering?"

"I've got a bit of gold brocade," Judy said, "that'll knock your eye out, and—"

"Er—will you put it on, please? Quickly?"

"Shakespeare, are you still going to try Cannae?"

"M'yes," Leonidas said. "You're going to be the Princess Alicia, in person. Now, we must do something with Myrna. They've seen her in that wimple. Myrna must have another costume."

"How's for a sarong?" Judy said promptly.

"M'yes. I wonder if we could. Isn't it a little chilly for a sarong, Judy?"

"If she's going to play Zora, she needs a sarong," Judy said. "Don't worry about the chill. As Frenchy said, I feex!"

"Er—do," Leonidas said. "Do. First, however, I shall have to see if I can—er—feex, myself. Wait just a moment."

He entered the living room.

Evelyn looked up.

"Why, Mr. Budenny!"

"It's simple telepathy!" Leonidas said, as he briskly shook Evelyn's hand. "How I have been wishing for you, dear fellow! I said only five minutes ago to Mrs. Beaton that if only I dared, I should telephone you and ask your aid! It's the play, you know! The play! My beloved play!"

"Play?" Evelyn said. "*Your* play?"

"That's what I've been trying to tell you about," Topsey injected hurriedly. "It's the play. His play!"

"Let me explain to him," Leonidas thrust Evelyn on the couch and sat down beside him. "While taking me home, Mrs. Beaton and I were chatting, and I told her about my beloved play, my own beloved play, on which so much rests!"

"You mean, you write plays?" Evelyn said. "I thought you were a most unusual auctioneer! I thought when I first saw you, you had the look of a literary man."

"M'yes," Leonidas said. "Of course, you understand that I was not always an auctioneer! There was a time, dear fellow, when my life was very different. M'yes, how very different! But one cannot always tell, can one? To have been born with a silver spoon in one's mouth is not enough, in these intensely chaotic times. Dear me, no! But," he added staunchly, "one can try! That is why, for these last ten years, I have worked on my beloved play, hoping—even praying, that some day it would retrieve my lost fortune and enable me to live, once again, as I used to live. A gentleman, surrounded by my books! And tonight, dear fellow, tonight my hopes and dreams are almost within my very grasp!"

"Gee," Myrna said, "gee, this is thrilling!"

"Tonight," Leonidas went on, "Mrs. Beaton told me that Ivan Vassily, the producer whose ear I have been trying to get for these many, many months, is here! Mrs. Beaton met him yesterday, at a meeting!

Think of it, dear fellow! Here! As near as Tilbury!
Think what that meant to me!"

"Gee!" Myrna said. "I'm all of a ladder! Go on!"

"And then," Leonidas lowered his voice, "then
the blow! Vassily is leaving by transcontinental plane
tomorrow! Think how my heart sank at that news.
And then came Mrs. Beaton's suggestion. We would
get his ear! We would force him to see the worth of
my beloved play!"

"Say," Myrna said. "That's what you was talking
about, huh? It was your play. Not the picture at
Keith's!"

"The play," Leonidas said, "that we hope will be
a picture, if only we can get Vassily's ear! I was so
enthusiastic, so excited that I forgot all else! At once,
we decided to assemble a cast—and when we discovered that Myrna was on the stage, we hired her at
once! Didn't we, Myrna? We paid you at once!"

Myrna nodded.

"Hastily, in a frenzy," Leonidas went on, "we
have assembled our little cast. We were about to start
out. And now, providentially, you come! Ah, dear fellow, say that you will help!"

"Of course he will, won't you, Evelyn?" Topsey
said. "You were marvelous in the Guild's play last fall.
Your voice is so wonderful! It's just what we need!"

"Why—" Evelyn obviously wanted to help, but
he was obviously confused.

"Sure you will!" Myrna said. "Just like Spencer
Tracy. What am I going to be?"

"You know Zora, in Lieutenant Haseltine?" Leonidas said. "Er—rather like that."

"Oh, boy!" Myrna said wistfully, "if I only had a solong!"

"Er—Judy will take care of that," Leonidas said. "Judy! Take care of Myrna now, please. Are *you* all ready, John? Come in, come in! I want dear Mr. Leicester to meet every member of our little cast!"

"Mr. Robbins!" Evelyn said. "Why, Mr. Robbins, *you!*"

"Ah, of course, you know him!" Leonidas said. "To be sure! In my excitement, I had forgotten! How fortunate! Now you two can chat, while I gather together the rest of our—er—cast. John, what was that new development you were telling me about in concrete?"

"Huh?"

"Architectural concrete slabs," Leonidas said. "M'yes, that was it. Architectural concrete slabs. I'm sure that Mr. Leicester, with all his building plans for his church, will want to know all about them. Tell him, John, all about architectural concrete slabs. Er— the whole story of them. Now, Topsey, please!"

She followed him out into the hall.

"Bill! This isn't going to work out! Evelyn is momentarily silenced, but we can't keep him from catching on, sooner or later! He'll start asking questions—"

"Your principal chore," Leonidas said, "is to see that he has no chance to. Now, d'you have your pad and pencil? Myrna will take the Zora part. Judy is the

Princess Alicia. Link—come here, Link. You are an outraged husband. John is to be a press photographer. Frenchy, you are a cop, as you used to be in the—er—good old days, when you racketed around with your brother. Topsey, you are a woman reporter. A sob sister. Now, listen!"

Five minutes later, Leonidas returned briskly to the living room.

"Have you told him about the concrete slabs, John? A significant development, I personally think. Now, dear fellow, you have but one line. Here. I have written it out, and Topsey will coach you en route. Er—so will Myrna. I might add that everything hinges on the force and sincerity with which you say it. You understand?"

Evelyn looked worried.

"I'm afraid I don't understand just *what* you plan to do," he said.

"Why, dear fellow, we're going to put on—actually act out—a part of my beloved play, for Vassily! We're going right now to Tilbury, to do it!"

"So much hinges on it!" Topsey said. "If we can just put this over, Evelyn, Mr. Budenny's future will be assured. And I think it's our duty to put it over, when you think how tremendously he helped us at the church tonight! Come along!"

Out in the hall, Evelyn stared blankly at Judy, resplendent in gold brocade and Mrs. Beaton's best velvet evening wrap.

"Aren't I gorgeous?" Judy said. "And would you

ever know Myrna, with her hair loose and that brown
powder? She's pretty gorgeous too, under my sweater
and skirt. She has on a solong—I mean, a sarong—that'll
knock your eyes out. It's a pity to cover her up, but
we don't want her to die of pneumonia on the way.
How do we divide up, Bill?"

"Myrna, Evelyn, Topsey and you in John's car,"
Leonidas said. "You know where to stop, John? Fine.
I will go with Link and Frenchy in the beachwagon.
We have some—er—alternate lines of action to discuss.
Ready?"

It was shortly after three o'clock when the two
cars pulled up on the turnpike in the town of Tilbury.

"Now, Link," Leonidas said as he got out of the
beachwagon, "you and Frenchy know what to do in
case this does not work out. But we'll try, in so far
as is possible, to follow the prearranged plan."

"Good old Bill!" Frenchy said. "Bat always used
to say if you wasn't straight, you'd run the city blind-
folded. Don't worry, Bill! We'll make it work!"

Leonidas walked to the sedan.

"Evelyn's simply wonderful!" Judy said. "He's
going to give that line everything he's got! Now,
Bill?"

"Now. You, and Myrna. John, you and Topsey
and Evelyn are to stay right here until you get the
flashlight signal. You understand, John. This is Hilltop Road, here to the right. The Birches is about half
a mile in. There are no houses this side of it, or beyond

it. Keep your engine running, and come at once when you see the signal."

"S'pose things go sour?" John said. "What then?"

"Wait for positive proof," Leonidas told him, "and then drive with great speed elsewhere. Come, Myrna. Come, Judy!"

Link and Frenchy fell in step with them, and the five proceeded along in the shadow of the dense woods that bordered Hilltop Road.

"Myrna," Leonidas said, "have you got it all straight? Do you know your part? Tell me, exactly, so we'll be sure you're letter perfect!"

Myrna told him.

"I got it," she said. "I can always pick up a routine quick. Gee, this is thrilling! Real lines! That is, real lines only I don't have to say nothing."

"M'yes," Leonidas said. "And a fur coat if you do it well!"

"Honest?"

"Honest," Leonidas said. "Now, Judy, run through your part."

Ten minutes later, the group was hidden in the bushes bounding the lawn outside Carl Colfax's darkened house.

"Remember," Leonidas whispered to Myrna, "back to your clothes the instant you're through!"

"Say!" she wiggled out of her skirt, "this is warm compared to some of the wings I stood in! Now?"

"Now!"

Myrna, in her sarong, strolled into the open stretch of lawn.

A second later, her voice rose in that hideous crescendo.

She yelled again.

Then a third time.

A light went on in an upstairs window. A second light instantly appeared.

Myrna opened her mouth wide and let out another scream.

Two heads appeared framed in the lighted windows.

"Wahhh!" Myrna screamed, and ran to the bushes at the left of the house.

Then she turned, and ran to the front door, letting out another screech as she ran.

"They're falling for it!" Link said in Leonidas's ear. "They're falling! They're coming downstairs! Look, hall lights, Bill! They're coming down!"

"Wahhh!" Myrna's voice rose again.

"She better hustle," Judy said. "They're opening the door!"

But as the front door opened, Myrna darted away.

When she reached the center of the lawn, Leonidas touched Frenchy's arm.

At once, a shot rang out.

Myrna seemed to stumble. Then she yelled once more, poignantly, and disappeared into the bushes.

But even before she reached them, Judy was rushing wildly towards the lighted doorway.

Screaming hysterically, she dove between the two figures silhouetted in the light, and fled into the house.

"That's got 'em," Link said. "They're all confused. See, they don't know what to do!"

"Ah!" Leonidas said. "But they're taking the bird in hand. There they go! There goes the living room light!"

"Judy's no slouch at screeching, herself!" Link said. "My God, hear her! They've both followed her. They're both in there. See? Time for me, don't you think?"

"M'yes. Well done, Myrna!" Leonidas told her as she came back. "A fur coat tomorrow! Get clothed, quickly. Watch for any distress signals, Frenchy. All right, Link. You go straight in. I'll circle around the bushes and slip into the hall. Signal for John the minute I'm in, Frenchy."

He arrived in the hall just in time to hear Link's infuriated bellow.

"My wife, I tell you! She's my wife, you skunk! Mine! Who are you?"

"Don't! Don't!" Judy screamed. "Don't! He's not the one! It's the other!"

Leonidas heard the sound of an excited scuffle, and then a yelp and a thud.

"You've killed him!" Judy cried out hysterically. "You've killed him! Speak to me, darling! Speak to me, Victor!"

Leonidas nodded.

It would appear that the nephew had gone down, according to plan.

"Don't you dare touch him!" Link snarled. "I'll knock you out! You, too! Who is this baboon? Is this another of your lovers?"

"Don't touch him!" Judy said. "Don't! Here! I'll save you! I'll save you!"

There were sounds of another tussle.

If the plans were proceeding as they should, Leonidas knew that Judy should be wrapping herself around Colfax, and Link should be attempting to tear her away.

John, his hands full of cameras, and his pockets bulging with flash bulbs, panted into the hall.

Winking at Leonidas, he marched to the doorway of the living room.

"Hold it!" he said. "Cuddle up closer, sister! Hold it! Got it. Now you, brother. Hold it! Got it. Now the two of you! Hold it! Got it."

The flash bulbs kept popping.

He was still taking pictures when Topsey, pad and pencil in hand, crowded past John.

"Now another one of her, John!" she said briskly. "Now this man. Now one with me and them!"

"I can't take any of old sourpuss till he gets that dumb look off his face! Smile, brother!"

"See here—" Colfax spoke for the first time.

"Smile, for God's sakes! Smile, can't you?"

"See here!" Colfax only just managed to make himself heard. "What is the meaning of—"

"Smile!" John said. "Smile! Smile! Smile! Smile! Topsey, get that fool to smile!"

"Smile!" Topsey shrilled, above the clamor of Judy's hysterical howling and Link's ear-splitting bellows.

That went on for several minutes.

Then Frenchy, bearing a gun in either hand, appeared in the hall and strode on into the living room.

There was a sudden, absolute silence.

"Okay, break it up!" Frenchy said. "You Colfax?"

"Yes, I am!" Colfax sounded completely bewildered. "And I wish you'd explain to me the meaning of all this!"

"I arrest you, Carl Colfax, for the murder of Marcus Meredith! Hey, father!"

Leonidas gave Evelyn, who had just entered the hall, a little shove toward the living room door.

"Father," Frenchy said, "this the man you saw?"

"Before God," Evelyn's bell-like tones rang out, "that is the man!"

"I'm not! You're crazy! I didn't!"

"Yeah?" Frenchy said. "You see that guy on the floor? He told us at nine o'clock tonight. We known since then. Come on, Colfax. We got the place surrounded."

"What? *He*—he told?"

"Yeah. He squealed on you. We'd been here after you before, but we had to get this witness. Thanks, father. You can go back to the car. Come on, Colfax!"

"He told!" Colfax's voice was trembling with fury. "He double-crossed me, did he? Well, I'm going to tell you about *him!*"

"Here's a pencil and paper," Topsey said eagerly. "Write it!"

"Keep your hands up, Colfax!" Frenchy said. "Dictate!"

Colfax, in tones that seethed, dictated.

"Okay," Frenchy said. "Slip them bracelets on him, Link. Now, sign that, Colfax. Now, write underneath that you killed Meredith. Go on. Save yourself the rubber hose. Write it!"

"This fellow's coming to," John said.

"Who's got that cord? Tie him up. Quick. Now, Link, gag Colfax, and blindfold him, and hobble his ankles. Here. Let me. You help John."

"Okay," Link said. "Hold still, doctor what's your name, and wait till we do you up nice, and then we'll let you listen to uncle's nice statement, and see if you want to make any additions or corrections. He says you killed Meredith."

"What!"

"He's just signed a statement about it. Want to make a statement, yourself?"

"The dirty-double crossing—"

"Do you," Link said, "or do you not wish to dictate a statement setting forth your part in this, before I gag you and take you back to the station for the boys to have fun with?"

"Who *are* you?"

"Detective Inspector Haseltine," Link said curtly. "Going to talk? Make up your mind!"

"I'll talk."

Fifteen minutes later, after he and Frenchy had loaded Colfax and his nephew into the rear of the beachwagon, Link strolled over to where Leonidas and Judy stood watching.

"To quote our friend John, I hand it to you with bells on, Shakespeare!" he said. "The way you figured it, down to the last detail! And to think Colfax doesn't even know you're behind it!"

"He mustn't," Leonidas said. "You must take care not to mention my name on the way home. Tell Frenchy. I shall maintain a discreet silence."

"Don't you think," Link asked Judy, "that this is incredible, all of it?"

"It was a pretty good Cannae," Judy said. "As good as any I ever played. Pretty good performances by the entire cast, if you ask me. Where did John take the others? Where did you send them?"

"I told John to drive slowly back to Topsey's," Leonidas said. "Evelyn obediently departed for the car when Frenchy ordered him to, but he's beginning to think embarrassing questions. They're written all over his face."

"He'll never get a chance to ask 'em," Judy said. "He made a couple of feeble attempts on the way over, but Topsey headed him off. She can head off a delegation like him. She can chairman anything. And Myrna's keeping him pretty occupied. Bill, I never saw a man so bewildered as Colfax was! You had him, the minute things began to pop! He looked so funny, standing there in his pyjamas, when John began to take pictures! By the time Frenchy came, he was completely licked. What now?"

"You and Link," Leonidas said, "will be dropped off at the church—"

"Suits me," Link said. "Of course, she'll probably turn out to be a shrew, and she can't afford dresses like that on what you make out of hardware, but I'm willing."

"To the church," Leonidas said, ignoring Judy's snort of indignation, "and take Topsey's sedan—here are the keys—and return those ducks to their rightful owner. Then come back to Topsey's. Er—don't take the short cut through the reservoir, will you?"

"Shakespeare, what about those cops!" Link said. "What are you going to do about all those trussed up cops?"

"Frenchy and I," Leonidas said, "are going to deposit Colfax and his relation at Marcus's. Then Frenchy, in his role of state cop, is going to discover and free those poor creatures in the closets."

"I get it!" Link said. "They'll be madder at being found by a state cop than at being put in by us!"

"That," Leonidas said, "is my hope. They will tell Frenchy that the murderers are a man with a beard and a young fellow with brown hair, and Frenchy will wave those confessions in their faces, and tell them that he has the criminals, and their confessions. Then, before they have apoplexy, he will add that if they do him the favor of staying there and guarding the pair, he will forget about their being locked up in the closets, and—er—cut them in, as the saying goes, on the credit."

"Then Frenchy leaves them!" Link chuckled. "Bill, will it work?"

"We can," Leonidas said, "only try it and see."

Dawn was breaking over Bald Pate Hill when Frenchy ran down the steps of Marcus Meredith's house, jumped in behind the wheel of the beachwagon, and drove hastily away.

"It worked," he said. "I slung your rubbers in back, Bill. It worked fine. Bat always said you had the brain! Say, I got the leg on all right first! Before I let 'em out."

"Er—how long do you think they'll stay there quietly?"

"I said I'd be half, three-quarters of an hour," Frenchy said. "They'll wait an hour, anyways. Maybe two. Bill, Colfax and that other guy'll talk!"

"It is my impression," Leonidas said, "that no one will pay much attention to them if they do. There are their confessions, Frenchy, in black and white. I feel we can leave the rest to the Carnavon police. After all, Colfax did not see me, or hear me. He never saw any of the rest of you before, and I doubt if he ever does again. He can't identify any of you. No, Frenchy, if those two talk, there is very little they can tell."

"Yeah. But suppose they say they didn't write those confessions and all?"

"Their statements," Leonidas said, "are too complete for them to attempt repudiation. They went into too great detail, in their respective efforts to involve the other more deeply. No, Frenchy, whatever problems which may arise are solely between that pair and the police."

The beachwagon rattled into Mrs. Beaton's driveway.

"Now," Leonidas said as they got out, "I think we had best proceed without fanfare by some rear door—where are Mrs. Beaton's servants, I wonder?"

"To the St. Alphonsus party, Judy told me. They're safe out of the way!"

"M'yes. Then let us proceed to restore that officer's uniform—did you take those handcuffs of his from Colfax? Good. And—er—you have some whiskey?"

"Yeah. I feex. Say, Bill."

"M'yes?"

"I know Myrna. She don't recognize me, but I know her. She's Chuck Riley's kid sister. Remember, the Riley gang?"

Leonidas looked at him.

"Frenchy, really? Frenchy, will you help me solve a problem that's been bothering me?"

"Why, sure, Bill! You know I'll do anything you say!"

"Frenchy, would you be willing to take her home, and get her away from Evelyn?"

Frenchy grinned.

"Say," he said, "I thought you wanted me to do something hard! Come on. Let's feex the copper."

Some twenty minutes later, a thoroughly confused and disheveled state cop blinked unhappily at the ceiling of Mrs. Beaton's kitchen.

"Simply disgusting!" Topsey said.

The cop looked at her.

"What happened, lady?"

"You slipped and fell, and we tried to revive you with whiskey, and the doctor," she pointed to John, "says you'd been drinking. You *had* been drinking, hadn't you?"

"Just a beer."

"Just a beer indeed! Smell yourself! It's simply disgusting! What's the matter? Can't you stand up? What are you making those faces for?"

"My head!"

"Disgusting, that's what it is!" Topsey said. "And I called the rector, and he didn't know a thing about any ducks! Now, I don't want to make any trouble for you, though heaven knows you've made *me* enough trouble! But you were very patient about my finding my registration, and you seemed to be perfectly gentlemanly. But I must say, if you make any further mention of ducks, or my car, I shall certainly report my side of the story to my son Cabot Beaton, and he will personally take it up with his good friend Ben Parker, your head commissioner!"

The cop swallowed, and winced.

"Lady," he said, "you win!"

Topsey shut the door behind him with a little sigh.

"Now," she said wearily, "what?"

"Call Myrna out here," Leonidas said. "She's still in the living room, talking with Evelyn. John, you go talk cement with Evelyn while we settle Myrna."

"Cement, again?" John said. "And say, where's Link and Judy?"

"They murmured something about getting breakfast at a dog cart," Leonidas said. "Go on, John. Talk cement. Ah, Myrna. Tomorrow at two—are you free, Topsey? Tomorrow at two, we will meet you at Katz's Fur Store—wasn't that the one you mentioned? And get your coat. Er—don't bring Rosalie."

"Honest!"

"M'yes. And now, run along with Frenchy. By the way, he used to be called Easy. D'you remember hearing of Easy?"

"Honest?" Myrna gave a little squeal.

"Come on, kid," Frenchy said. "I'm taking you home. First I got to shovel William and his old lady back, and then we'll get along."

"Easy!" Myrna said. "Say! But *he*," she jerked her head toward the living room, "he was going to take me!"

Frenchy grinned.

"Him? That stiffneck? Come on, kid, we'll still get a look-in at the St. Alphonsus party!" He hooked his arm through hers. "So long, Bill! Be seeing you!"

"That," Topsey said with a yawn, "leaves Evelyn. I'll just sit here while you settle him. If you can. I have my doubts."

Leonidas twirled his pince-nez for a moment, and then walked slowly into the living room.

His feet dragged across the blue broadloom, and he sighed as he slumped into a leather chair.

"A failure!" he said. "The work of years. Lost!"

"I didn't understand," Evelyn said anxiously. "Topsey didn't give me a chance to ask. Which man was Vassily?"

"We didn't understand either!" Leonidas said. "He'd gone. He went yesterday. All our work in vain! All our work, all my hopes, all my prayers, all in vain!"

"Come, come, dear fellow!" Evelyn said. "A little defeat, one little setback—what does it mean? Let me tell you!"

"What you mean," John said sleepily when Evelyn finally stopped talking, "is for him to buck up. Buck up, Bill!"

Leonidas got up from the leather chair.

"How much," he said, "do you need to complete your Building Fund?"

"Quite a lot, I'm afraid," Evelyn said. "Fifteen hundred dollars before we can start the new wing. I was discussing the price of concrete with Robbins—"

"In return," Leonidas interrupted, "for the new spirit you have instilled in me, I shall complete that fund! No, don't say a word! I ask of you only that you shall never refer to this evening again, to me, or to anyone else! Never mention, never renew this painful experience. John, take him home. I wish to be alone with my thoughts."

"But—"

Leonidas waved him away.

"Not a word! That is my condition. Good night!"

"He means it," John said. "Come on. Now, what's the rockbottom estimate you got? Well, come on, and I'll tell you what I'll do. I'll—what? Who? That girl? *Her?* Say, she went off with that other guy, long ago. What you care? You got fifteen hundred bucks out of this night's work, and you can start that wing tomorrow. Now, you get me a copy of those figures, and I tell you what I'll do—wait a sec. Forgot a camera."

John came back into the living room, gravely saluted Leonidas, and departed.

A minute later, Leonidas heard the long black sedan leaving the driveway.

Twirling his pince-nez, he returned to the kitchen and stood for a moment in the doorway.

Topsey, seated at the kitchen table, was sleeping soundly.

"M'yes," Leonidas said, "indeed!"

He found his rubbers and his cane and his leg-shaped package and his green-handled sickle, put on his coat, and left.

It took him half an hour and several bus changes to reach the Carnavon Four Corners, grey and sad-looking in the early morning drizzle.

It had been, he thought, a tiring and an expensive night, but there was much material which Lieutenant Haseltine could use. He now had a plot for the new Haseltine novel, due on the tenth of the next month. All he needed was a title.

He raised his cane to hail the orange Boston-bound bus, and stepped over the pile of snow to the door.

A second later, he landed squarely on the base of his spine in the slush of the gutter, while the same burly bus driver stood above him.

"I told you what'd happen if you ever got on my bus again! The nerve of you!"

The door slammed, and the bus drove off.

"Ha ha."

Leonidas looked around.

John, with his camera in his hand, was leaning out the window of his black sedan, rumbling with laughter.

"Ha ha!" John said. "Look at that fool package sticking in the snow! Like a leg. The left leg! Ha ha!"

"M'yes," Leonidas said. "An excellent title. M'yes, indeed. The Left Leg!"